LESSONS *from* MY GRANDMOTHER

LESSONS *from* MY GRANDMOTHER

Every Life is a Guided Journey

Martha Mutomba

NEW YORK

LONDON • NASHVILLE • MELBOURNE • VANCOUVER

LESSONS *from* MY GRANDMOTHER
Every Life is a Guided Journey

Published in New York, New York, by Morgan James Publishing. Morgan James is a trademark of Morgan James, LLC. www.MorganJamesPublishing.com

The Morgan James Speakers Group can bring authors to your live event. For more information or to book an event visit The Morgan James Speakers Group at www.TheMorganJamesSpeakersGroup.com

ISBN 978-1-68350-466-5 paperback
ISBN 978-1-68350-467-2 eBook
Library of Congress Control Number: 2017902471

Cover design by:
Rachel Lopez
www.r2cdesign.com

Interior design by:
Bonnie Bushman
The Whole Caboodle Graphic Design

Front cover art by:
Mary Pablo

Author photograph by:
Sungmi Um

In an effort to support local communities, raise awareness and funds, Morgan James Publishing donates a percentage of all book sales for the life of each book to Habitat for Humanity Peninsula and Greater Williamsburg.

Get involved today! Visit
www.MorganJamesBuilds.com

In memory of my beloved grandmother

CONTENTS

Present Day

T he buzz from my phone's alarm clock woke me at five a.m., same as every day. I reached over the bedside table and grabbed my phone, silencing the alarm. I peeled the bed covers away and climbed out of bed. Lazily, I stretched my body, arms extended outward, back slightly arched. Then I shuffled into the bathroom. After a quick shower, I dressed and came down the stairs to my living room. I walked to the big bay window opposite the staircase and opened the blinds, letting in the gentle morning light. I then sat in my favorite chair for my morning meditation. Meditation has become a daily practice for me. I meditate once in the morning and again toward the end of the day. This morning, my *mbuya* (grandmother) appeared to me in a vision that came toward the end of my meditation session.

I began this morning's meditation by setting an intention to sit in communion with Source and to rest in its love. I didn't sit to ask for anything or to surrender any challenges in my life to Source. I sat to give myself time to appreciate Source and to receive appreciation from it. For I have come to know that this short time I spend in Source nourishes and sustains me as I go about my day.

I closed my eyes and focused my attention on my breath, to quiet my mind, calm my emotions, and relax my body. I followed the breath as it gently came into my body and gently left my body. After several breaths, I focused my attention on my heart space in the middle of my chest. Within a few moments, I experienced a familiar perceptible shift. The experience felt like slowly diving into a deep bottomless hole in my heart space and simultaneously expanding outward beyond my body, beyond my mind, beyond the room, beyond the house, beyond the sky, beyond the earth, into a vast empty space. I felt myself floating in a void with no objects or life forms in sight, enveloped in complete silence, utter stillness, and deep peace.

I felt like I was cradled in the warm embrace of an invisible being. I felt protected, safe, and secure. I surrendered into the warm embrace, relinquishing the feeling of a personal existence for a while.

As my awareness started coming back into my mind, I caught a glimpse of an image that started as a blur in the distance and then slowly moved closer into focus. I saw myself in the image. I was sitting beside a gently flowing stream. The gurgling sound of water tumbling over pebbles combined with the sweet chirping of birds in the distance added to the tranquility of the surroundings. When I looked across the stream, I saw nothing at first. As I peered closer, something began to emerge, first a stirring and then a blurry image that eventually materialized into an old woman. I instantly recognized the old woman; it was my grandmother, my father's mother. She was gesturing with her arm, asking me to join her on the other side of the stream. I immediately rose and floated across the stream. My grandmother offered me her hand, and when I took it, she led me into a deep forest.

This is the point where the vision ended and I slowly became aware of my body sitting on the chair in my living room. I said a short prayer of gratitude and appreciation for what had transpired and for what was to come during the day, and then I slowly opened my eyes. Glancing at the clock on the wall, I realized that time had passed. I rose from the chair and walked across my living room, past the kitchen, and through the French doors leading to a stone patio and my backyard. Then I settled on this wooden bench by the edge of the patio, where I am sitting right now as I recount my story to you this Saturday morning.

It is a gorgeous Southern California spring day. The breeze is light and crisp, and I can smell citrus blossoms from the orange trees that form a privacy wall on the north side of my yard. Clusters of brilliant white blossoms peek through the lush green foliage on the trees.

I live in a small town about forty-five minutes from downtown San Diego going north on Interstate 15. Being inland, the weather is perfect for growing fruit trees and vegetables. I have many fruit trees in my backyard, and I have a garden where I grow most of the vegetables I need for my kitchen year-round.

This is the third time that my grandmother has appeared to me in a vision at the end of a meditation session. The first time I had this vision, it ended as I recognized the old woman who appeared across the stream as my grandmother. The second time, I recognized my grandmother and saw that she was beckoning for me to cross the stream. I tried to get up and cross the stream, but for some reason I wasn't able to rise from where I was sitting. In today's vision, I finally rose and floated across the stream to join my grandmother on the other side. Together, we walked into the forest.

I am not sure why my grandmother has been appearing in my visions recently, but I suspect it may have something to do with the landmark date of December 21, 2012, that has just passed. According to the ancient Mayan people, a catastrophic event was supposed to end our physical world as we know it on this particular date. For months prior, news about the end of the world was everywhere—on TV, the radio, and the Internet. However, December 21 came and went with no incident, and life continued as usual. The only changes I have noticed in my own life are these recurring visions of my grandmother, which started on the morning of December 21—the very day that disaster was supposed to strike. The second vision came in mid-February, and here we are in mid-March of 2013.

My grandmother died nearly twenty years ago. She was known to most people as *Mbuya* Debwe, but in the family we simply called her *Mbuya* (Grandma).

Grandma was the deep and silent type. She only spoke when spoken to, and she only gave her opinion when asked. But the words that came from her in those rare moments she chose to speak revealed profound wisdom. Sadly, not many of us were ready for what she had to say in her time.

Now gone with her is the sacred knowledge she had carried in silence—the wisdom I had glimpsed on a rare occasion that turned out to be the last time I spent with her. I clearly remember those particular few days I spent in her company. I remember her soft, wistful gaze as she stared at the distant horizon. I remember her gentle, knowing smile that revealed the lone tooth in her mouth. I remember her wise, loving eyes that twinkled when she had something important to say. I remember her lyrical voice. And most of all, I remember the life lessons she shared with me—the lessons about the origin of human beings and everything in creation.

Grandma said human beings and all that is in creation originate from a source that is like a bubbling spring with innumerable spouts that simultaneously spew life into the world. She called this origin *Mavambo* (Source).

I will now tell you about Source, because this is the one thing I would love for you to walk away with from the story I am about to share. I consider the lessons about Source to be the most valuable piece of wisdom that my grandmother passed on to me—really, the most valuable piece of wisdom that anyone has ever passed on to me. In my opinion, this wisdom holds the secret of life here on earth.

That is a very bold claim, you might say. Yes, it is. But please allow me a few moments to explain why I make this claim.

You see, at the level of Source, all of creation—all that is seen and unseen—is one large interconnected being. As human beings in our physical bodies, we originate from Source and disappear back into Source. Each of us arises from and is permanently connected to Source.

A unique feature of our lives as human beings is our ability to deliberately access Source and allow the life force from it to flow through us and manifest—that is, appear in a form that can be perceived—in the physical world. But not many of us are aware of our existence as a part of Source, let alone know how to deliberately access it and allow it to fuel our lives.

Most of us go through life only aware of the physical or material world. This is the world of the human body—as flesh, blood, and bone—and the physical forms and material objects that we as human beings interact with on a daily basis during our lifetimes. We limit ourselves to what we experience with our five physical senses—what we see with our eyes, hear with our ears, smell with our noses, taste with our tongues, and feel with our skins. However, a large part of our lives exists in a realm that is not detectable by these physical senses. A large part of our lives exists in Source, in the deeper dimension called the spiritual realm. This spiritual realm is also sometimes called the nonphysical or the formlessness—to distinguish it from the world of physical forms and material objects that we discern with our physical senses.

At any given moment that we are expressing in this physical world, we arise from this nonphysical, formless Source as spirit, as a flow, as a radiant light that is our individualized soul. This light, the formless spirit that we are, is a flow of unconditional love and creative energy that is first discernible in our hearts and then flows into our human forms—our minds, our emotional energy systems, and our physical bodies.

As we move through our daily lives, we can deliberately access Source through our own hearts and allow our spirits, our souls, to flow from Source and express in the world. To do this, we first have to quiet our minds, calm our emotions, and relax our bodies, and then focus on our hearts and become aware of our souls inside our hearts. We have to become aware that we are radiant light. We have to become aware that we are spirits housed in physical bodies. Once we gain this awareness with our minds, our spirits rooted in Source flow through our hearts as the unconditional love and creative energy—the life force—into our human forms, to guide and fuel our lives. And it is this life force that holds the power and potential to manifest our hopes, our desires, and our dreams, so that we can witness them come into reality in our physical lives.

On the other hand, when we go through our lives oblivious to our spiritual nature—only aware of our physical bodies and the material objects around us—we are blind to the existence of the realm of spirit and Source. And we live our lives stumbling in darkness. We live our lives not knowing that we have the creative power to manifest our hopes, desires, and dreams. And, for the most part, our hopes, desires, and dreams go unfulfilled.

Human beings who are aware of their eternal connection to Source are said to have awakened or to have attained a state of consciousness or to have come to a realization of their fundamental nature. Those who have not yet gained an awareness of their true nature as spiritual beings are said to be unawake or to be living in a state of unconsciousness or to be unrealized.

Various practices can be used to cultivate an awareness of our spiritual nature and access Source in any given moment, under any given circumstance. Meditation is one such practice, which is why I make meditation a part of my daily routine.

Well! Where are my manners? Here I am already going on and on, and I haven't even introduced myself yet.

Forgive me. I have such a strong passion to share with others what I have come to know and understand about our true nature as human beings, and sometimes I lose myself and forget my manners.

My name is Yeukai. Yeukai Mandizvidza.

Yeukai is a common girl's name in my native Shona language, spoken by a large proportion of the population of Zimbabwe. Yeukai means "remember" in English. This name is usually given in the context of a family that is being urged to remember something of specific importance to their situation or history. Perhaps they are urged to remember to be thankful for the joys of past good times or to remember to connect to the spirits of deceased ancestors (*vadzimu*) who protect the living every single day. As is often the case with Shona names, one usually has to inquire about the family's situation and history to understand the contextual meaning of Yeukai. I didn't even know the real reason why I was given the name Yeukai until I was in my late twenties. That piece of information came to me as part of the life journey I want to share with you.

In retrospect, I realize that the journey I have traveled was motivated by my desire to end the suffering I was experiencing in my life. I now realize it was the chaos and confusion born out of a lack of understanding of my true nature and purpose in this physical world that caused the suffering. Because of that suffering, I started seeking answers to the most basic questions of life: Who am I? Where do I come from? Why am I here? On some intuitive level, I knew that finding the answers to these questions would bring an end to the suffering I was experiencing.

Through my journey in search of the answers to the questions of my life, I began to understand that mysticism, in the context of our human lives, is nothing more than the simple moment-to-moment awareness of our spiritual nature and the recognition that we are individualized expressions of Source flowing as spirits— as unconditional love and creative energy—into our human forms to guide the choices we make and fuel the actions we take. And in this awareness, we focus our actions on sharing our gifts with other human beings and with the world. The gifts we share can be anything that we love to do: taking care of families, teaching, singing, writing, running businesses, inventing new forms, and many such endeavors.

When we deliberately allow the life force from Source to flow through us as we share our gifts and serve others, we are fulfilling our purpose for passing through this physical dimension that we call the world. Then we are doing what we came to do here on earth.

It is that simple!

Yet it seems to be the most difficult thing to grasp, because not many among us understand this very simple tenet of life here on earth. As such, many people continue to live in the dark as it were.

I came to know about Source and my true nature as a human being through the life lessons I received from my grandmother, and my knowledge continues to deepen as I journey through my life. My life has gone through several transitions, all of which, I believe, have been catalysts for my spiritual growth.

Born in the mid-sixties, I grew up in a small rural area in what was then British-colonized Rhodesia, which is now Zimbabwe. I was a budding teenager at the height of the so called Bush War. This was the liberation struggle that eventually ended colonialism and white supremacy in my country, and in 1980 ushered in an independent Zimbabwe that has been ruled by a black-majority government ever since.

I was brought up a Catholic and received all my early formal education at Catholic mission schools, where I completed my primary and secondary education. I then obtained a bachelor's degree in a science discipline at the local university in Harare, the capital of Zimbabwe. After that, I left my country to study for a doctorate degree at a university in England. I finally came to California where I have lived for nearly twenty years. Initially, I came to the United States to work as an academic research scientist at a university, but I soon joined the workforce of the biotechnology industry as it was booming in the mid-nineties.

My early Catholic upbringing within the missionary system offered me an opportunity to receive a wonderful education that opened numerous doors in my life, and for that I am grateful. Yet the religious lessons taught to me within the missionary system at that time left me believing in a God who dwelled in the sky somewhere, judging, passing out sentences, and punishing us human beings—the sinners. The punishment, as my young and impressionable mind understood it then, was living a life of strife and struggle on this earth, followed by a life of eternal burning in hell when we die. Not much of a life to look forward to, I often thought.

It was in my late twenties, just after I completed graduate studies, that I was first exposed to the true nature of our lives. This is when I spent time with my grandmother and when she, in her kind and humble way, had introduced me to Source—the well from which all creation arises.

Through her lessons, I came to know that the entity my grandmother called Source was the same entity the missionaries had introduced to me as God. But there was a difference between the teachings. The missionaries had taught me about a God I had to fear, and who was waiting to punish me for my sins. On the other hand, my grandmother introduced me to the entity of Source as a loving, caring, nurturing, forgiving, healing, and harmonizing life force behind all of creation. She taught me about Source as the architect of all creation, the Presence found in all forms seen and unseen.

Grandma talked about Source as the power behind all of life's manifestations: the rising of the sun, the birthing of a child, the sprouting of a seed, the flowering of a plant, the soaring of an eagle, the flowing of a river, the tranquility of a lake, the stillness of the night sky, and the silence of death.

It has taken me a lifetime to fully grasp the meaning of the teachings my grandmother shared with me then, and I have had many detours along the way. However, to this day, I still continue the learning process to build upon the foundational lessons from my grandmother. I combine her teachings with the wisdom I glean from various sources: other cultures that I have encountered in my travels around the world, teachings of modern-day spiritual and motivational teachers, and ancient teachings in the Bible and other spiritual texts. I enjoy reading and discussing spiritual texts, not from a religious point of view as such, but from the perspective of understanding ancient wisdom that can guide our lives in today's modern world.

I also enjoy learning about the different practices that various cultures use to maintain contact with Source. I love learning practices from African cultures, Native American cultures, and Eastern cultures. What I have learned to do over the years is to adopt only those practices that resonate with me. Each time, I focus on the practices that give me the best opportunity to live a life of love, joy, and creativity.

Through my journey, I have also come to understand that Source—the origin of life my grandmother taught me about, the God the missionaries preached about—is referred to by different names across cultures, traditions, and religions: the Creator, Spirit, Highest Spirit, Great Spirit, the Lord, the Almighty, the Mighty Power,

Adonai, Allah, the Supreme Being, Divine Presence, Divine Love, Divine Energy, Divine Power, the Life Force, the Benevolent Provider, the Infinite Intelligence, the Invisible Energy, and many others. In the telling of this story, I will use any one of these terms to refer to Source.

I have also come to understand that Source is recognized and acknowledged in different ways and through different practices across cultures. In some cultures, mostly the indigenous cultures around the world, recognition and acknowledgment of Source is an integral part of the way people live—seamlessly incorporating the spiritual realm into their everyday activities. In most so-called developed societies, however, recognition and acknowledgment of Source tends to be through more structured and organized religious practices and belief systems. Whether the recognition and acknowledgment of Source is through ritual indigenous practices or through structured religious practices is, in my mind, only a minor point. To me, the important element to realize is that it is the same Source we human beings are already rooted in, regardless of the practices we may or may not use to recognize and acknowledge it.

I feel compelled to share my story to encourage others to seek answers to the basic questions of life. My experiences fuel my belief that the power to restore love, joy, and creativity in our physical world lies in the answers we find in our hearts, and practice in our lives.

One more person searching to understand his or her true nature and role in this world and ultimately taking action and sharing his or her gift with the world is one person closer to the realization of humanity's oneness with each other, oneness with nature, and oneness with everything in creation. It is one step closer to a world in which love, joy, gratitude, appreciation, kindness, generosity, and creativity are the dominant human expressions. I believe this will happen as we, one by one, consciously access Source and allow it to fuel our lives.

Without this shift in consciousness, the human race, I believe, is destined to continue to manifest the chaotic conditions we currently see around us, which threaten to destroy the world that we know. We see chaos everywhere in its various gradations: disrespect, unkindness, inconsiderateness, self-importance, malice, greed, corruption, hostility, hatred, callousness, bullying, aggression, destruction, cruelty, violence, rape, murder, genocide, all the way to wars between nations. The suffering that this chaos fosters cannot go on. It is up to each and every one of us to do our part to end the chaos and the suffering.

One more thing I want to say: It doesn't matter at what stage of life we awaken—that is, become aware of our true nature as spirits arising from Source to express in the world. It doesn't matter whether our awakening comes in our youth, middle age, or twilight years. It also doesn't matter what we have or haven't done in the past, what we have or haven't achieved in our lives, or what we have or haven't accumulated as part of our possessions. It doesn't even matter whether we, or those around us, judge our lives to be successes or failures. The important thing to grasp is that from the moment of our awakening, from the moment of our recognition of Source as our true home, we realize what we are and why we are here in this physical world at this particular time.

From the moment we awaken, we are redeemed. In that moment, we have the opportunity to let all the mistakes and misgivings of our past fade away, to let all the burdens that we carry disappear, and to let all the grudges we hold within dissolve into the nothingness that they are. In that moment, we have the opportunity to heal. In other words, we have the opportunity to start new lives with new identities as spiritual beings rooted in Source. If we choose to heal—that is, if we choose to let the past fade away, the burdens disappear, and the grudges dissolve—then we will begin to see how we fit into the picture of the whole, and we will come to know and appreciate our uniqueness and the value of our lives in the scheme of creation. At every step of the way, we will know that we are traveling on a guided journey to the tomorrow we desire.

Aren't we all seeking this type of clarity for our lives?

Perhaps I am jumping ahead of myself again. Let me step back and share the journey I have traveled thus far. It has not been an easy road, or a direct one for that matter, but it has been a journey worth traveling.

THE HOMECOMING

In September of 1992, I flew home to Zimbabwe. I had just completed my doctoral degree in England, and my next adventure was to travel to the United States where I would continue my quest for knowledge. At twenty-seven years of age, I was full of hope and optimism for my future. I thought the research fellowship I had secured at a university in San Francisco was exactly the right opportunity for this time in my life. I was thankful for the doors that were easily opening for me to pursue my dreams. Before going to America, though, I went home to visit my family. I had been away for about four years, and I missed them terribly.

The overnight flight from London to Harare was uneventful. The British Airways Boeing 747 jet that ferried us from London Heathrow Airport landed at Harare International Airport at around eight in the morning. I collected my two carry-on bags from the overhead compartment, hoisting the bigger bag over my right shoulder and dangling the smaller bag in my left hand. I followed the other passengers as we filed out of the plane. As I stepped through the aircraft doorway onto the landing area of the boarding stairs, I felt a dry still heat—a sharp contrast to the cool humid conditions of London that I had just left behind.

I heard shouts coming from a viewing area on the rooftop of one of the airport terminal buildings, and I turned my gaze in the direction of the shouting voices. Shading my eyes from the glistening sun with my right hand, I spotted a large group of people frantically waving from the rooftop, and then I heard my name called out.

"Yeukai Mandizvidza!" one voice shouted above the rest.

"Yeukai!" followed another.

"Auntie Yeu!" a child's voice squealed.

Squinting my eyes for a better focus, I recognized the people waving and shouting my name—they were members of my family. A large grin broke across my face, and I lifted my right hand high above my head and waved energetically. I continued to smile and wave as I descended the staircase onto the tarmac and walked toward the main building of the airport terminal.

I went through immigration and then walked to the baggage claim area where I retrieved my baggage—one small suitcase with my belongings and two oversized suitcases with gifts for my family. At customs, the officer—a smartly dressed young woman about my age—completed examining my bags and bade me a warm welcome home.

I pushed the cart with my luggage along a wide corridor leading to the arrivals hall. Turning a corner at the end of the corridor and passing through a doorway, I found my family waiting for me. My mother—*Mai*—and father—*Baba*—stood at the front of the group, beaming smiles radiating from their faces. Behind them were my two sisters—my elder sister Mary (Sis Mary) and my younger sister Mugumo. A few paces behind my sisters were my elder brother Martin, his wife Sara, and their three boys who were sporting matching bob haircuts. The older boy, about seven years of age, was the spitting image of Martin. The identical twin boys, about five, seemed to take after Sara.

My six younger brothers—Matthew, Maxwell, Maurice, Melvin, Marshall, and Mark—stood in a group just behind Martin and his family. Sis Mary's husband Jonah stood to the side, holding a beautiful baby girl to his chest. Latching on to Jonah's trouser leg was his son, a shy, handsome boy of about five.

My gaze took in the rest of my family members standing around: several aunts, uncles, and cousins. Of course, the word "cousin" here is as it is used in Western cultures. This is different from my culture, where my male cousins are considered my brothers for all intents and purposes. The same is true for my female cousins—they are my sisters.

Amid shrills of excitement, I greeted each of my family members in turn, some with hugs, some with handshakes, some with a pat on the back. We must have appeared like a spectacle to the other people in the arrivals hall. That didn't bother me, and it didn't seem to bother any of my family members either.

My brother Matthew took the cart with my luggage and started for the doors leading out of the airport terminal building. We all followed him. Outside, we filed into cars and drove from the airport in a convoy that was about eight or nine cars long. I was in the fifth car of the convoy, a sedan that belonged to Sara—I called her *Maiguru* Sara, using the relational term for addressing the wife of one's elder brother. She was at the wheel. In the passenger seat beside her was Martin—I called him *Mukoma* Martin, using the relational term for addressing one's elder brother. I sat between my parents in the backseat. A thought came to my mind: If someone were to add a motorbike or two to our convoy, then I would be forgiven for feeling like a dignitary. I hadn't expected this many people to show up to welcome me at the airport. I was touched and grateful for my family's display of support.

I drank in the passing scenery as we drove from the airport toward the city. The immaculately maintained paved roads were lined with neatly trimmed trees, manicured lawns, and pruned collections of colorful flowering shrubs. In the distance, shiny tall buildings dotted the skyline of the city center. We bypassed the city center and headed toward the northern suburbs of Harare where *Mukoma* Martin and his family now lived.

When I had left the country four years earlier, *Mukoma* Martin and his family were still living in a tiny apartment in one of the multi-residential complexes closer to the city center—in the area called the Avenues. About two years after I left, I received a letter from him informing me that he and his wife had finally bought their dream home in the affluent northern suburbs of Harare. Before Zimbabwe gained independence, these northern suburbs were reserved for white people only. But now, after independence, a lot of young black professionals could afford to buy houses in these exclusive neighborhoods.

Both *Mukoma* Martin and *Maiguru* Sara were successful professionals. He was a lawyer and she was a bank executive. I was happy that they were now enjoying the fruits of their hard work. When we were growing up, *Mukoma* Martin had always been a hard worker and did exceptionally well in school. He had earned a law degree at the local university and started working for one of the prestigious law firms in Harare, then finally opened his own law practice—fulfilling his long-held dream. I had looked up to him as my role model.

I was impressed by the homes in my brother's neighborhood. Looking through the wrought-iron gates in front of the properties, I got a peek at what lay behind the six-foot block dura walls. Gravel driveways led to single-story bungalows surrounded by lush lawns and colorful flowerbeds.

Maiguru Sara turned the car from the main street, following the convoy of cars through wrought-iron gates and along an expansive driveway lined with low-lying green shrubs. The main house was straight ahead. It was a modern ranch-style brick building with a red tile roof and a covered front patio with mahogany railings to match the mahogany of the front double doors. A trimmed green lawn covered most of the grounds, bordered by flowerbeds. A vegetable garden sat behind the house slightly to the right. Past the vegetable garden, at a distance of several yards behind the main house were two separate smaller dwellings—living quarters for the housemaid and gardener.

The car rolled to a stop in front of the main house. As we were getting out of the car, the front doors burst open and more relatives spilled onto the driveway. Another round of greetings started, repeating the scene at the airport. Among the relatives were two women, one introduced as Matthew's wife and the other as Maxwell's wife. I noticed both were pregnant.

The front doors opened into a small foyer that led to a large sunken living room with elegant furnishings. An eight-piece L-shaped leather couch set ran on two sides of the room, framing a sitting area with a long glass-topped table in the middle. An entertainment center made of dark wood took up one wall of the room, holding a twenty-seven inch TV, a multi-component stereo set, and a huge collection of music cassettes and videotapes. Lamps with wide shades stood on end tables. Framed photographs dotted the freshly painted walls—portraits of my brother and his wife on their wedding day, my brother in his graduation gown, his wife in her graduation gown, and their three boys at various stages of their lives.

Although the living room was large, I didn't think it could hold all the people present. More chairs were brought from other rooms; even the patio chairs were brought inside. People started finding spots to sit down. Most women sat on the carpeted floor, leaving the chairs and couches for the men. I spotted my mother, who had sat on the floor at the front of the room, and went over to sit by her side. My two sisters joined us on the floor. The crowd spilled over into the dining area adjacent to the sitting room.

I knew everyone was getting ready for the traditional greeting ritual that involved exchanging a set of standard statements. I could see that it was going to take a while for members of my family to settle down. Children were running around tripping over things, and even some adults would settle down in one spot and then get up to find a different spot to settle. As I quietly watched what was happening, I took the opportunity to mentally go over the traditional greeting ritual.

I recalled what we were taught about the greeting ritual when we were small children growing up in the rural areas. We were taught that for Shona-speaking people, this ritual exchange of greetings is a form of showing care, concern, and respect for one another—applauded virtues in our culture. The other revered virtues in our culture are appreciation, compassion, kindness, generosity, and hospitality. We were taught that these virtues are a part of a larger vision to promote harmonious living among our people and the people of the rest of the world, thereby making the world a better place for everyone to live.

In the Shona-greeting ritual, we follow a certain protocol when inquiring about someone's well-being. As I had grown up performing this ritual all my life, I knew exactly what to do. I knew that I had to start by asking after the well-being of my father, followed by asking after the well-being of my mother, and then work my way through my uncles, aunts, and so on. As a sign of respect, I would address my father as *Moyondizvo,* which is the principal praise name for the people of our clan, whose totem is *Moyo*.

Let me briefly explain about principal praise names and totems.

In our culture, each family belongs to a clan, which is a group of people who can trace their paternal lineage to the same ancestor. Our family, the Mandizvidza family, belongs to the Rozvi clan; therefore, I am a Rozvi. Each clan has a social marker called a totem, a *mutupo,* which was adopted by the founding ancestor of that clan and is inherited by every member of the clan—both men and women. The *mutupo* can be an animal, but it can also be an object or an organ of the body. In the case of our Rozvi clan, our *mutupo* is *Moyo* (the heart). In a traditional setting, members of a clan—both men and women—can be addressed by their *mutupo* as a term of respect or endearment. For our clan, men can be addressed as *Moyo* and women as *maMoyo*.

The organizational structure can get a little intricate, as oftentimes there are different clans with the same *mutupo*. This is because, even though families may share an ancestor, somewhere along the paternal lineage there was a split into two or more factions due to feuding within the family, migration patterns, or the clan becoming too big. Clans that share the same *mutupo* are differentiated by an additional social marker called a principal praise name, a *chidawo*. The *chidawo* for our Rozvi clan is *Moyondizvo*. There is also the *Njanja* clan whose *mutupo* is *Moyo*, like ours, but their *chidawo* is *Sinyoro*. Only men, but not women, can be addressed by their clan's *chidawo* as a sign of respect or endearment. That is why I would address my father as *Moyondizvo* in the greeting ritual.

The noisy clearing of a throat broke my reverie. I looked around and noticed that my family members had settled down and were now looking at me with anticipation. I knew someone was giving me a signal to start the greeting ritual, so I addressed my father, who was sitting on a couch across the room from me.

"*Makadini, Moyondizvo?* (How are you, *Moyondizvo*?)" I said, looking at my father and clapping my hands softly and rhythmically, a gesture of respect when addressing one's elders.

"I am well, *maMoyo*, if you are well," my father responded in our language.

"I am very well."

"How did you leave the place where you are coming from?" my father asked.

I replied that everyone and everything was well where I was coming from.

Then I turned to my mother beside me, saying, "*Makadini, Shava?*" My mother is from the *Chihera* clan, whose *mutupo* is *Shava* (eland).

"I am well, *maMoyo*, if you are well."

"I am very well."

"Were you treated well and were you happy in England, my child?" my mother asked. I replied that I was treated very well and that I was very happy in England.

I proceeded to exchange greetings with my aunts, and their respective husbands. Next, I exchanged greetings with my brothers, my male cousins, Sis Mary and her husband, and my female cousins who were older than me. After we completed this phase, it was time for me to give an opportunity to those who, by custom, were expected to ask after my well-being. My sister Mugu—we called her by the shortened version of her name Mugumo, which means last born—asked after my well-being first. And then my brothers' wives, my younger cousins, and the children followed suit.

Even the baby, my sister's eight-month-old, seemed to get the idea. Smashing her hands together and clapping, she looked in my general direction and blubbered, "Ta-a, ta-a! To-o, To-o! Ta-a, ta-a!" Sis Mary translated the baby talk, saying that the baby was asking after my well-being. So, I responded appropriately. There was laughter all around.

It took about fifteen minutes to complete the greeting ritual. It felt good to be surrounded by family and to take time to connect with every individual present through the familiar greeting ritual. I felt like I was back in the fold of my family again.

After the greetings, I distributed the gifts I had brought. Two weeks before my journey home, I had visited a London flea market and bought items in bulk at a huge discount. I had expected to give presents to many people, as this was customary, but I hadn't expected such a huge turnout. I was glad that it seemed almost everyone received something—even if it was a pair of socks or a small matchbox car. People seemed happy with what they received and thanked me for the gifts. There were even a few gifts left over for the other relatives I would be meeting in the coming days. After the gifts were distributed, the party started. As I had expected, my return home was a cause for celebration.

My parents announced that they had invited more relatives and friends for a celebration at our rural homestead, our *musha*, which was located in a village in the communal areas of Buhera District, in the southeastern region of Zimbabwe.

It wasn't just my homecoming that we were celebrating. My father said that many good things had happened while I was away to warrant a big celebration. The family had grown. My younger brothers, Matthew and Maxwell, had gotten married, and both their wives were expecting babies soon. Sis Mary had welcomed her second child, the baby girl. Together with *Mukoma* Martin's three boys, my parents already had five grandchildren. With two more on the way, this was a good head start on the many grandchildren that my parents had their hearts set on. The rest of my siblings, who were still in school, were all doing very well—my younger brothers Maurice, Melvin, Marshall, and Mark and my sister Mugu.

Indeed, there was cause to gather and rejoice, and my family had waited till I was home so that I could share in the festivities. It seemed, in the next few days, there would be more relatives to greet and rejoice with.

For the Shona-speaking people, and especially in the rural communities, the word "relative" can mean anyone who lives within a few miles' radius of your homestead. More often than not, you find that you are related to everyone you know. The custom used to be that when you met someone for the first time, you greeted each other and then discussed your family trees to figure out how you were related. By the time you bid each other farewell, you would no longer be strangers; you were long-lost relatives who had just found each other again. At that rate, one could find themselves with a lot of relatives in pretty short order, and everyone was invited to family gatherings.

I was excited about going to our rural homestead because I knew I would see my grandmother. Grandma didn't like to travel, especially on long journeys such as the one from our village to Harare. She used to say that car rides jarred her old bones.

Later that afternoon, *Mukoma* Martin invited me to accompany him into the city center to buy groceries to take to the village for the celebrations, and some of my brothers and male cousins came along for the ride. We drove to the city center in *Mukoma* Martin's twin-cab truck. My brothers and cousins kept a jovial conversation going, mostly about sports. I didn't pay much attention to their conversation, my focus was on the passing scenery. As we approached the city center, I noticed that the traffic was a little heavier than I remembered. Cars, trucks, taxis, commuter minivans, and city buses clogged the roads, slowing us down.

I didn't mind the delay, as it gave me time to take in the familiar surroundings of downtown Harare. We had passed the residential apartment complexes in the Avenues area and were now surrounded by tall buildings housing storefronts, restaurants, banks, and offices. A few men in blue uniforms rode bicycles, weaving in and out of the slow-moving traffic. I knew these were messengers who delivered packages between buildings. Men smartly dressed in three-piece suits and women stylishly dressed in skirt-and-jacket suits walked in and out of office buildings. Shoppers emerged from shops lugging bags. Vendors hawked their wares to passersby.

My brother parked the truck and we took a leisurely stroll along the streets of Harare, before heading to the supermarket. As I looked around, I was impressed by how clean and well maintained the city center looked. The jacaranda trees and the flowerbeds that lined the streets blended in well with the modern buildings.

The supermarket, housed in a long rumbling building at the heart of the city, was bustling with people. *Mukoma* Martin picked a shopping cart, and we walked through the aisles lined with packed shelves and overflowing produce bins. The supermarket was just as well stocked as any of the high-end supermarkets one found in England. The only difference was perhaps the limited variety of each item. Whereas one was likely to see ten or more varieties of coffee on display in a supermarket in England, here one had perhaps only two or three varieties to choose from.

We filled up the shopping cart, paid for the groceries, and went back to the truck and drove toward the south side of the city, heading to the industrial complexes that housed various manufacturing operations. We stopped at one company and bought several crates of bottled beer—Castle and Lion Lager. Then we stopped at another company and bought several crates of bottled sodas, a mixture of Coca-Cola, Fanta, and Sprite. *Mukoma* Martin mentioned that it was cheaper to buy the beer and sodas directly from the bottling companies at wholesale prices than to buy from the supermarkets. Of course, it helped that he had friends at both companies who gave him favorable discounts. With the grocery shopping completed, we drove back to his house to continue with the celebrations.

The next day, we left the city about midmorning in *Mukoma* Martin's truck, heading southeast on the Harare-to-Mutare highway on our way to the village. The truck was packed to capacity. *Mukoma* Martin was driving, with my father sitting in the front passenger seat beside him. I was sharing the back seat with Mugu, who was sitting in the middle, and my mother, who was sitting on the other side. More family members sat in the cargo section of the truck, packed among the bags of groceries and crates of beer and sodas that we were taking to the village.

A convoy of cars was going to leave Harare later that evening, bringing more family members who had to work that day. Sis Mary and her family were going to drive down in their mid-size sedan. *Maiguru* Sara was bringing her boys and other relatives in her car. A few more cars would bring the aunts, uncles, and cousins. Still more relatives would travel on long-distance buses that ferried people between the city and the rural areas.

As we left Harare behind, I took in the familiar Zimbabwean countryside. A prominent feature of these parts was the large stretches of commercial farms bordering both sides of the paved highway. Meticulously kept pastures rolled for miles and miles, with numerous sprinklers puffing sprays of water, keeping the grass green. Herds of fat cattle grazed lazily, not paying much attention to the passing traffic. On occasion, a rider and his horse galloped in the distance.

On some farms, the main residences were visible from the road—rambling ranch houses surrounded by brightly colored bougainvillea shrubs and sprawling lush lawns. Most of these residences had large glistening swimming pools and paved tennis courts, and some even had racetracks for horses—a prominent display of the affluence of the farm owners. These farms belonged to the rich European colonial settlers, the white people—the *varungu*. At the periphery of the farms, barely visible from the road, one could see shanty shacks—the farm compounds where black farm workers and their families lived.

In between the commercial farms was low-lying bush dotted with granite boulders jutting from the earth and standing like regal sentinels. Further back, grayish-blue hills graced the horizons. This was beautiful countryside.

We passed the towns of Rusape and Nyazura, turning off the Harare-to-Mutare highway to head south toward the small mining town of Dorowa. After driving a few miles out of Nyazura, the rich farmlands interspaced with low-lying bush gave way to the open communal areas inhabited by the majority of the population of my country. Sparse vegetation—yellowish-brown grass, scruffy thorn bushes, and scattered leafless trees—dotted the arid stretches of mostly sandy soils.

Amid this desolate landscape sat clusters of dwellings, homesteads for the people living in these communal areas. About a decade or so ago, the dwellings in the communal areas were mostly collections of tiny round grass-thatched huts on small cleared parcels of ground—two on one homestead, three on another, and perhaps even up to five round huts on a few homesteads. Now, another type of structure had been added to some of the homesteads—a four-cornered brick house with a zinc, asbestos, or tile roof. Most were tiny, perhaps just one or two rooms. But a few homesteads had large four-cornered houses—each with perhaps three or four rooms. Some had fire-baked red brick walls; others were plastered and painted yellow or blue or green, with black trim. I knew that a four-cornered house at a homestead was a status symbol and a sign of progress. It marked the dwelling of a successful family.

By some of the homesteads, children stood in the dusty yards, cheerfully waving to passing vehicles. Adults could be seen tending small vegetable gardens on the outskirts of the homesteads. Groups of young boys watched over small herds of cattle and goats that were scrounging for scraps of grass and the rare foliage on the bushes.

We passed several newly built schools, hospitals, and rural township expansions— popularly known as growth points. I viewed these building developments as one of the many visible signs that life for people living in communal areas was changing for the better.

I gave credit for the positive signs of development to the black-majority government that had ruled our country since independence. I thought that the government was leading the country in the right direction with regards to raising the living standards of people in rural communities. The optimist in me thought that perhaps in another ten years or so, the plight of the villagers whose homesteads we were passing would be much improved, and that perhaps the economic gap between the white farmers and black villagers would start to narrow.

As we drove across the countryside, my father kept us entertained with accounts of his adventures in the old days when he used to travel these parts of the country as a young man. On a couple of occasions, my mother gently corrected my father on a few facts. You see, my father had a tendency to embellish, all in the spirit of telling a good story. We had a good laugh at the stories my father told.

Mukoma Martin turned the truck off the paved highway onto a wide gravel road. After traveling for about six or seven miles on the gravel road, he took another turn onto a narrow trail that looked more like a footpath than a road. This was the trail that led to our village. The truck slowly negotiated around the many obstacles in its way—tree stumps, remnants of broken-down wagons, and even goats and their herders.

After about half a mile on the trail, the truck crested a small elevation and I got a full view of our homestead across the river valley. As if he was giving me a moment to take in my childhood home, *Mukoma* Martin hit the brakes and brought the truck to a stop for a minute. A flutter pulsed in my stomach as I stared at our homestead in the distance.

Our home stood on a clearing of beaten earth, a little less than half an acre. I saw the familiar collection of building structures, each serving a specific function. The largest building was a four-cornered brick house with a red tile roof. The big house served as the main sleeping quarters. To the left of the sleeping house was a large grass-thatched round hut made of brick. This was the cooking hut and also served as a gathering place for family meals. Another large round hut stood next to the kitchen—sort of a "spillover" sleeping hut whenever a lot of people stayed at the homestead.

To the right of the sleeping house was a storage hut that stood on four huge stone stilts, raising the hut about three feet off the ground. Called a *hozi*, the storage hut was a sort of granary used to store harvested crops like shelled maize (corn), peanuts, roundnuts, and beans, for feeding the family during the year. Next to the *hozi* stood my grandmother's little brick, grass-thatched hut that she used both for cooking and sleeping. Located some distance away on the western side of the homestead were the toilets—two rooms, one for men and the other for women.

I took in the surrounding neighborhood. To the north of our homestead was a hill that served both to break the strong winds of the dry seasons and as a source of firewood for the community. To the east were our nearest neighbors' three building structures—a cooking hut, a sleeping hut, and a *hozi* just like ours. To the south was another neighbor's place, and beyond that was a homestead belonging to my uncle, my grandparents' eldest son.

Mukoma Martin slowly rolled the truck down the slope to the makeshift bridge that traversed the river and pushed it up the incline to our home, coming to a stop in front of the wooden gate that marked the entrance to our homestead. I took a moment to just sit and observe the scene in front of me.

The place was bustling with activity. It looked like a busy marketplace on a Saturday morning. It seemed as if half the community was already there, no doubt to help prepare for the festivities.

Men were driving teams of yoked oxen hauling logs for firewood, some were chopping the logs to stoke the fires, and some were constructing makeshift bathing areas to be used by the crowds. Women were cooking, some were cleaning dishes, and some were carrying buckets of water from a borehole located a few hundred feet from the edge of the yard, bringing the water to a temporary outdoor cooking area set up beside the cooking hut.

The outdoor cooking area was the staging place for brewing the traditional local beer, known as *ngoto* in our part of the country. It took about seven days to brew the *ngoto*. The process was initiated by mixing cornmeal porridge with a meal made from ground, sprouted millet. My mother was well known for brewing the best-tasting *ngoto* in our area. If memory served me well, on that day, the women were "burning the beer," which essentially means boiling the beer mixture for hours to reduce its water content and get it to the ideal alcohol concentration before it was further processed to be ready for drinking the next day. Steam rose from two forty-four-gallon steel drums set beside burning logs spitting roaring flames. The air was filled with the familiar earthy aroma of the brewing beer.

The crowd flocked toward the truck as we piled out, and a round of greetings and introductions ensued. It was a little overwhelming seeing everyone all at once—the familiar faces from my childhood, new faces of relatives who had joined the family by marriage or other means, and children born while I was away. In all the confusion, we gravitated toward my grandmother's hut.

I entered Grandma's hut first, followed by the rest of the family members who had arrived from Harare with me and a few family members who had been waiting at the homestead. Even though it was the middle of the day, the inside of Grandma's hut was slightly dark. The hut had no windows, and the narrow door didn't let in much light. I knew Grandma preferred it that way.

As my eyes adjusted to the poor lighting in the room, I saw Grandma's small frame. She was sitting in exactly the same spot where she had been sitting when I said goodbye to her four years earlier as I left to go overseas, huddled in front of the fireplace in the middle of her hut. And she appeared just about the same too. A crocheted woolen hat, which she called her *nguwani*, covered her head. An old shawl, now paper thin and faded, draped around her thin shoulders. As I looked at her wrinkled face, I saw her eyes peering at me from deep within their pockets. Upon recognizing me, she lifted her frail arms in welcome, and I knelt down so she could reach my shoulders. I felt the distinct tremor in her body as her arms folded me in a gentle embrace. She started sobbing in joy; I did too. After a while, Grandma let go of my shoulders and lifted one corner of her shawl, wiping the tears streaming down her face. She held up another corner of the shawl to me. I reached for it, wiping the tears streaming down my face.

As people crowded into the small hut, I sat down on the floor next to Grandma, looking at the familiar surroundings. A black clay pot sat on the fireplace, a configuration of three mud blocks joined by crisscrossed metal bars. At the front of the hut, opposite the doorway, was a built-in earthen platform—a *huva*—a common feature in cooking huts in rural areas. My grandmother's *huva* was about two feet high, one foot deep, and four feet long, running along the walls of the round hut. Large decorated clay pots with short necks and outward-slanted openings sat on top of the *huva*. The clay pots were arranged in three columns, each column with three pots delicately balanced one on top of the other. A built-in earthen bench, less than a foot high and about a foot deep, ran the perimeter of the right side of the hut, from the *huva* to just before the doorway. That was the seating area for men, and I could see a dozen or so men and boys squished together on the bench. The women sat on the cement floor.

Grandma's bedding was neatly piled behind the door—two goatskin mats, three blankets, and a ragged-looking tied bundle that my grandmother used as her pillow. She called the pillow her *mutsago* and she made it by scrounging around for scraps of cloth and tying the pieces to the bundle. I smiled to myself, remembering the running family joke when we were growing up: If you couldn't find an item of your clothing, you first went to check Grandma's *mutsago*. If you found the item tied to her *mutsago,* that meant Grandma thought the item was too worn out or was in some way inappropriate for you to still be wearing it. And that was the end of it—once a clothing item joined the *mutsago*, you knew you would not get it back.

I asked after my Grandma's well-being, addressing her by her *mutupo* of *Mhara* (impala) of the *Mbuya Chikonamombe* clan. My grandmother responded that overall she was well, but that she tended to get back pains in the mornings and leg pains at night. She asked me if I had been treated well in the foreign lands where I had been, and I responded that I had been treated well.

"I am glad that you were led to find your way back home," Grandma said in our language, her voice soft and shaky. She was smiling, her already wrinkled face creasing even more and the lone brown tooth in her mouth sticking out. Her eyes still sparkled with tears.

The greeting ritual continued until everyone in the hut had connected with everyone else, according to custom. When the greeting rounds completed, the conversation turned to a discussion on whether the rains would arrive early that year. Some people were of the mind that the rains would arrive early, but others believed that the rains would arrive late. I knew this was a discussion with no definitive ending, so I took the opportunity to do one more thing. I had one more stop to make. I stood up, excusing myself, and went outside and walked a few yards from Grandma's hut to visit the grave of my grandfather, *Sekuru* Mandizvidza. The grave was on a low-lying flat granite surface—a *ruware*—at the edge of the yard, opposite the temporary outdoor cooking area. I sat down on the warm rock surface, facing the grave, and paid my respects in silence, with my eyes closed.

After I said what I needed to say, I opened my eyes but continued to sit beside my grandfather's grave. Memories of my childhood came to me, one at a time, weaving in and out of my mind.

As far back as I could remember—perhaps to when I was about four or five years old—Grandma had always lived at our homestead and watched over it for us. At first, it was her and *Sekuru* Mandizvidza. After *Sekuru* passed away many years back, it had just been Grandma.

My parents were primary school teachers, and they mainly worked at Catholic mission schools. Over the years, they worked at different schools across the country. As young children, my siblings and I had traveled with my parents and attended primary school wherever they were stationed at any given time. When each of us completed primary school, we were sent to Catholic boarding schools for our secondary education. Later on, each of us attended the university in Harare. So we had lived in many different parts of the country, and had many exciting adventures. But what I had cherished the most growing up was coming home to the village during the school holidays. This was our home base, and Grandma watched over it for us.

By our estimation, Grandma was in her late nineties. We weren't sure of her exact age as records were not kept during the period that she was born. We knew she was born and grew up during the time when European white settlers, *varungu*, were claiming land across what later became colonial Rhodesia, which is modern-day Zimbabwe. In the rare occasions that Grandma chose to talk about the past, she recounted her experiences as her family, and many other families, were driven away from the settlements in the lush valleys of the country. She said the valleys had fertile soils for growing crops, green pastures for grazing animals, numerous rivers abundant with fish, and expansive plains teeming with game. She said that in those days, people only took what they needed to survive and there was always plenty for everyone.

Then Grandma would describe how the white settlers came with guns and chased the native families from the valley settlements and drove them to barren areas with no fertile soils, no green pastures, no fish, and very little game. It didn't matter that the tribes had lived in the valleys for generations and had the graves of their dead to prove it, she said. Grandma would tear up when she recounted the turmoil within the tribes as they had watched the white settlers destroy sacred burial grounds, dam up rivers, and burn down forests. It seemed the whites had no reverence for the sacredness of the land and its people; all they cared about was making way for their sprawling ranches.

As I had learned the history of my country in school, I had found out that with time, indigenous people were finally restricted, by law, to live in these infertile land parcels that later came to be called native reserves. According to the colonial laws, blacks were not allowed to own land anywhere else outside these native reserves. This is something I knew very well because I grew up within the native reserve system, which was abolished only after Zimbabwe gained independence, following the liberation war. In fact, land was one of the major reasons for the armed struggle that liberated our country from white-minority rule.

Despite my grandmother's advanced age, she was of sound mind and had an excellent memory. She had given birth to ten children, but only six—five boys and one girl—had survived to marry and have their own families. My father was the fourth of the surviving siblings. He had elected to take care of his parents from the time he started working, since he was the most educated of the six children, having completed a teacher's training course—which, in those days of white-minority rule, was considered a great achievement for a black person. Additionally, both he and my mother worked and earned good salaries, which had afforded our family a decent life by village standards. When we were growing up, my parents could afford to feed and clothe us, and could also afford to pay for each of us to be educated at good schools.

Grandma insisted on living alone though, assuring my parents that she didn't need them to pay anyone to look after her when they were away teaching school. In her opinion, the young boys and girls who were paid to look after her caused her more trouble than they were worth. My parents had finally struck a compromise with my grandmother. Grandma had agreed that while she was alone at the homestead, one of my cousins, the daughter of my uncle who lived nearby, would come to help her with some of the harder chores such as fetching water from the borehole. Grandma still tended her small plot of land and grew her own corn and vegetables. She also gathered her own firewood, and she cooked and cleaned for herself.

I was startled out of my reverie by the voices of women raised in song. As I listened, I recognized the familiar song. I turned around and saw that the women had just started filtering the beer, working in an assembly line.

The steel drums in which the beer had been boiled had been removed from the fire and moved to the "filtering station" set up under the eaves of our cooking house. One woman was pouring the beer mixture into a large hessian sack that two other women held over another steel drum. The thin brew flowed through the sack into the holding steel drum, and the dregs remaining in the sack were collected in buckets and dumped onto the compost heap behind the toilets. The filtered beer was poured into clay pots that were carried into the *hozi*. I knew that in the *hozi*, the beer was left overnight to complete the final maturation step before it was ready for drinking the next day.

The song the women were singing was to help keep up the rhythm and morale as they worked. It was a song of *mushandira pamwe*, a song of working together. I joined in the sing-along with the women, mouthing the words that roughly translated to:

Mothers and fathers of this land
Let us unite and work together
Girls and boys of this land
Let us unite and work together
Children of this land
Let us unite and work together
For when we unite and work together

The job becomes light and life becomes light
Oye-e! Oye-e! Oye-re-re-e-e!
Let us unite and work together
Oye-e! Oye-e! Oye-re-re-e-e!
Let us unite and work together

I watched the assembly line for a few more minutes. Then I got up and walked back to the crowd. I joined everyone in preparing for the next day's celebration. I helped clean and prepare the entrails of a goat that had been slaughtered to feed the crowd that evening, and I helped cook and serve the evening meal. More relatives arrived from Harare and other parts of the country. The evening meal was a boisterous affair, with food plates being passed back and forth. It was hard to keep track of it all. Amid the chaos, everyone got fed and everyone was happy.

After dinner, I joined the other women in cleaning the dishes by the moonlight. When the evening chores were finished, we sat down to rest. It was time for my relatives to ask me about my adventures in England, and I was happy to share my experiences with them.

I related some of my early fumbles as I tried to fit into the English society. Even though I had grown up under white rule in Rhodesia and was aware of some of the "dos" and "don'ts" of the English society, I still made some mistakes as I tried to adjust to life in England. I recounted the first time I met my graduate advisor, the professor in whose laboratory I was to conduct research for my doctoral thesis. We had exchanged letters before my arrival in England. In those letters, I had told my advisor that I was looking forward to working in his laboratory under his guidance. He had responded warmly, saying he was looking forward to my joining his group. In my naiveté, I thought the ice had been broken—so to speak. I was wrong.

My first face-to-face encounter with my graduate advisor was at a social event the department held for the incoming class of students to meet their faculty advisors. I had arrived at the venue early, found my name tag, and stuck it to my chest. Then I started searching for my advisor. Upon spotting him by his name tag, I walked over and extended my right hand to him for a handshake.

"Hello, I am Yeukai Mandizvidza," I said, "your new graduate student. I am very excited to meet you."

My advisor slowly looked me over from top to bottom and, with his left hand holding a glass of wine and his right hand stuck in his pocket, he finally met my gaze and said, "Have we been formally introduced?" Then he broke the gaze and glanced to his left, taking a sip of wine from his glass.

I was taken aback by my advisor's response. A retort formed in my mind. *This is what I'm trying to do. I'm trying to introduce myself to you so that we can consider ourselves formally introduced.*

But of course I didn't utter the retort in my mind—not out loud anyway. I just smiled sheepishly and awkwardly withdrew my hand and stuck it in my skirt pocket. Luckily, a smartly dressed lady standing nearby had witnessed this embarrassing exchange. She took a few steps toward me and leaned over to read my name tag.

"Can you tell me how to correctly pronounce your name?" she said, with a kind smile on her face.

Speaking slowly, I enunciated my full name for her, and she repeated it back to me.

"Did I get it right?" she asked. I nodded with a warm smile, surprised by how well she had pronounced my name.

Then she turned to my advisor and performed the formal introductions. Now that we had been formally introduced, my advisor shook my hand and said he was delighted to make my acquaintance and welcomed me to his laboratory.

On hearing his words, I had to struggle to keep my eyebrows in place as they threated to shoot to the top of my head. Instead, I gave him an appropriate response. When I turned to thank the lady who had come to my rescue, I noticed she had moved on and was engaged in a conversation with a group of people. I settled for murmuring a silent thank you in her direction.

I did get used to my advisor's sometimes cold and dismissive mannerisms. I was assured that his standoffish attitude was a product of good breeding or something to that effect. To my surprise, I ended up enjoying working with him and the other students in his laboratory.

I also related an incident that happened the first time I took a commuter bus from the university campus to one of the outer suburbs where I was visiting a friend. As I was about to get on the bus, the driver—an elderly man—greeted me warmly.

"Hello, *luv*. Where to this morning?"

As I stood still with my mind racing at a hundred miles an hour, I thought: *Who does this man think he is, calling me love? Who does he think I am? Is he mistaking me for someone else? I have never met this man in my life before, and here he is acting as though he knows me affectionately.*

"Hurry up, *luv*. I will take you where you want to go," the driver said, a broad smile lighting up his face and revealing a prominent gap between his top front teeth. His genuine and open friendliness won me over, and I got on the bus.

"Here, *luv*, you look lost, come sit by me," said an elderly lady who was sitting in a seat directly behind the driver. She scooted over, patting the seat next to her.

As it turned out, the driver was married to the woman who had invited me to sit by her side. I got to know the couple, Harold and Theresa, very well. We became good friends. Of the three Christmases that I spent in England, they invited me to their home, and I had Christmas dinners with their family.

I shared many other stories from my time in England. My relatives loved the stories and kept asking for more. We stayed up till the wee hours of the morning. In the end, I thanked those who had written me letters when I was away. I told them how those letters had kept me going in moments I had felt homesick. By the time I went to bed, I was exhausted and collapsed into a deep sleep. I knew I was home.

Village Celebration

I woke up to the crow of a cockerel. My body ached from the physical exertion of the day before, but I got up ready for more work. I exchanged morning greetings with relatives, some of whom had been awake and hard at work for hours already.

The day started with the most important event of the celebration—a thanksgiving to our ancestral spirits and a recognition of *Musiki*—the Creator—one of the many names used by Shona-speaking people to refer to Source.

My brothers fetched an ox from the cattle kraal and tied it to a tree next to my grandfather's grave. People gravitated to the graveside, and within a few minutes almost everyone present had settled down around the grave. As I strolled over to the gathering place to take my seat with everyone else, I took a moment to observe the colorful scene.

The crowd sat in a rough semicircle facing the grave and the tree to which the ox was tied. Women, dressed in colorful clothes and most with headscarves or hats covering their heads, sat on straw mats inside the semicircle. Most held toddlers in their laps or had babies strapped to their backs. Men sat at the outer edges of the semicircle, surrounding the women. Local officials dressed in formal attire—the area chief, councilmen, and village heads—sat on plastic chairs on one side. The rest of the men—mostly dressed casually in T-shirts and jeans or shorts—sat on wooden benches, logs, stones, or bricks. Boys and girls of all ages sat intermingled in the crowd. Everyone was quiet, no doubt in reverence of the ceremony about to commence.

My uncle, the eldest of my grandparents' children, rose to lead the ceremony, as was his duty as head of the family. A tall, thin man, with a clean-shaven head, he was smartly dressed for the occasion in a black suit, white shirt, and black bowtie with white dots. On his feet, he wore black homemade sandals crafted from the treads of a worn tire—a signature attire for my uncle as he never wore store-bought shoes. He made the sandals himself and ran a brisk business selling the sandals to others in the community. My uncle also made woven mats and baskets that he sold. He was good at making things with his hands.

My uncle's given name was Pasipanodya, but, in following with our cultural tradition of respect, he was not referred to by his given name. Instead, he was referred to as *Moyondizvo,* just like my father. If one wanted to specifically refer to my uncle among many *Moyondizvos,* as were present at that day's gathering, then they would call him *Baba va*Tatenda, meaning father of Tatenda—Tatenda (we are thankful) was the name of his first-born son.

My uncle walked to the front of the crowd and crouched on his knees, facing my grandfather's grave. Directing his comments to the grave and clapping his hands softly and rhythmically, he called out to the spirit of my grandfather, by name and *chidawo*. Then he continued on to call out to the spirit of my great-grandfather and the spirit of my great-great-grandfather. For each of the spirits he called out to, my uncle also mentioned the gift that each of these ancestors—*madzitateguru*—shared during the time they were in this physical world.

He described how my grandfather was a medicine man who had healed many people, how my great-grandfather was a revered hunter who had been well known for the game he caught to provide abundant food for his tribe, and lastly how my great-great-grandfather had killed a lion with his bare hands, saving his family from being devoured alive.

Growing up, I had learned that this custom of recounting the accomplishments of each ancestor was for the benefit of the younger generations and served two purposes. The first was to let the youngsters know that they were descendants of people who had achieved great things in their lifetime. The second was to motivate youngsters to rise to greatness in their own lives and have accomplishments that would be remembered and recounted long after they were gone from this earth.

Still crouching, my uncle turned to face my grandmother and asked her to call to the spirits of her ancestors. My grandmother, who was sitting on the ground, surrounded by four generations of descendants, softly called out, by name and *chidawo*, the names of her paternal ancestors going back three generations. And she announced that each of them had been an accomplished craftsman with creative hands that they had used to fashion reed baskets tight enough to hold water for the kings. Gazing softly at my uncle, my grandmother said she was glad that he took up the craft of weaving and continued to bless people around him with the gifts of the mats and baskets that he made.

My uncle nodded to his mother in acknowledgment of her compliment, and then shifted on his haunches to face my mother, who was sitting to the right. He asked my mother to call to the spirits of her ancestors. In a strong and steady voice, my mother called to her ancestors. She announced that her ancestors had been accomplished farmers who were well known across many territories for their large *hozis* full of provisions sufficient to feed many families for many years. As I glanced at my mother, I could see the pride in her eyes and hear it in her voice. Then my uncle, pointing to the large *hozi* on my parents' homestead, remarked that my mother herself was an accomplished farmer just like her ancestors. I heard murmurings in the crowd and saw heads nodding in agreement.

My uncle then proceeded to invite the ancestral spirits and all the spirits of the land to join in the gathering. Raising his hands and face to the sky, he called out to *Musiki*. And he asked the spirits to help convey his gratitude and appreciation to *Musiki* for the good things that had happened to the family. He said that he was thankful for my safe return from foreign lands, for the new family members who had joined the clan and for those on the way to joining the clan, for the success of the youngsters of our clan doing well and making meaningful contributions in the world and uplifting the name of our clan, for the general good health of all the people gathered, and for the ample rains and good harvests in the past years. And then he asked the spirits and *Musiki* to guide and protect us through the celebration.

Finally, my uncle turned to the ox tied to the tree and, staring it in the eyes, thanked the animal for giving its life to feed the crowd. He asked that each of us feeding from its body receive blessings and strength to do what was required of us. He then stood to his feet and gently patted the ox on its forehead and nodded to the crowd. A thunderous applause broke, with men clapping and whistling and women ululating—expressing their joy in high-pitched vocal sounds. After the applause, we all went back to our chores, and the men slaughtered the ox for the day's feast.

Young boys carried fresh meat to the outside cooking area. I watched a small boy, about six years old, as he hoisted an ox leg on his shoulder, tottered about for a few seconds, regained his balance, and then dragged himself and his load across the yard. He plopped the ox leg on the ground in front of the women standing by the cooking area. The crowd cheered, some people praising the boy by his *chidawo*. "Good job, *Sinyoro*," they shouted.

The boy's face burst into a smile, revealing a gap where two front teeth were missing. Suddenly, the boy was overtaken by a wave of shyness that quickly turned into panic. He frantically ran through the crowd searching for his mother and, upon finding her, grabbed hold of her leg and hid his face in the folds of her flowing skirts. The crowd burst into laughter; people understood the boy's need for his mother's protection when he unwittingly found himself the center of attention. Yes, this was the home of my childhood. This was how I had remembered it in all the time I had been away.

It was still quite early, but most guests had already arrived for the celebration. Breakfast was served—for each person, a cup of tea with milk and sugar already added, two slices of white bread, and a small serving of onion and tomato soup. This was to hold the stomachs until the main feast in the afternoon.

My mother, a devout Catholic, had invited the resident priest of a nearby mission hospital to give Mass at the gathering. The priest arrived at the homestead in time to join everyone for breakfast. Then he started Mass just a little after ten o'clock. He gave a sermon on the prodigal son and his return home to be given a feast by his father. I found that to be an interesting topic for the gathering, and I wondered how it applied to the occasion.

Mass was followed by brief speeches from my father and mother, my brothers Matthew and Maxwell, and two of my cousins. In their speeches, each of them thanked everyone for coming to celebrate with our family.

In the meantime, preparations for the feast were in full gear. The cooking area that had been a makeshift "beer-brewing facility" the day before was now central command for preparing food for the day. The crowd that needed to be fed kept growing—over five hundred people at my last estimate at the Mass service, and more people continued to arrive.

The cooking area was now manned, not by women alone as on the day before, but by both men and women working in teams—each team assigned to prepare a specific dish. On large gatherings like this, men joined in the duties of preparing food. As I watched the scene, I saw a group of men stirring cornmeal into two steaming forty-four-gallon steel drums, the same drums used the day before to concentrate the beer mixture. The men were cooking *sadza*, the traditional staple of Zimbabwe, which is prepared by adding cornmeal to boiling water to make a thick porridge with a consistency similar to polenta. Another group of men was roasting chunks of fresh beef from the slaughtered ox. Several groups of women were preparing numerous side dishes to go with the *sadza* and beef.

The meal was served around 2 o'clock in the afternoon. Those who dared to brave the heat sat inside the buildings. However, most of us sat outside—taking refuge from the sun under the eaves of the buildings and the shade of the trees dotting the homestead.

I had forgotten the blessings that come with caring for each other and sharing—be it feasts or meager pickings. I was glad that we were sharing a feast that day. Several dishes were served: *sadza*, open fire-roasted beef, chicken stew, fried fresh greens from the garden, cabbage-and-carrot coleslaw, boiled pumpkin, and ash-baked sweet potatoes. As I discreetly observed the crowd, I saw people digging into the food on their plates with open enthusiasm and appreciation. Using their fingers, people pinched off big chunks of *sadza*, rolled the chunks into balls in the middle of their palms, dipped the balls into relish, and popped the relish-smothered balls into hungry mouths. Teeth tore into roasted beef and crushed chicken bones. The sounds of smacking lips and swallowing throats filled the air. I turned to my plate and dug into the food with the same enthusiasm and appreciation.

The meal was washed down with drinks that were in plentiful supply. The choices of non-alcohol beverages were Coca-Cola, Fanta, Sprite, or Mazoe Orange Crush. The beer drinkers, mostly men, had a few choices as well. There was the clear bottled beer that we brought from Harare. There was the commercially brewed opaque beer called Chibuku that came from the local beerhall packaged in brown plastic containers that had an eerie resemblance to Russian-made scud missiles; and thus, were popularly known as Chibuku "scuds." Then there was the freshly brewed *ngoto* prepared from locally sourced ingredients. A few men drank bottled beer or "scuds," but most of the men drank *ngoto*.

The rich aromas from the food mixed with the heady fumes from the fermenting *ngoto* created a familiar dizzying effect. I used to think that with *ngoto*, you didn't necessarily need to drink it; you could easily get a buzz from breathing in the fumes. I could tell by the heady feeling I was starting to experience that my mother and the women of the village had made a particularly potent batch of beer this time. My uncle, *Baba va*Tatenda, considered the expert on traditional beer in our area, confirmed my suspicions when he took a sip of the *ngoto* and declared it the best batch of *ngoto* he had tasted in a long time. He praised my mother and the women who had helped to prepare the beer. My mother graciously accepted the compliment with a warm smile and encouraged everyone to enjoy the feast.

Lunch was followed by more speeches, mostly from uncles and aunts, and from some of the local officials. Each of them expressed joy at being invited to be a part of the festivities. Entertainment was provided by a local group that performed traditional dances. The feast continued all day and into the early part of the evening.

In the evening is when the *kwasa kwasa* dance craze took over. *Mukoma* Martin drove his truck to the edge of the yard and started blasting music over the truck's stereo speakers. The crowd went wild when the opening guitar rhythms to the song "Zing Zong"[1] by Kanda Bongo Man blared over the speakers. Erupting into an impromptu sing-along, people shouted the lyrics of the song along with Kanda Bongo Man. What was curious to me was that even though people joined in the spontaneous sing-along, I doubted anyone knew the meaning of the lyrics of the song they were shouting. The lyrics were neither in English, Shona, Ndebele, nor any one of the local dialects. The lyrics were in Lingala—a language spoken in regions around the central part of Africa. Looking at the shouting crowd, one wouldn't know this. It seemed people were just making up their own words to go with the tune.

As I glanced around, I noticed people stopping what they were doing and gravitating to the makeshift dance floor that had formed in front of the truck. Women abandoned dishes they had been cleaning by the borehole; men relinquished beers they had been holding close to their mouths; the elderly extinguished pipes they had been clutching in their hands; children abandoned hide-and-seek games they had been playing. It was clear there was an invisible force taking over the crowd.

Kwasa kwasa is a dance rhythm that originated in the Democratic Republic of the Congo—formerly Zaire—in the seventies and spread across the African continent in the late eighties and early nineties. *Kwasa kwasa* is more than music and dance; it's almost like a cultural movement. It's about breaking free from the inhibitions of everyday life and expressing oneself through song and dance—even if it is just for the short time that the music is playing.

The music is from the *soukous* genre that is sometimes also referred to as African rhumba. It's an intricate blend of lyrics and instruments—one or more electric guitars, acoustic bass guitar, drums, and sometimes even flutes, saxophones, and trumpets. The music often starts in a slow rhythm that progressively transitions to a fast-paced beat, reaching a climax in the middle of the song. In most of the *soukous* songs, a chanter joins in to dial up the emotions with hints of a yearning for something. Not understanding Lingala myself, I don't always know what the yearning is for. I often think it must be a longing for a lost love, a desire to be acknowledged and appreciated, a return to the good old times, or just a short reprieve from the daily grind of everyday life. At least those are the emotions that the music evokes in me. The fusion of melodies, musical instruments, and chanters' voices into a perfect symphony seems to give the music its hypnotic powers, often possessing the body to move to its rhythm. This was what was on display in front of me that evening.

"Zing Zong" is one of those songs that starts at a fast pace and goes to an even faster tempo. The "change gear"—that is, the rhythm transition—happens very early in the song. The transition had happened at the end of the first verse that had aroused the crowd, and the song had already shifted into high gear. Everywhere I looked, people were moving in rhythm to the music. Old men and women seemed content to flay their arms in the air, and toddlers bounced up and down on their mothers' laps. On the dance floor, children and adults were gyrating their bodies as if they had no joints.

My eyes were drawn to a woman who seemed to have completely lost control of her body, letting the music direct her movements. She appeared to be middle-aged, but was moving as if she had the body of a teenager. Her hips were swirling in fast circular motions in rhythm to the music—rotating in a clockwise direction first, then changing and rotating in a counterclockwise direction. With her legs spread wide, she slowly lowered her body until she almost touched the ground with her bottom and then quickly bounced up like a coiled spring. Raising her right hand in the air in front of her and putting her left hand on the small of her back, as if it was hurting her, she made a slow three-hundred-and-sixty degree turn with her whole body, all the time keeping the gyrations of her hips going. At that point, a middle-aged man flew onto the dance floor and started to mirror the woman's movements. In unison, the man and woman performed intricate dance moves.

More people joined in the dance, taking the lead from the couple at the center of the dance floor. The dancers moved as a unit, giving in to the joy of song and dance and freely expressing themselves with their body movements. Just for a short while—perhaps a minute or two—all their troubles, trials, and tribulations appeared to be forgotten or set aside.

I continued to watch the dancers. As the music swelled, I closed my eyes and uncharacteristically found myself joining in the dance. I could not perform any of the intricate gyrations I was witnessing on the dance floor—my body was too stiff for that. With arms flailing in the air, I swayed my body in rhythm to the music, taking a few short steps in front of me and then back again. That seemed to be an adequate expression of the feelings the music was inducing in me. I became one with the crowd, united by the music.

We danced most of the night away.

In the morning, my relatives from the surrounding communities left to go back to their homesteads. My family members stayed one more day, and then, by the evening of the following day, everyone left. My married siblings, my aunts, uncles, cousins, and their families went back to the towns and cities where they lived and worked. My parents went back to the school where they were stationed at that time, and my younger siblings went back to the boarding schools or colleges they were attending. Everyone bid me goodbye and assured me that they would come to see me again before I flew off to America.

After everyone left the homestead, I went into Grandma's hut and shut the door. I pulled a goatskin mat and sat down in front of the fireplace. The fire had died down, the glowing embers left behind providing the only lighting in the room.

Grandma was sitting on the other side of the fireplace, in her usual spot. She looked at me for a few moments, nodded her head in silence, and added two logs on top of the glowing embers in the fireplace. The dry logs crackled and sputtered for a few moments and then finally burst into yellow flames, sending dancing shadows across the walls of the small hut. We sat in silence. As the fire burned, silent tears slowly coursed down my cheeks.

The fire finally died down and the room grew dark. I dried my cheeks. Without a word, Grandma unwrapped her shawl from around her shoulders and handed it to me. Accepting the shawl in silence, I wrapped it around my shoulders and lay down on the mat. Within a few minutes, I heard Grandma's soft snore from the other side of the hut. I shut my eyes and listened to the sounds of the night—the occasional bark of a neighbor's dog, the hooting of an owl in the distance, the soft racket of rats scrambling down the walls of the hut in search of food. Eventually, I fell asleep.

I woke up to a gentle prod in my ribs. Rubbing my eyes open, I saw Grandma stooping over me, poking me with her walking stick. Yawning, I rose to a sitting position on the mat, pulling Grandma's shawl from around my shoulders and handing it back to her.

"*Mangwanani, Mbuya,*" I said, offering the morning greeting to my grandmother.

"*Mangwanani,* Yeukai."

"*Mamuka sei?*" I added, inquiring if she had slept well and had woken up feeling rested.

"I woke up well, if you woke up well."

"I woke up well."

"Let us stretch our legs before the sun wakes up," Grandma said. "It is good to greet the sun as it comes back from its resting place."

I was familiar with Grandma's morning walks. She woke up around half-past four in the morning every day and left the homestead to go to the hill near our village. She would be gone for about an hour or two and return with a bundle of firewood. None of us at the homestead paid much attention to Grandma's morning ritual. We all assumed that she went into the bushes on the hill to relieve herself since she didn't much care to use the toilets at the homestead, afraid that she might fall through the hole in the floor.

For all those years, none of us was ever curious enough to ask Grandma about her morning walks up the hill. Whenever we were at the homestead during school holidays, there was always so much commotion going on, especially in the mornings. There were cooking fires to start, yards to sweep, water to fetch, huts to clean, firewood to gather, food to prepare, animals to feed, clothes to wash, fields to plow, crops to plant, harvests to bring in, and vegetable gardens to tend. It was a wonder we managed to do it all, and repeated it every day. The significance of Grandma's ritual walk was lost in that commotion, until that day when I woke up to the prod of her walking stick in my ribs.

We started the trek up the winding path to the hill. The village was still sleeping. Grandma, shawl wrapped around her shoulders and the ever-present *nguwani* covering her head, led the way in her bare feet with the aid of her walking stick. I followed behind. As I watched my grandmother, I realized, for the first time, that there was a pattern and rhythm to her walk. Stooping over her walking stick held in her right hand and with her left arm draped over her back, she cast her walking stick a few inches in front of her and stuck it into the ground. Then she lifted her right leg and planted it just a little behind the walking stick, followed by her left leg which she planted parallel to the walking stick. She lifted the walking stick and cast it in front of her again, repeating the cycle—propelling herself forward. She made these movements in such rapid succession that it was hard to notice the pattern and rhythm; but as I listened, I could hear the thud, thud, thud of her walking stick as it drove into the ground at constant intervals.

The walking stick was Grandma's companion, and not only because it aided her walking. I knew it meant much more to her than that. My grandfather, *Sekuru* Mandizvidza, had made that walking stick for my grandmother just before he died. It was a simple walking stick carved out of the trunk of a mopane tree. Tapered at the bottom end for an easy drive into the ground, it progressively widened at the top, ending in a hook-shaped handle for a comfortable grip. I remember it took my grandfather several tries before he finally fashioned this walking stick and polished it to a glossy shine. I even remember the day he presented it to my grandmother. She had received the walking stick with tears in her eyes. It was as if she knew that the walking stick was my grandfather's parting gift to her. And from that day on, she had kept the walking stick by her side.

Grandma's pace slowed slightly as we started climbing the gentle incline of the hill. About fifteen minutes into our walk up the hillside, we came to a small clearing with a few stones arranged to form a loose circle. The ground looked parched, as it always did at the end of the dry season. Dried yellowish-brown grass interspersed with crinkly thorn bushes surrounded the clearing. A few trees dotted the landscape. In another month or so, the rains would arrive, and once again the grass, bushes, and trees would come alive.

Grandma slowly walked to the center of the clearing. She poked the ground with her walking stick and, finding a soft spot, drove the stick into the ground for support and then slowly lowered her body to sit down. She gave a huge sigh of relief when her bottom touched the ground, as if she was glad she made it to the ground without toppling over. I sat down next to her. Grandma stretched her legs in front of her, facing east. I did the same.

"I am going into silence for a few moments," Grandma said, looking at me. Then she rested her hands on her thighs and tilted her head slightly up to the sky, her eyes closed. I waited in silence.

The soft song of a dove in the distance reached my ears. With the song in the background, I turned to the view.

From my vantage point, perched on the hillside, the beauty of the valley that was home to our community stretched before me. The open landscape was dotted with homesteads. Smoke twirls rose up from the cooking huts at a few of the homesteads, disappearing into the morning air. To the west were small plots of land where people in the community cultivated most of their food crops such as corn, millet, sorghum, peanuts, roundnuts, and beans. The remains of the last harvest had been reduced to dry stalks, ready to fuel the fires that would sweep through the area before the first rains arrived.

My eyes drifted to the long winding gully that was home to the river that served our community. I traced the gully's path as it cut its way through the elevated plains in the northeast, gradually dropping in altitude as it snaked through the valley, and eventually disappearing behind the hills to the southwest. The river itself had now dwindled to shallow water pools connected by weak trickles.

Then my gaze settled on the rising sun, a yellow glow nestled between two hills in the east. The song of the dove died, and there was only the silence of the morning.

Grandma finally opened her eyes. She turned to look at me, a soft smile on her face. "I am glad you chose to stay behind with me, Yeukai," she said in our language. "I am glad that we have this time together," she continued. "I believe this time was arranged by Source, the origin of all life. And I believe this time has a purpose that comes from Source. I hope that together, we can fulfill this purpose."

A puzzled expression covered my face as I looked at my grandmother. But I didn't say anything, and she continued to speak. "You will be going away from this land soon, and so will I. Even though we will both be traveling, the journeys we will travel are different. You will return here to be with the family at the end of your journey, which is as it should be. However, my journey is the kind that no one returns from. My journey is to go back into Source, to go back to the origin of life. That is where I arose from many years ago. That is where all of us arise from when we are born into this world. I have been in the world long enough, and it is time for me to return into Source, our true home. I will be long gone by the time you return from your journey, so we will not see each other again in this world." I now knew that my grandmother was referring to her death.

"I also know that I have one more task left before I complete what I came to do in this world," Grandma said. "I have been wanting to speak with you because I have something to share with you." I continued to look at my grandmother, still not saying anything.

"Your life is very different from the simple life that I have lived," Grandma continued. "But, no matter how educated one can be, no matter how traveled one can be, no matter how rich one can be, there is something that remains the same in all human beings; that is, we are all spirits that come from Source and in the end we all return into Source."

It was unusual for my grandmother to open up like this, so I immediately knew that she was about to share something deep. As I continued to look at her, she took off her hat and scratched her clean-shaven head a few times, and then put the hat back on her head.

"I have watched you grow up," Grandma said. "And I admire the way you have handled yourself. You have grown into a fine young woman with a lot of potential, and I know you will accomplish many things on your journey in this world. I am very proud of you." She picked up her walking stick and, using its pointed end, started scratching the ground, drawing irregular shapes in the loose soil.

"I fear I did not do my duty in teaching you the ways of our people," Grandma said, staring at the shapes she had scratched in the dirt. "I did not teach you the ways of our people because I felt that with your education, you may not have much use for them. But now I see that you do."

My grandmother lifted her head from the ground and looked directly at me, considering me with her kind eyes. I kept quiet, returning her gaze. After a few moments, a smile tugged at my grandmother's lips.

"If you are willing to listen to an old woman, I will share with you what I know," she continued. "My ways are the old ways of living in the world. I think you may find these old ways to be of some use in your modern life, especially in the strange lands where you are going." Grandma shifted her eyes to stare at the horizon. It was as if she was imagining what my life would be like in the distant lands I was soon to visit.

"I will listen to what you have to teach me, *Mbuya*," I said. I was brought up to respect my elders, and I was also very fond of my grandmother.

"When you were born, I was the one who chose a name for you," Grandma said, her gaze still fixed at a point in the distant horizon. "I was delighted when your parents agreed to give you the name Yeukai."

I knew that Grandma had chosen my name; my parents told me this when I was growing up. But I didn't know the reason why I had been called Yeukai (remember). I had received the Christian name Mavis when I got baptized in church. Like most people of my age growing up under the missionary influence, I had a Christian name and a Shona name. But I had never used my Christian name. As a child I was called Yeukai to respect my grandmother's wishes, and when I grew up I chose to keep Yeukai as my first name because I felt that it was special. Each one of my brothers and sisters had both a Christian and a Shona name, but only Mugu and I chose to keep our Shona names as our first names.

"I knew then that you were the one who would take over from me, so I chose the name Yeukai to remind myself that when the time came, I would teach you the lessons I need to pass on to you. This knowledge I speak of is not something you will find in books," Grandma said, reminding me that in our tradition, ancient knowledge was stored in people's hearts, not in books. "I can only pass this knowledge to you through conversations. This is knowledge passed down from *madzitateguru edu* (our ancestors): from our forefathers and their forefathers before them."

Grandma paused and swallowed, turning to look at me.

"You may not be able to apply everything that I teach you to your modern life, but I ask that you think of applying those parts of the teachings that will help you live a life that has purpose."

My grandmother was an old woman, but a wise one too. I didn't know how wise, though. I soon found out.

The lessons started the following day and continued for a few days; thus began my journey to discover the mystical being who inhabited my grandmother's body. In those days that we spent together, I discovered a side of her that I didn't know of, a being I think none of us in my family ever knew.

OUR CONNECTION TO SOURCE

On the second day following everyone's departure from the homestead, Grandma and I woke up before dawn and walked to the clearing on the hillside. We sat down facing east with our legs stretched in front of us, as we had done the day before. Grandma went into silence, with her eyes closed. I sat and waited.

I felt a sense of excitement—the kind one gets when starting a new adventure. I didn't quite know what was in store, but I was ready to find out.

I stared at the eastern horizon, letting my mind drift.

Grandma cleared her throat, bringing me back to the moment. I turned my head to look at her, my eyes meeting her gentle gaze.

"Yeukai," Grandma began to speak, "I will now share with you the lessons that were passed down to me so that, when the time comes, you can pass these lessons to others." Grandma kept her steady gaze on my face.

"The first important thing is to learn to listen to Source," Grandma continued. "I am not speaking of listening with your ears. I am speaking of listening with your heart," she said, lifting her right hand and resting her palm on her chest. "It is the heart that can communicate with Source. Learning this kind of listening will help you to understand what I am going to share with you. I will teach you how to listen with your heart. It is very easy to do." She paused, taking a deep breath and closing her eyes.

"I want you to take a deep breath, like what I just did," Grandma continued, opening her eyes and staring at a point on the eastern horizon, her hand resting back on her legs. "Then in the moments following the deep breath try not to think of anything, say anything, or do anything. I ask that you go into silence, and then observe the rising of the sun in silence. As you observe the rising sun, I ask that you stay alert and notice any feelings or sensations or emotions that may arise in your heart, and then put your attention on that which arises."

I nodded, closing my eyes and taking a deep breath. I opened my eyes, turning my head and looking toward the east.

The sun was a pale yellowish globe as it climbed out of the valley nestled between the two hills in the east. Its glow colored the eastern horizon a vivid yellow, interspersed with patches of ruby red and burnt orange. As I gazed at the magnificent display of colors, I heard a soft humming lament. The haunting sound was coming from my grandmother. The combination of the majestic display of colors in the east and my grandmother's melancholic humming in the background penetrated my mind to a depth I had never felt before.

The colors grew more vibrant, almost leaping out of the sky. A yearning rose in my heart. As I kept my attention on my heart, the yearning deepened into such a distinct longing—a longing to be one with the sun, a longing to be one with the sky. I wanted to step out of my body and join the scene that I was witnessing. I wanted to be a part of the sun, a patch of the sky, a speck of the vivid colors. I wanted to be anything as long as I was a part of the whole. I didn't resist the urge, and the feeling intensified. Finally, something swelled in me, and I had the sensation of moving closer and closer to the sun, until I was lost in it.

Grandma startled me as she cleared her throat, and I turned my head to look at her. I had been so engrossed in my experience that I didn't notice she had stopped humming and was now sitting quietly, watching me.

She gave me a moment to collect myself and then began speaking, her gaze now turned back to the eastern horizon. "I will now continue with the lesson," she said.

"What you are witnessing right now, Yeukai my child, is the sun obeying the guidance from Source. Source in its totality is invisible to our eyes, but we can feel it in us as energy, as a life force. This energy arises from Source and creates everything that we see in the world and a lot more that exists in a form we cannot see with our eyes. The energy arising from Source runs everything in creation, including the sun. Every day, the sun rises from the valley between the hills in the east, moves across the vast expanse of sky, and sets behind the hills in the west." She made a sweeping gesture with her hand to illustrate the movement of the sun from the east to the west. "Whether there is rain or sunshine, the sun follows this same pattern every single day; it travels this journey around the world every day. The sun is guided by Source in every step of the way as it makes its journey around the world."

Grandma paused to clear her throat again and then continued. "The sun is connected to Source and allows the energy from Source to flow through it and guide it in its daily movements. In this way, the sun follows a natural rhythm from Source, and this rhythm forms forces that support life in the world. The birds of the skies, the plants of the forests, the fishes of the rivers, and the animals of the land all depend on the rhythm of the sun."

Then she said, "Now I shall ask you this: What do you think would happen if the sun decided not to follow the guidance from Source?" Grandma swallowed, turning to look at me briefly, then shifting her eyes back to the horizon. "I shall tell you what would happen. The life that we know would change. Life goes on in the world as it does because the sun follows the guidance from Source, and in doing so, the sun establishes the rhythms that sustain the world and everything that we see and a lot more that we do not see."

Grandma paused, her eyes still fixed on the horizon. I remained silent, fascinated by what I was hearing. I could see the truth of what she was saying; I just hadn't thought of life in quite that way before. I wondered where the conversation was headed. My curiosity was piqued. I waited for Grandma to continue, excited to hear what she would say next.

"The birds, just like the sun, are connected to Source and are guided and fueled by the energy from Source in every moment of their existence," Grandma went on. "They instinctively know what to do to survive and flourish in their environments. So do the plants, the fishes, and the animals. The creatures of the world know how to connect to Source and receive all that they need to survive. The creatures of the world have a pure connection with Source."

Grandma glanced at me, checking whether I was listening. I smiled and nodded, letting her know that I was paying attention. She returned my smile, and then looked back at the horizon as she continued to speak. "This is the way it is meant to be for us human beings as well. In human beings, this pure connection to Source can be seen in babies. Newborn babies instinctively follow a natural rhythm. They cry when they come out of the womb, they breathe air in and out, they suckle on their mothers' breasts, and they sleep. In a matter of months, they learn how to roll over, sit, crawl, and walk. Their development from one stage of life to the next happens naturally because they are fully connected to Source and follow the guidance from Source with no hindrances in the flow of the energy that sustains their lives."

A soft smile spread across Grandma's face as she continued to speak.

"The connection in babies is so pure that it can be seen as the joy and enthusiasm for life that they display. Next time you are in the presence of a baby, observe how it smiles, how it wiggles about in joy with no cares in the world, and how it burbles, making meaningless noises. Notice how it freely gives its love to everyone around." Grandma paused. It was as if she was giving me time to imagine what she was saying.

"When in the presence of someone in pain," Grandma continued to speak, "a baby instinctively knows how to reach out with compassion. We, as adults, may see the baby break into a smile as it gazes deep into our eyes. We may see it as the reaching out of an unsteady hand to grab at our mouth, our chin, our ear, our nose. That is the pure expression of Source through the baby. If you take a moment to observe the feelings that stir deep in you during these interactions, you will witness your own response to the pure expression of Source through the baby. That is how human interactions are supposed to be in this world—Source in one reaching out to Source in another." Moisture gathered in my eyes as I listened to my grandmother's beautiful words. Something in her words rang true deep down in me.

"Even as adults, we are connected to Source because our spirits are located in it. Once we learn how, we can feel the energy of Source flowing through our hearts into our human forms. That is the natural flow of the creative energy that sustains our lives." I turned to look at my grandmother. Her eyes were shimmering. An expression of pure joy covered her face.

"As human beings, we start as spirits in Source and we yearn to come into the world to anchor the energy of Source and to be a channel for Source to express in the world. We ask for bodies from the soil to house our spirits, and we ask for our parents to bring us into the world. With the agreement of the soil to give us bodies and the agreement of our parents to bring us into the world, our spirits emerge from Source and come through our hearts to create our minds, which in turn create our emotional systems and our physical bodies. You see, our bodies and emotional systems are connected to our minds, our minds are connected to our hearts, our hearts are connected to our spirits, and our spirits rest in Source." Grandma paused, looking at me.

"Are you following what I am saying?" she asked.

I took a moment to mentally repeat what Grandma had said, checking to see if I had understood her.

"I think so, *Mbuya*." I finally nodded, satisfied that I had grasped her teaching.

"Good, then I shall continue," she said, shifting her gaze to the valley below.

"We are born into the world as the babies that are seen and heard. Each of us starts as a baby, which is essentially a spirit that originates from Source and that has come into the world in human form. The baby is fully connected to Source, and all its activities are governed by Source. That is the way it is meant to be."

Grandma lifted her face to look at me. In that moment, I noticed a shift in her expression. The joy on her face faded, turning into a deep sadness. Then she cast her eyes to the ground as she continued to speak—her voice now solemn.

"Unfortunately, as the babies go through the stages of becoming full adults in human society—developing into toddlers, then young boys or girls, and finally mature men or women—something happens that causes the connection of the human minds to the human hearts to break. And it is the breaking of this link between our minds and hearts that creates the sense of disconnection from Source. It appears there is a gradual blocking or limitation in some way of the ability of our minds to access our hearts; thus, we feel disconnected from Source." Grandma paused, her eyes still downcast.

"My child, this sense of disconnection from Source is the root cause of the chaos, confusion, and suffering that we witness in our world," Grandma quietly added.

I was stunned. I leaned toward my grandmother. I knew I was being told something of profound significance, and I didn't want to miss a word.

"What do you mean, *Mbuya*?" I asked. "What do you mean that the connection of the human minds to the human hearts become broken? What do you mean this sense of disconnection from Source is the root cause of the chaos, confusion, and suffering in the world?"

Grandma lifted her eyes to meet mine. "Yeukai, my child," she said, "that is what I want to share with you during this time we have together."

Then Grandma closed her eyes and took in several deep breaths, as if summoning energy to continue her teaching. Opening her eyes, she looked directly into mine again and said, "In its endless wisdom, Source allows the gradual blocking of the stream of its energy through the human hearts to the human minds, emotions, and bodies. For what purpose we don't yet know." Grandma paused for a moment.

"But what we know," she continued, "is that if humans do not seek, find, and reunite their bodies, emotions, and minds to their hearts and to Source on a daily basis, they lose their way."

Grandma must have noticed the confused expression on my face and known that I wasn't quite getting the point she was making. With gnarled fingers, she rubbed her chin in quiet deliberation—her eyes appraising me. Settling her hand back in her lap and shifting her gaze to the horizon, she expanded on what she had just said.

"By simply observing people's behavior, you can easily separate the people who have a sense of connection to Source and are fueled by its energy from those who have no idea they are immersed in Source. People who live with a sense of connection to Source share love freely. They are kind, generous, compassionate, considerate, and respectful. Their deeds are about serving others, encouraging others, uplifting others, and inspiring others. Because the energy of Source freely flows through them and they continue to follow the guidance from within, they instinctively know what to do in any situation they encounter." She paused, shifting her body to a comfortable sitting position. The ground was a bit hard, and even I was beginning to feel the strain of sitting down on it for a long time.

"When they see a hungry person, they share a portion of their food. When they see a troubled person, they listen to the troubles without passing judgment.

When they see a person in need, they offer help without asking for compensation, recognition, or reward." She paused again before continuing to speak.

"And they do all these things with joy and an enthusiasm for life. Their life is about giving to others, not taking from others. And in their giving to others, they receive all they need in their lives. Their energy comes from Source, and they know that the energy will not run out. Their minds and hearts are connected. Because of that connection, they feel the energy from Source flowing through their hearts into their minds, emotions, and bodies to guide and fuel all their actions."

Grandma paused, turning to look at me, her eyes regarding me intently. I knew she wanted to know if I was now following her teaching. I nodded my head, letting her know that I was starting to get the point. She turned her head to stare at the horizon again.

"People who have lost their sense of connection to Source lose the joy and enthusiasm for life." Grandma continued to speak. "There is a sense that their minds and hearts are no longer connected. Because of that sense of disconnection, they no longer feel energy from Source flowing through their hearts into their minds, emotions, and bodies to guide and fuel their actions." Grandma paused, catching her breath.

"Some people go through their days angry and full of hate. Some become mean, selfish, and inconsiderate. Some lie, cheat, and steal. Some manipulate, bully, dominate, control, and belittle others. Some are consumed with greed. In extreme cases, some may even rape, maim, or kill others and not see anything wrong with their actions. They can easily defend such evil acts. Somehow people lose the ability to feel compassion for others. And they lose the capability to feel the pain, hurt, and suffering that is caused by their actions. All because their minds are no longer nourished by the energy from Source."

Grandma continued to speak, her gaze still on the horizon. "Because this world is full of human beings running around with minds that are no longer connected to their hearts and are therefore blocked from the free flow of life energy from Source, we see chaos around us. You only have to look around to see the evidence of what I am talking about." She shifted in her seat again.

"We used to see brothers killing one another over ownership of family cattle, and we used to see tribes killing members of other tribes to gain control of fertile grounds. Things became worse with the coming of *varungu* from faraway territories to take away land that belonged to *madzitateguru edu*." Grandma shook her head as she said this.

"In our way of living in the old days, elders knew how to bind the human minds back to the human hearts and back to Source to maintain the sacred communion with Source that sustains peaceful coexistence of human beings with each other and with nature. The elders passed down this knowledge as part of the lessons they taught their young on how to grow up and become mature, contributing members of the society. Elders taught their young practices for respecting elders and their teachings, for protecting and caring for one another, and for taking care of the land that gave them sustenance." A faint smile played across Grandma's face as she spoke.

"Elders also taught their young to say a prayer of gratitude to the land when planting seeds that grew into crops that would feed families, when gazing at flowers that would become fruits to nourish their bodies, when collecting tree branches that would become shelter to protect their families, and when gathering leaves and roots that would become medicines to heal the ailments of the sick. And above all, elders taught their young to live in harmony with nature. They taught their young only to take from nature what was required to sustain life, and no more."

Turning her head to look into my eyes, she said, "That is how knowledge was passed down from one generation to another. That is how this knowledge was preserved, and that is how the sacred union with Source was maintained."

Her gaze wandered away from my face and back to a point in the distance, the smile disappearing from her face. "This knowledge has now been lost because of *varungu* and their ways and teachings. The way children are raised today takes them further away from Source. Children are taught to read and write, but they are not taught the ways to maintain a sense of connection with Source and the sacred bond that sustains peaceful living. Not only that, nowadays, children are also taught to reject the knowledge passed down from their elders. They are told that our ways of worshiping Source through *vadzimu* are pagan and evil. They are taught to reject the ancient teachings that contain the sacred knowledge for preserving our sense of connection to Source. They are taught to reject the very knowledge that helps us to keep our sacred union with the power that sustains our lives. So the children grow up not knowing how to maintain a sense of connection to Source, which is there to guide and fuel their lives so that they can grow into loving, kind, generous, compassionate, considerate, and respectful human beings. When they have children of their own, those children do not receive the sacred knowledge of life, and the cycle of ignorance continues. Thus, we get more and more people living in the world with no knowledge of how to maintain a sense of connection to Source. Then we wonder why there is so much chaos, confusion, and suffering in the world."

Turning her head toward me, Grandma said, "Please do not misunderstand. I am not saying that in the past every child grew up to be a compassionate human being. Even in the old days, some children listened and followed the teachings taught by their elders and grew up to be compassionate human beings, but some did not listen and heed the messages and grew up to be troublesome adults. Even then, we still had people who deceived or committed crimes against other human beings—people who lied, cheated, stole, or killed. As I said before, we witnessed brothers killing their brothers over cattle. There were husbands who beat their wives and children as if they were animals. There were tribal chiefs who led raids against other tribes to steal fertile lands and cattle and to kill men, women, and children. We still had people who lived in complete ignorance of their true nature as human beings connected to Source and fueled by the energy from it."

Grandma stopped talking for a moment, casting her eyes to the ground, lost in thought. Then she continued speaking, saying, "The point I am making is that at least in our old way of life, the elders had the chance to teach their young the ways of Source. And because of those teachings, more of our children grew up with the sacred knowledge of their true nature as a part of Source. Now that chance for elders to teach their young is gone, and it seems it is gone forever. Now the young are left to wander on their own, and many get lost in the process. They grow up to be adults with no direction; even worse, some grow up to be adults who destroy the good they see in the world."

Grandma stopped talking again. I kept quiet. Time passed and she still remained silent. When I looked at her, she was sitting very still with her eyes closed. I was beginning to think she had dozed off, but then she opened her eyes, fixing her gaze on the horizon, and started to speak again. In an almost inaudible whisper, she said, "If *varungu* had been willing, they could have taught us the good aspects of their way of life, and we could have taught them the good aspects of our way of life. Together, perhaps we could have created a new way of living. I would have liked to live in a world created by bringing together the good from their way of living and the good from our way of living, to create a new way of living."

Shaking her body as if to bring her attention back to the present, Grandma looked at me and said, "But no, that is not what happened. When *varungu* first came to our land, they did not take the time to understand our ways of living and worshiping. They did not ask us questions about how we maintained our connection to Source. They did not even think that we knew about Source."

A sadness crept into her voice as she continued to speak, returning her gaze to the horizon. "What they did instead was to preach the word of their God and his goodness and mercy during the day. But in the cover of night they plotted against us and came to burn our houses, steal our animals, and chase us from our lands."

Grandma was quiet for a few moments, lost in her thoughts again. "I think," she finally said, "the *varungu* who came to our land were those who had lost their sense of connection to Source and no longer had love in their hearts. They could lie, cheat, steal, and kill and not see anything wrong with their actions. They stole our land and killed us like animals. They did all these horrible things to us because they had lost their ability to see that we were human beings like them, and that we originate from Source just like them. They no longer felt compassion for us, and because of that they no longer felt our pain and suffering." She shook her head again.

"On top of that, *varungu* began teaching our children lies, leading them to lose their sense of connection to Source. They taught our children about their God who had to be feared. They taught our children that they deserved to be punished by God and that they would burn in hell when they died. These kinds of teachings drove more of our young further and further away from Source and from the truth." There was another long pause.

"Then the terrible war came," Grandma finally said. Her voice was now low, with a slight tremble to it. "I think about the war that was fought to take our land back from *varungu*, and the evil acts committed by both sides of the armed struggle during that war. We witnessed the world going mad right before our eyes. We lived through a world where murders were committed in front of jeering crowds.

We were forced to watch as men were hacked to pieces with axes and their blood squirted over the people gathered to watch the butchering of human beings. We were forced to watch as soldiers dragged dead bodies behind trucks as if they were dead animals. Women and children were raped, and no one said or did anything to stop it. Families were wiped out—father, mother, children, and grandparents— gathered in their huts and the huts set on fire. The screams of human beings burning alive are not something that is easy to forget."

A short silence followed, and then she said, "We heard their cries for help."

Grandma dropped her head to her chest. "We lived through it all. It seems like a bad dream now, but we lived through it. The madness, the evil, the cruelty . . ." Her voice trailed off as she started sobbing quietly, tears streaming down her wrinkled cheeks.

It hurt in my chest to see my grandmother cry. Tears welled in my eyes as I watched her relive the atrocities she had witnessed in the war to liberate our country from white colonial settlers. I sat there and I let my grandmother cry. When her sobs subsided, I helped her to her feet, put my arms around her shoulders, and slowly led her down the hill back home. She looked very old and very weak. She was silent for the rest of the day and went to bed in silence. I spent another night huddled on the straw mat across the fireplace from my grandmother. I wanted her to know I was there if she needed anything.

As I lay awake, my mind wandered to the subject of colonialism. I thought it was just as well my grandmother didn't know the whole story of the atrocities brought to humanity and to nature by that scourge. I had learned about some of the atrocities of colonialism through my education, travels, and exposure to other cultures. I had learned about the chaos that colonialism brought to the whole of Africa, not just to our country. I had learned about the colonization of the American continent following Christopher Columbus's voyage, and the atrocities visited on the indigenous tribes and nations who had lived in those lands. I had learned about the slave trade, the capture of people on the east coast of Africa and how they were sold as free labor to plantation owners in the Americas. I had learned about the greed that seemed to be the driver behind it all. I thought of the injustice and the senseless cruelty visited on human beings by other human beings. It brought fresh tears to my eyes.

A Cry for Humanity

Divine Presence
I cry to you in anguish
And I know you hear the prayer in my crying
My prayer is for all humanity as we cry for salvation
For those of us who inflict pain on others
For those of us who endure the pain
For those of us who bear witness to the atrocities
May we find relief and refuge for our distressed minds
As relief and refuge are not to be found in the things of the world
They are to be found only in you
And in you I surrender this prayer

Divine Power
I yearn to connect to that which you are
And I know you hear the prayer in my yearning
My prayer is for all humanity, as we seek salvation
To stop those of us who inflict pain on others
To comfort those of us who endure the pain
To dissolve the guilt of those of us who bear witness to the atrocities
May we find relief and refuge for our disconnected minds
As relief and refuge are not to be found in the things of the world
They are to be found only in you
And in you I surrender this prayer

Divine Love
You are the invisible energy that heals my mind
You are the invisible energy that heals all minds
May you, with your unconditional love
Heal the minds of those of us who inflict pain on others
Heal the minds of those of us who endure the pain
Heal the minds of those of us who bear witness to the atrocities
May we find relief and refuge for our wounded minds

As relief and refuge are not to be found in the things of the world
They are to be found only in you
And in you I surrender this prayer
Amen

EVERY LIFE IS A GUIDED JOURNEY

O n the next day, Grandma and I woke up before dawn, climbed up to the sitting area on the hillside, and settled in for our morning quiet time. I could see that Grandma had regained her composure and was back to her strong self again. She went into silence, with her eyes closed. I sat still, witnessing another majestic sunrise.

I gazed at the striking beauty on display, with Grandma's teaching from the day before running through my mind. Grandma had said that the sun was connected to Source and was guided by Source through its daily journey around the world. I remember wanting to tell my grandmother that it was actually the world that revolved around the sun, and not the other way around. Just as well I had stopped myself in time. This was not the time or place to argue such a minor point. I chose to focus on the big-picture lessons that my grandmother was conveying to me.

Grandma had said that all forms in the world, including human beings, depended on the sun for existence. And that should the sun choose not to obey Source, then life as we know it would end. I could clearly see the truth in what Grandma had said. It all made sense to me now.

Then something dawned on me. I realized that Grandma was using simple language to pass on her knowledge to me. She wasn't imparting her knowledge shrouded in the thick symbolism of parables, idioms, and proverbs—the style favored by most elders and the style she sometimes liked to use. Grandma was talking to me in a very simple and plain manner, clearly spelling out the points she wanted to make. I very much appreciated my grandmother's consideration, given that she was communicating a lifetime of wisdom and it was a lot for me to absorb. There was a lot to absorb, not only in volume, but also in meaning and significance. No doubt, my grandmother knew that if she tried to pass her knowledge to me shrouded in symbolism, I would probably get lost and miss the points she was trying to convey.

Not that I didn't value the richness of our language and the tradition of telling stories in parables and enriched by idioms and proverbs; quite the contrary. I very much enjoyed listening to elders pass on teachings of morality and ethics disguised as fairy tales of *sekuru gudo* and *tsuro* (grandfather baboon and the hare), of *shumba ishe wesango* (the lion, king of the forest), and of *njuzu yemumvura* (the mermaid of the waters). I had grown up hearing these kinds of stories as part of our tradition, and had gleaned many valuable life lessons through them. But I sensed that the knowledge that my grandmother was passing on to me this time was somehow different. I didn't quite know how different yet, but I sensed it.

Reflecting on another key fact that Grandma had shared, I wondered: What is it that we as human beings can do to maintain our sense of connection to Source at all times and stop the chaos, confusion, madness, and suffering that she had spoken of?

It seemed as if Grandma had sensed the question on my mind because at that moment I felt the gentle poke of her walking stick in my ribs. I had been so absorbed in my ruminations that I hadn't realized she had completed her time in silence and was waiting for me to emerge from my reverie. I met my grandmother's gaze, smiling. Then I nodded to let her know that I was ready to start the day's lesson. She nodded back and proceeded to speak, shifting her gaze to a point in the distance.

"Yeukai, my child, nature can teach us many lessons, if we take the time to observe it in silence. This is because in nature we find evidence of the creative energy of Source in action. Yesterday I spoke of how the sun maintains its connection to Source, which is why its every move is guided by Source. If we choose to, we human beings can follow our way back to Source by observing the sun. We can put our attention on the sun and ask it to help us to reunite our human forms back to Source. The sun can be the channel that we travel through to find our way back to our permanent home in Source."

As Grandma said this, I realized the significance of why she had asked me to witness the sunrise in silence the day before.

"When we regain the sense that we are connected to Source," Grandma continued, "our minds are healed of the chaos and confusion that cause the madness that we see around us. With the minds of humanity healed, there is no more need to destroy, no more need to dominate, no more need to control, and no more need to hurt or harm other human beings. With the minds of humanity healed, order is restored, and so are peace and harmony."

I continued to listen as Grandma expanded on her teaching. "It is not just the sun that can be our guide to reuniting our minds to our hearts and to Source. Any object that has maintained its connection to Source can guide us back into unity with this origin of life. Whenever we put our undivided attention on an object with a connection to Source, that object becomes a channel for us to reunite with Source. The object can be the sun, as I said; but the object can also be the sky, the moon, a star, a river, a plant, a flower, a bird, a butterfly—it can be anything." She paused and swallowed.

"Even other human beings can be our channels back into Source, as long as their own sense of connection to Source is maintained. Looking at a baby, especially a newborn, is a powerful way to connect to Source. Focusing on a loved one and appreciating their good aspects is another powerful way to connect to Source." She paused again, before continuing.

"Another easy way to connect to Source is to perform a task that is of service to others and to the world, and as we perform that task, to give our complete attention to it," she added. "And yet another way is to just sit in silence, with our minds clear of any thought," she said. "So you see, there are countless doorways for us human beings to regain our sense of connection to Source, if we choose to."

Grandma leaned down to rub her legs, dislodging grains of sand stuck in the crevices of her wrinkled skin. Age had taken its toll on her body. She reached for her walking stick, drove it in the ground for traction, and then slowly hoisted herself up. She stood with her back stooped, leaning against her walking stick. I knew that she liked to stand up often, to keep the circulation in her legs going. She often remarked that at her age, it was important to get up and move about so that the body didn't forget how to function.

I could tell that my grandmother had been a remarkably beautiful woman in her younger days. Now, even though her posture was permanently stooped, her skin sagged, her fingers curled from arthritis, and her face thin and gaunt, the beauty that lay beneath still remained. Grandma had a way of holding herself with poise and grace that gave her a presence that age could not rob. Yet another feature that aging had not diminished in my grandmother was the glint in her brown eyes. She had the most striking eyes, especially when they twinkled because she had something important to say, the way they were twinkling now.

Resuming her teaching, standing with the rising sun as a backdrop, Grandma said, "The most important thing is to wake up each morning and reunite your body, your emotions, and your mind, to your heart and to Source. The most important thing is to wake up and surrender your human form to Source. You start the day with the recognition that you are a creation of Source, and declare your willingness to be the eyes of Source, the ears of Source, and the arms and legs of Source in the world. When you deliberately make this connection to Source at the start of your day, everything you do will be guided by Source. As your spirit, the energy from Source will flow through your heart as the life force that animates your being, will flow through your mind as the thoughts you think, will flow through your emotions as the feelings you experience, will flow through your voice as the words you speak, and will flow through your body as the actions you take throughout the day. When other people look at you, what they will see is the image of Source—whether they know this or not."

Grandma sat back down, pulling her shawl around her shoulders. She continued to speak, her eyes still looking at a point in the distance.

"I take time every single morning to be with Source here on this hillside. This is the time I establish my sense of connection to Source. It is the time I give my day and my life to Source." She paused for a brief moment.

"You can be with Source in any place that is quiet," she continued. "You can stay in silence with Source, with your mind still and not focused on anything. You can close your eyes or leave your eyes open, it really does not make a difference.

The important thing is not to let thoughts run through your mind and take your attention away from Source."

Closing her eyes she added, "You can just stay calm, with your heart filled with gratitude and appreciation for Source, and in turn letting the energy from Source fill you and nourish every part of your being. You let yourself bathe in the energy of Source." She took several slow, deep breaths, a serene expression on her face. After a short while, she gave a small sigh and then opened her eyes, slowly taking in her surroundings.

Then she turned her gaze to me as she continued to speak.

"Another way is to use the time to say your prayers to Source, letting your mind stay active. When you choose to use your time for prayer, you can pray about anything that rises in your mind. You can ask any particular questions you have for Source and you can bring up any particular issues that might be in your life. You can ask for blessings for your family, your relatives, your friends, your neighbors, your crops, your animals, or even the whole world. This is the time you speak to Source. It is the source of your life energy, and also your supply for all that you will ever need to live the life that is in store for you. Let your prayers be a conversation with Source." Grandma paused.

"And when you pray, learn to pray with your whole being," she added.

I was a bit intrigued by my grandmother's last statement, so I asked, "*Mbuya,* what do you mean when you say learn to pray with your whole being? I don't quite understand that."

My grandmother had a knowing smile on her face, as if she was expecting that question. "I will tell you what I mean, my child," she said, returning her gaze to the distant horizon.

"You can say your prayer in the privacy of your mind," she said, "you can speak your prayer quietly, or you can shout your prayer from the top of your voice. What is important though is not just the words—whether you speak them out loud or in silence. What is important is to pray with your whole being. You may utter the words of your prayer out loud or you may say the words of your prayer quietly in your thoughts, but let the voice of your prayer rise from your whole being."

Glancing back at me, Grandma noticed that I still wasn't clear on what she meant. She closed her eyes, absently rubbing her wrinkled forehead with her fingers. Then she opened her eyes again, looking directly at me.

"I want you to close your eyes and remember the way you felt as you were watching the sunrise yesterday," she said. "Imagine we are back to yesterday and you are watching the sunrise again. Recall the feelings you experienced yesterday."

I closed my eyes, recalling the image of the rising sun in my mind. Immediately, I felt a slow but distinct rise of energy in my body. The feeling grew into a sense of joy in my heart, euphoria even. My body relaxed into the sensation.

"Do you feel it now?" Grandma asked. I nodded my head in response, my eyes still closed. "What you are experiencing is how it feels when your whole being is connected to Source. Now you are ready to say your prayer with your whole being. Anything that you pray for in this state is directly heard and acted upon by Source." A moment of silence followed Grandma's words.

"Do you now understand what I am saying?" Grandma finally asked.

I opened my eyes and looked at my grandmother, who was regarding me intently.

"Yes, I understand what you are saying now," I replied. "As I recalled the scene from yesterday, I felt an energy spreading throughout my whole body. I felt a heightened sense of aliveness and this incredible joy in my heart." Talking more to myself than to my grandmother, and turning my eyes toward the blue sky, I continued to speak, saying, "It means that I can recall the memory of the sunrise at any time and any place to induce the powerful feelings that I experienced yesterday, and then say my prayers with that feeling as my backdrop. It means that I can bring this same feeling up by focusing on an object that has maintained its connection to Source." I looked back at my grandmother, a wide grin on my face. She was smiling and nodding at me. She knew that I had finally grasped the point she was making.

Grandma dropped her eyes to the ground, poking the dirt with the index finger of her right hand. "Every single day," she said, "I pray for all my children—those who passed on and those who continue to live. I pray for eternal peace for those who left this world, and I pray for blessings of good health and prosperity for those still with me in the land of the living. I pray for all my grandchildren to live worthwhile lives. I pray for good rains and bountiful harvests. I pray for peace in our country and for peace in the world, and I pray that more people find their way back to Source."

Grandma looked down at her hands, studying her fingernails that had been hardened and browned by old age. "So you see, you can pray for anyone or anything. Let the prayers rise up from your heart and offer them with your whole being," she said.

"But there is something you have to remember," she continued. "After your prayer, you must be in silence for as long as you can, so that you can listen for guidance from Source. This is the time to listen for the answers to your prayers." Grandma paused and became very still for a while.

"The answers from Source do not come through your ears as would a voice from, say, your mother or your father," she finally continued, lifting her eyes from her hands to look into the distance. "The answers to your prayers surface from deep within you. Sometimes you feel a thought rise up in your mind, a string of words formulating in your head. Sometimes a deep emotion rises in you and, in that moment, the solution to a challenge you have been facing suddenly appears in your mind. You may, all of a sudden, know what to do in a situation where you have been burdened with indecision. Sometimes you get a vision of what you need to do next." Another moment of silence followed.

"What you have to know is that Source responds through our hearts, our minds, our emotions, and our bodies," Grandma added. "Source responds to us through our human forms."

Turning her head to look at me and putting her right hand on her chest, Grandma said, "When people say listen to your heart, this is what they mean. You have to listen to the messages and watch for the signs that come to you through your heart, through your body. When the answers come to you, you will know. The answers will feel right for you and for your life at that moment."

Returning her gaze to the distance, Grandma said, "Now, before concluding your prayer, you need to give thanks and be grateful as if Source has already answered your prayers. Even as you pray, you must remember to praise Source for the guidance and the blessings you receive in your life." A brief pause followed.

"Starting your day in communion with Source is a powerful way to live your life," Grandma said. "When you start the day by asking Source to guide your activities and when you follow your heart and take action according to that guidance, then you are living a guided life. Your life becomes a guided journey. You realize that, indeed, every life is a guided journey."

Grandma fell silent for a while. The silence was broken by the growling of my stomach. I felt a little embarrassed, but Grandma smiled and said, "We better be heading home. I think it is time to nourish our bodies."

We got up and wandered into the surrounding bushes on the hillside, gathering firewood to take home. Grandma untied the rope around her waist that doubled as a belt to "keep her dress in place," as she called it and to tie bundles of firewood. She tightened the rope securely around her firewood pile. I took the belt from the skirt of the matching two-piece set that I was wearing and used it to tie one end of my firewood bundle. I then unwrapped the scarf I had around my neck and used it to tie the other end of my firewood bundle.

Grandma unwrapped her shawl from around her shoulders and twisted it into a coil pad, a *hata,* and handed it to me. I smiled at my grandmother as I reached for the *hata*. I placed the *hata* on top of my head as a cushion, and then I hoisted my firewood bundle to rest on the *hata*. My grandmother took off her hat, folded it in half lengthwise and placed it on her head to use as her *hata*. She then lifted her firewood bundle onto her head.

We hiked down the hill, our firewood bundles on our heads. Grandma was in front with her right hand on her walking stick and her left holding onto her bundle of firewood. I followed right behind her heels, my firewood bundle carefully balanced on my head.

The village was now awake and teaming with activity. Men cracked whips at the bellowing cattle and bleating goats, driving the animals to pasture. Dust puffs rose at homesteads as women swept the yards.

When we arrived at the wooden gate to our homestead, I glanced over at the homestead next to our place. The neighbors, an elderly couple, were sitting under the eaves of their cooking hut, taking refuge from the morning sun that was already blazing. The woman sat on the ground and the man sat on a wooden stool, both resting their backs against the brick walls of the hut. I shouted my morning greetings, and the couple shouted back their greetings in unison.

Grandma and I walked through the gate and unloaded our firewood bundles in the yard. I made a fire in Grandma's hut and prepared a breakfast of cornmeal porridge with peanut butter. And we ate in silence.

After breakfast, my grandmother took a goatskin mat and spread it under the shade of a fig (*muonde*) tree at the edge of the yard, then she lay down on the mat to rest. This was her favorite spot to take naps during the day—under the shade of the *muonde* tree. After I washed and put away the breakfast dishes, I joined my grandmother under the shade tree.

Grandma must have sensed my presence, because she opened her eyes and slowly sat up. She cleared her throat, looking up at the sky.

"It is very hot today. It feels good to sit under the shade," she said.

Then Grandma looked at me for a moment. I smiled and nodded my head. She returned my nod and started to speak. "There are times when one can clearly feel the guiding hand of Source in the unfolding of one's life events," she said, her voice strong and steady. "One of my clearest experiences of receiving guidance from Source happened in the first few years I was married to your grandfather. As you know, we were married for a number of years before I could give your grandfather children," she paused, casting her eyes to the ground.

"In those days," she continued "it was a big shame to the family if a woman could not bear children for her husband. Women were shunned for that. But your grandfather stood by me and told me that we would have children if we were meant to raise a family," she paused again.

"I finally bore him a son," Grandma said. "*Maiweee*!" she exclaimed.

Continuing to recount her memories, she said, "Your grandfather must have been the happiest person I had ever seen. He loved that child as I had never seen a man love a child before. There was nothing he would not do for that child."

Grandma raised her eyes to look at me, a sadness clouding her face.

"As life would have it," she said, "one morning I woke up to find our son dead beside me. He was barely a year old. I neither heard a cry nor felt a movement during the night. It was as if he quietly slipped away from us."

Grandma closed her eyes and continued to talk, her voice calm. "Your grandfather was inconsolable in the days and weeks following the death of our son. He walked around as if in a daze, sometimes muttering to himself. He blamed himself for what had happened. He said that as a medicine man, he should have been able to save our son. He could not understand how he could be given the powers to heal other people and save their lives, but could not save his own son. He seemed angry that he had not been given the chance to heal our son, because we did not even know that our son was ill. Your grandfather kept asking what his medicine was good for if he could not save his own son. I had never seen a man so brokenhearted before in my life. I didn't know which pained me more, the loss of our son or watching your grandfather grieve. It took him a long time to recover from the loss."

Opening her eyes and staring into the distance, she said, "A little over a year after our son died, we were blessed with another child—a little girl this time. Your grandfather loved that girl and treated her like a princess. It seemed as if he had forgotten all the pain and heartache of losing our first son. And again, we lost that child when she was just over a year old; like her brother, she left us quietly in her sleep. This happened again with our third child, another boy, and our fourth child, another girl. Both died before they reached the age of one."

Still staring in the distance, my grandmother went on. "When my fifth child was born, another son, I prayed to Source every single day and asked it to show me what it was I had to do to keep my baby alive. And I sat and listened for the answers; I listened for long periods of time."

Grandma turned toward me, our eyes meeting. The veil of sadness had lifted off her face, replaced by a serene expression. "One morning as I listened, I received my answer in the form of a vision. I saw myself carrying my baby on my back and going to visit an old woman who lived alone in the next village. Most people considered this old woman a witch, and therefore avoided her. But my vision was so clear and I was desperate to keep my child alive that I was willing to try anything." Grandma shifted her gaze to the horizon, I did the same as I continued to listen.

"That evening," Grandma continued "I told your grandfather that I was visiting my sister who lived in the same village as the woman I had seen in my vision. When I left your grandfather, I went to the old woman's homestead. I found her standing by the doorway of her hut. As she hurried me in, she told me that she had been expecting me for a long time. She took the baby, undressed him, tightly wrapped him in a clean cloth, and poured a concoction of herbs down his throat. In a very short time, the baby started vomiting violently and sweating profusely. I was overwhelmed by fear, I thought my baby was going to die. All this time, the baby did not cry, not even a whimper." A short pause followed.

"My poor baby was heaving and emptying his insides, but he did not cry." Grandma added, shaking her head from side to side.

"Then the vomiting stopped," she continued. "The old woman bathed the baby in warm water laced with herbs. Then she wrapped him in a clean cloth, handed him back to me, and told me to go back home. I went to see my sister as I had told your grandfather, and then returned home. I never told anyone about my visit to the old woman, not even your grandfather."

Grandma was quiet for a long moment.

"My boy lived," she said eventually. "That boy is your uncle, Pasipanodya. I named him *Pasipanodya* (the ground consumes) as a reminder of the powers of Source to take away that which it gives. I buried four of my children in the ground, and the ground consumed them."

Continuing on, she said, "After that, I took all the babies I bore—your aunt, your father, and your three other uncles—to that same old woman, and she performed the same ritual she had performed on your uncle. And my six children are all still living to this day. I never questioned Source as to why my first four children died. I never asked what the old woman was doing to keep the ones I had alive, and she never told me. Each time I took a baby to her, I found her waiting by her doorstep, and after each ritual she handed the baby back to me and told me to go home." Grandma paused again.

"I thank Source every day for leading me to that old woman," she finally said. "And I thank Source every day for the joy of the six children that I raised. They are the blessings of my life to this day. And Source has blessed me even more by giving me many grandchildren."

I had known about the deaths of my grandparents' children but had never heard the complete story. Grandma's voice, as she narrated the events, had such a comforting sense of acceptance of the way things were meant to be. She seemed to know, at a deep level, that what had happened was part of her journey. And she seemed to know that she had received the blessings of raising her children and seeing her grandchildren because she had followed the guidance from Source.

After a lengthy pause, my grandmother continued with her lesson. "As I mentioned earlier this morning, we come into the world on a journey. Everyone has a choice to travel the journey alone or to be guided by Source. Most of us end up traveling alone out of ignorance, because no one taught us how to seek the guidance of Source as we live our lives. Yet this is the simplest thing to do. When you establish your sense of connection to Source every single day, you will receive blessings at every turn of the way. It starts by committing to connect to Source first thing in the morning—as the sun rises. This is one of the most powerful rituals you can adopt to change your life for the better."

Continuing on, she said, "But also remember that as you go through your day, you must keep a part of your mind rooted in Source. It doesn't matter what you are doing—you should perform all your tasks connected to Source. When you are fetching water, cleaning dishes, gathering firewood, or performing other chores, be aware that Source is making possible your every move and give thanks for that blessing. Then at night, right before you go to sleep, take a few moments to give thanks to Source for all the events of the day. When you do this, you will train your mind to always keep a sense of connection to Source, and in doing so you allow the energy from Source to freely flow through you at all times. If you remember to do this, then your life becomes a channel for Source to shine through you for all others to see."

She went on. "As human beings, we don't need money, power, or influence to live a life of joy in this world. All we need is to maintain a sense of our connection to Source. And in that state, we can ask for blessings for ourselves, for others, and for the world."

With that, the day's teaching ended. Grandma said that she felt rested and was ready to work in the vegetable garden. We left the shade of the *muonde* tree and went to weed and water the small vegetable garden that stood beside the borehole. We worked until it was time for lunch. I made a light lunch of *sadza* and fresh vegetables we had picked from the garden, making sure to boil the vegetables until they had almost crumbled so that my grandmother could eat them. With no teeth left in her mouth except for one, Grandma mostly ate things that did not require chewing, so most of her food had to be boiled to a soup.

After lunch, I went outside and washed the dishes. And as I continued with the chores for the rest of the day, I kept my grandmother's lesson from that morning in my mind, and I tried to see Source in every action that I was performing.

As the sun was starting to set, I saw my uncle, *Baba va*Tatenda, coming toward the homestead. I knew that he frequently came to check on Grandma.

"*Tisvikewo!*" my uncle announced his arrival, opening the wooden gate and walking into the yard.

"You may arrive, *Moyondizvo*," I responded to my uncle's salutation. "*Masikati!*" I added, saying the afternoon greeting to my uncle.

"*Masikati maMoyo!*"

"How did you spend the day, *Moyondizvo?*"

My uncle replied that he had spent the day well.

He was wearing an old pair of denim dungarees spotting holes at the knees, paired with a faded brown T-shirt that had seen too many washings. His dusty callused feet were clad in his signature homemade sandals. His clothes had muddy spots all over, so I suspected that, like us, he had spent part of his day in his vegetable garden.

"I saw you coming down the hill with your grandmother this morning," he said. "I am glad that you are joining your grandmother in her morning walks. Going up the hill every morning is very important to her. It seems to make her happy and to add years to her life." I nodded my head in response and smiled, but didn't say anything.

My uncle walked toward Grandma's hut and disappeared inside. As I watched him, I wondered whether he knew what his mother did when she went up the hill every morning. I wondered whether he knew the real person behind his mother. I wondered whether he knew how she had received and followed the guidance that had probably saved his life, the guidance that had probably saved the lives of all her surviving children. Then I thought about the mystery of life, the supernatural aspect of it that we miss as we go about our busy days. I thought about how we, as human beings, walk in the world totally oblivious to the true nature of our lives. I thought about how we are blind to the richness of our lives that exists beyond the perception of the physical senses.

Communion

I breathe deeply
And quiet my mind, still my emotions, and calm my body
Reaching my heart
The part of my being connecting me to you, Divine Love
Your unconditional love rises in my heart
And flows into my mind, emotions, and body
A cleansing balm to my human form

I am filled with a sense of well-being
Cradled in your arms, I feel supported
I let go and relax in your warm embrace

My awareness stays focused
On the energy of unconditional love in my heart
I let the love
Wash away the bonds holding me back from you, Divine Love
I access the knower who knows the truth about my life
I am lifted up and out of my old life
Releasing the past
Leaving all my mistakes and transgressions behind
The burdens that weigh me down are dissolved
And I am light and afloat again

As I continue to go deep into my being
Reaching a depth
Where you dwell in my heart
I feel a sense of complete freedom, Divine Love
I am free from chaos and confusion
I am free from fear, anxiety, doubt, and worry
I am redeemed and made new again
I am fresh
I am whole and complete
Ready to be a vessel for you

I feel the energy
Flowing from you through my being
Bringing with it a sense of an all-encompassing love
A comforting sense of calmness and serenity
And a peace beyond all understanding
From this place of love and peace
I set the intention for you, Divine Love

To flow through me and out into the world
Blessing all the forms that I encounter
Today and every day of my life
Amen

WE ARE HERE TO
CO-CREATE WITH SOURCE

A pleasant breeze greeted us on our morning walk to the hillside the next day. When we arrived at our sitting area, we settled down for our time in silence. Grandma had her eyes closed and her head slightly turned up toward the sky. I sat with my eyes open and my gaze fixed on the eastern horizon, waiting for the sun to rise. A thought had come to me in the middle of the night. I would watch the sunrise and ask the sun to guide my mind back into my heart and into a sense of connection with Source. I would ask the sun to guide me on my way back home into Source. This was going to be my prayer.

The sunrise was another breathtaking display of colors. Layers of deep amber, reddish purple, and coral pink appeared over the hills in the east. As the sun slowly climbed out of the valley, the colors gradually spread until the sky above the eastern horizon became a live iridescent shimmer. I was hypnotized. Emotion rose up in me. It felt as if what I was witnessing on the outside was also happening within me. It felt as if the sun was moving inside me and painting the same dazzling images in my heart that it was painting in the sky. I closed my eyes. The sun was now inside my heart. With my focus on my heart, I prayed in a soft whisper.

I follow the sun in my heart. The sun is leading me back to Source. The sun is leading me back to my connection with the energy that guides and fuels my life. I am on my way home to Source.

I repeated this prayer several times, and then fell silent. My attention remained on the sun within my heart and on my intention for the sun to lead me home. My mind was quiet, my emotions still, and my body calm. A sense of peace settled over me, and I relaxed into the peace. I lost track of time and thought.

I slowly opened my eyes and noticed that Grandma was no longer sitting beside me. I must have dozed off because I didn't hear her get up and leave. As I surveyed the area, I caught a glimpse of my grandmother behind scruffy bushes a short distance away. She was tying a bundle of firewood to take home. When she looked up and saw that I had opened my eyes, she made her way back to the sitting area and carefully lowered her body to the ground, sitting down to start the day's lesson.

She took a few deep breaths and, with her gaze staring at the valley below us, started to speak. "In the beginning, Source created the world and everything that we see in it. Source continues to create every single day, and will continue to create until the end of time. It creates more birds from the birds that already exist. It creates more plants from the plants that already exist. It creates more fishes from the fishes that already exist. It creates more animals from the animals that already exist. And it creates more human beings from the human beings that already exist."

I could sense from Grandma's voice that she was getting excited as she continued to talk. "As I said yesterday, watching nature can teach us many valuable life lessons. We can learn from the seed as it travels on its journey to become a plant. When given proper conditions of soil, moisture, and sunlight, the seed wakes up from its deep sleep and sends its roots into the ground and its shoot above the ground. It grows into a plant that provides food or shelter. The plant flowers, bears fruit, and forms more seeds. And before it dies, the plant scatters its seeds on the ground. During the next season, more plants will sprout out of the scattered seeds, and these seeds will continue the cycle of life. In this way, the seed co-creates with Source."

Turning her head to look directly at me, Grandma went on. "It is the same with us human beings. We too are here to co-create with Source. We are born to our parents, who raise us the best way that they can. We go through our teenage years and eventually become adults. We bear our own children and do our best to raise them. Our children grow up to become adults who bear their own children. And when we eventually die, we leave our children and grandchildren behind to continue the cycle of life."

As I gazed at my grandmother, listening to the words she was speaking, I felt a now familiar emotion rise up in me. It was the same emotion I had felt as I watched the sunrise—a slow warm feeling coursing through my body. Then I saw the twinkle in her eyes and knew something important was coming, so I listened intently.

"But in human beings, Source gave something else!" Grandma exclaimed, raising her right hand and poking the air with her index finger. "In human beings, the ability to create is not only limited to producing other human beings. It also extends to creating ideas and acting on those ideas to bring new forms into the world. As human beings, we are capable of considering different options of what to co-create with Source. We can choose to create one thing over another. We can choose to follow one path over another. Source gives us free will." She rested her hand in her lap.

I could now see where Grandma was going with her teaching.

"We obtain ideas and act on those ideas to change a condition or a situation," Grandma continued to speak, her eyes returning to the view of the valley. "Each creative idea that comes through a human being is flowing from Source; it is a creative impulse rising from Source. Each creative idea is the life force seeking to be expressed in new ways—as new forms or new objects in the visible world." Grandma paused briefly, taking a few deep breaths.

"An idea that arises in the mind of a human being is the energy of Source guiding that person to create something that did not exist before." Grandma continued to speak. "It is Source breathing life into that person so that a new form can come into existence. We call such ideas insights. All human beings have the capacity for insight, but very few of us know that, and even fewer utilize this ability to access direct knowledge from Source. The ideas that we get through insight are meant to build on what already exists in the world. The ideas are meant to improve our way of living and to improve our environment."

Intrigued, I asked, "*Mbuya*, do you mean ideas such as inventions?"

"Yes, it can be inventions as you say, or any other new form. Think of the people who discovered how to make fire to cook food. Think of the people who discovered how to build shelter so the tribes could be protected from the harsh elements, and how to cultivate crops so there is adequate food for the tribes all the time. Those discoveries started as ideas that were perceived, through insight, and acted upon by human beings. Just imagine where the human race would be if those ideas had not been perceived and acted upon. I think we would still be living in the jungle like animals."

I was now nodding, completely understanding the points my grandmother was making.

"You also have to remember something," Grandma continued. "The insights we receive are not always great ideas that bring about big changes to the way the world works—like the inventions that you mentioned. Sometimes the insights may appear small and insignificant. As an example, let us say that one person in a tribe received an idea to plant sorghum and millet instead of corn during the rainy season, and he acted according to that insight when everyone else planted fields and fields of corn. Then let us say the rainfall is poor that year. In hindsight, that person would then realize that he was guided to plant sorghum and millet because, unlike corn which requires a heavy rainfall to produce, sorghum and millet bring in bumper harvests despite poor rains. The insight that this person received and followed would ensure that there is enough food for everyone in the tribe, even if the corn fails."

Giving another example, she said, "Or one person may have an idea to tell a story to the young. That story may turn out to be the inspiration that marks a turning point in the life of a youngster who was struggling to find a direction in life. That youngster might grow up to be the leader of a nation one day."

Grandma stopped for a moment, licked her dry lips, and then continued to speak. "As human beings, we need to understand that Source is always seeking to express through us in the form of ideas, messages, or insights. But the only time we can perceive this guidance is when our minds are quiet and resting in our hearts. The only time we can receive ideas, messages, or insights from Source is when our minds are not clouded by the little things that show up in our day-to-day lives and tend to absorb our attention."

She looked at me and said, "I shall ask you this question: When your mind is busy thinking about all the things you need to do that day, is there room for you to listen to Source?" I carefully considered Grandma's question, then shook my head.

"You are correct. No, there is no room to listen to Source," she said. "I shall ask you another question. What about when you are worrying about how you will get money to buy that new thing that you want; is there room to listen to Source?" I shook my head again, still looking at my grandmother.

"The answer is no again," she said. "And it is the same answer when you are thinking about the person who did something to hurt you. Or when you are thinking about what you dislike about this or the other. These types of thoughts distract your attention, and you turn away from Source and no longer listen to the very guidance that helps your life to unfold with ease."

I nodded, agreeing with what my grandmother was saying.

"When you carefully observe our lives as human beings, you will find that instead of listening to the messages from Source, we spend our time thinking and worrying about things that do not matter. We spend our time remembering the reason why we do not like this person or that situation, or judging this person or that situation, or replaying incidents that made us angry a long time ago, or replaying the tragedies of our lives. Source created our minds as mediums to communicate with us and let us know what we need to do next to create in the world, guiding us from moment to moment so that we can create according to its plan. But what do we do?" Grandma asked rhetorically. "Instead of listening for guidance from Source, we let our minds be preoccupied by small issues, and even harmful thoughts in some instances."

Shifting her gaze to a point in the distance, Grandma said, "When you take Source out of the human mind, you take away the ability of human beings to create for the good of the whole. In our tongue, we have a saying that captures this understanding very well. We say, *Simba rehove riri mumvura* (The strength of the fish is in the water)." She coughed, clearing her throat.

"When a fish is taken out of the water," Grandma continued speaking, "it will wriggle and writhe and flap its head and tail about. If it is not returned to the water, it will die. The same is true with us human beings. When we lose our sense of connection to Source, when we lose our sense of connection to our water of life, we enter a state of chaos and confusion. And if we do not regain our sense of connection to Source, this state of chaos and confusion eventually leads to our destruction." She paused, running her tongue over her dry lips again.

"On the other hand, when we are in the fold of Source, we are in our water of life. We maintain our sense of connection to Source. When we are in that state, we can directly perceive ideas, messages, and insights that flow from Source, and we can take action according to the guidance we receive. Any action that we take in a state of connection to Source positively contributes to what the world becomes."

Then there was silence.

I couldn't believe what I was hearing from this old woman I had known all my life as a beloved grandmother and protector. Grandma seemed to be speaking from a place I had never heard her speak from before—a place deeper than could be seen on the surface. She seemed to be channeling from someplace deep inside of her, someplace beyond her.

The silence stretched. Glancing at Grandma I saw that she had closed her eyes. I let her be. I got up and walked into the surrounding bushes. My mind was full of the information she had just shared.

What Grandma had said about creating made me think of human nature in a different way. I began seeing things with fresh eyes. I now could clearly see that the inventions that have contributed to the evolution of the human race began as ideas in people's minds. The ideas came through people who perceived them and acted upon those ideas to bring new forms in the world.

I thought of the idea of creating ships that sailed across oceans. This idea led to the expansion of the human race into further places. Trains, cars, and planes, which are even faster modes of transportation, came later to further enable the migration of humans from one place to the other. Then humans built spaceships that enabled travel into space and culminated in the historic moon landing. I wondered what mode of transportation would come next and, more importantly, where it would take humanity. Standing on the hillside, I stared into space as thoughts continued to roam in my mind.

From what Grandma had said, I understood that if I reoriented my mind to align with my heart and with Source, and I surrendered, then I would connect to the energy of Source and receive ideas, messages, and insights from this realm. And if I followed those ideas by taking action, I would be creating according to the plan of Source; I would be a co-creator with Source. In this way, I would be contributing to the growth and expansion of the world.

It sounded simple enough.

A question came to me: If it is this simple, why is it that I and most human beings don't make the effort to reorient our minds to align with our hearts and with Source, so that we co-create the good that would lead to the positive growth and expansion of the world?

More questions came to me: What if there were ideas waiting to be expressed through me, and I didn't even know about them? What if that is true for every human being on this planet? What if each of us is meant to bring something new and different into the world? What if each of us carry our own unique destinies within us, in just the same way that the seed carries its destiny within it? What needs to change for us as human beings so that we can start to freely express in the same way that the seed freely expresses?

I continued to think about what my grandmother had shared as I gathered firewood to carry home. After a short while, Grandma stood up and stretched and then said it was time to go back home. We carried our firewood bundles and went down the hill.

After breakfast, I kept myself busy washing dishes, cleaning the hut, and washing clothes while Grandma took another nap under the shade of the *muonde* tree. I made a light lunch of boiled pumpkin for us, which we ate under the shade. When we finished our lunch, Grandma suggested that we make some peanut butter as we had run out.

Making peanut butter from scratch is one of the chores I used to enjoy when I was growing up. After washing and putting away the lunch dishes, I climbed into the *hozi* to fetch a basket of unshelled peanuts. I took the basket to the shade where my grandmother was still sitting, and we started shelling the peanuts. The afternoon was hot and still, with hardly any noise except the gentle cracking of peanut shells under the pressure of our fingers and the bird songs in the distance. We worked quietly, each lost in thought.

As the afternoon heat died down, we went inside the hut where Grandma roasted the shelled peanuts in a *rwaenga,* a large piece of a broken clay pot serving as a roasting pan. She preferred to roast the peanuts over glowing embers rather than a burning flame, as the flame was likely to overheat the *rwaenga* and burn the peanuts—ruining the peanut butter.

I watched as Grandma deftly moved the peanuts around the *rwaenga* with her bare hands, taking care not to burn her fingers on the hot surface. The pink skins of the peanuts started turning a burgundy color and a pleasant aroma filled the hut. When the peanuts were roasted to her liking, Grandma transferred them to a *rusero*, a round-shaped tray-like utensil woven out of river reeds. She gently squeezed the peanuts with her hands to remove the flaky skins, blowing the skins away with gentle puffs of her breath. Then she handed the roasted peanuts to me.

I retrieved a wooden mortar and pestle set stored under the *hozi*. I cleaned the mortar and pestle by rubbing them with dry cornmeal. Then I poured the roasted peanuts in the mortar. Using rhythmic up and down strokes of the pestle, I pounded the peanuts until they had the consistency of a crunchy paste.

Next, I scooped the peanut paste from the mortar to finish the smoothing process with a pair of grinding stones that sat beside the *hozi*, the large rectangular grinding stone (*guyo*) and accompanying small stone (*huyo*). Kneeling at the back end of the *guyo,* I placed the peanut paste on the edge of the *guyo* near me and put a collecting plate on the other edge—where the processed peanut butter would flow out. Using both hands, I pressed down on the *huyo,* sliding it over the *guyo* with smooth forward and backward motions of my body, crushing the peanut paste into a fine smooth butter with each stroke. As I worked, I recalled the countless times I had ground peanuts while growing up, and I found myself settling into the familiar rhythm.

It took about thirty minutes of back and forth movements for me to finish grinding the whole batch of the peanut paste. By the time I finished, I'd had a good aerobic workout and was breathing hard. My knees felt a little raw from kneeling for such a long time. I got up and stretched and then took the plate full of peanut butter into the hut.

When I entered the hut, Grandma broke into a praise poem, expressing her gratitude for my help in making the peanut butter. She said:

"Maita, Moyo. Maita, Sahayi. Maita, Dhewa. Tinotenda, veDzimbabwe. VaRozvi vakapera nenda. Maita, vachirera nherera. Vanorera nedzisi dzavo. Munyaradzi wevanochema. Zvirambe zvakadaro, Sahayi. (Thank you, Moyo.

Thank you, Sahayi. Thank you, Dhewa. Thank you, those from Dzimbabwe. Those from the Rozvi clan who perished by lice. Thank you those who take care of orphans. Even taking care of orphans who do not belong to them. Comforter to those who cry. Let it always be like that, Sahayi.)"

I loved praise poetry, a hallmark of the Shona tradition. Praise poetry, as I had learned growing up, was used to express gratitude, appreciation, or sing the praises of another person who had been of service in one way or another. Each clan has a particular set of words and phrases that are recited for its members, addressing a person by the *mutupo, chidawo,* or other attributes for that clan. The poem recited to a person can be short or quite long, sometimes recounting the clan's history including the areas where the clan originated from and where the clan's ancestors were buried. Each phrase, idiom, or proverb used in the poem has a story behind it, which the elders taught to the young members of the clan. These stories were another way of reminding clan members of their rich heritage. The idea was to make the person being thanked feel a sense of connection to those who lived before him or her, and therefore a sense of connection to a bigger whole. In the traditional setting, it was common for someone to have a praise poem recited to them several times a day, each time that he or she performed a good deed.

A special feeling comes over one when they hear praise poetry recited to them. It's a kind of warm glow inside. This warm glow was rising in me now as I listened to my grandmother reciting the poem to me. I have heard it said that the warm glow that one feels rising up is the spirit dancing in ecstasy. The warm glow stayed with me as I cooked our dinner of *sadza* with a stew of dried deer meat in a peanut butter sauce.

I Am a Co-Creator with Source

Divine Love
The deep silence
The spacious stillness
The infinite formlessness
From which arises the energy of unconditional love
That brings into form that which was not there before

I root and anchor myself in that which you are

My source and my supply for all that I will ever need

I thank you for my life that you freely give to me

I am a part of the creative force that you are

I feel you as the energy that rises in my heart

And flows through my mind

Bringing the intuitions

That I perceive as ideas, messages, and insights

To guide my thoughts, my emotions, my words, and my actions

So that from this day going forward

I am a co-creator with you, the source of my life

Creating the forms that are needed in this world

For the world to grow, expand, and evolve to the next level

To glorify your name and sing your praises

I pray let this be the way that I live my life

Today and all the days that I am here on this earth

With this prayer I surrender into you, Divine Love

Until the day I return into you

Amen

RETURNING TO LOVE

T he nights spent curled on the floor of my grandmother's hut were taking a toll on my body. That evening, I decided I would sleep on a bed in the main sleeping house. After dinner, Grandma and I sat outside her hut, enjoying the moonlight and the gentle evening breeze. Grandma finally got up to go into her hut and I got up to go to the main sleeping house.

"*Ave mangwana, Mbuya!*" I said, bidding good night to my grandmother.

"*Ave mangwana, Yeukai!*" she responded in a soft voice, closing the door of her hut.

I walked the few yards from Grandma's hut to the sleeping house, unlocked the front door, and entered the small sitting room. Soft moonlight came through the open doorway, bathing the room in an eerie grayish light. Three doors led from the sitting room to the three bedrooms. The door directly in front of me led to my parents' bedroom, the one on my left led to the boys' room, and the one on my right led to the girls' room. I went into the girls' room and stretched on the comfortable bed that took up almost half the room, not bothering to get under the bedcovers.

Even though my body was tired, my mind was too restless for sleep. I lay awake for hours staring at the ceiling. Grandma's words had stirred a lot in me, and I had many things to ponder. I was still trying to wrap my mind around the profoundness of what Grandma was teaching me and, again, appreciated the way she kept her language very simple. She was communicating the key points in a very straightforward way, as if she were teaching a small child. Maybe that was the only way I could grasp the essence of what she was conveying. In many ways, my understanding of spiritual matters was like that of a child.

According to what Grandma had taught me so far, as human beings, we all have the ability to connect to Source at any time and under any circumstances, and to allow its creative energy to flow through us and bring new creations into the world. We don't need a fancy education, we don't need power and control over others, we don't need a lot of money, and we don't need to be born into privilege. All we need is our willingness to connect to Source.

What is even more amazing is what we can accomplish when we stay connected to Source. In that state, we can perceive ideas, messages, and insights coming directly from Source. And if we choose to act according to the guidance we receive from Source, any one of us could be the person who introduces a new invention to the world, a new way of being in the world, a new way of expressing in the world—a new song, a new dance, a new teaching, a new message. In this way, we become co-creators with Source.

Again, I asked the questions that had been plaguing my mind. If it is this simple, why don't we as human beings connect to Source and let our lives be guided by the energy from it? Why don't we choose to allow ourselves to be channels for new creations to come into the world? Why don't we choose to create conditions that allow us to live our lives in love, joy, and creativity?

The answers to these questions came with the next teaching.

The next morning, Grandma and I walked to our spot on the hillside. After our silent communion with Source, we settled down for the day's lesson.

"I can see by the look in your eyes that you have more questions," Grandma said, her soft gaze appraising me.

"Yes, I do, *Mbuya*," I responded. "I lay awake last night, and I kept thinking of the same thing. What is it that prevents us as human beings from connecting to Source so that we can create conditions that bring peace and joy to everyone in the world?"

"Aha!" Grandma exclaimed, pointing a finger at me, a wide grin spreading on her face. Resting her hand in her lap, she said, "That is the right question to ask, my child. I am so glad you are asking this question. It shows me that you are following what I am sharing with you."

Grandma closed her eyes, breathing in deeply, holding her breath for a second, then breathing out deeply. She repeated the breathing cycle one more time and then opened her eyes, resting her gaze on my face as she went into her teaching, which was her way of answering my question.

"Source created the world in love and commanded all that is in it to live in love. Source wants us to live our lives with peace in our minds, joy in our hearts, seeing and experiencing love in everything we do. Source wants us to live in harmony with nature—with the birds, the plants, the fishes, the animals, the mountains, the valleys, the forests, the lakes, the rivers. And it wants us to make creativity the main focus of our lives." Her gaze shifted from my face to the valley below us.

"The trouble is, many of us human beings are not aware of the intention of Source, the intention that we live our lives in love, peace, and joy. This ignorance is apparent when one takes the time to observe how most of us live our lives today."

Returning her eyes to my face, Grandma asked, "When you observe your life and the lives of those around you, what do you see?" she paused for a moment. "Do you see people living in love, peace, and joy?" I kept looking at my grandmother, but didn't say anything.

Shaking her head, Grandma answered her own question. "The answer is no!"

Returning her gaze to the valley, a sober look now on her face, she said, "What we see in our lives and in the lives of others around us is suffering of one form or another. We see people living in fear. We see people living in worry, doubt, and despair. We see people lashing out in anger, rage, and hatred. We see cruelty and violence directed against other people and against nature. We see people living not in love but in fear, not in peace but in confusion, and not in joy but in sorrow. And we see people not focused on creating, but focused on destroying the things that Source has created."

Grandma had accurately summed up the human condition as I had witnessed it so far in my life. I realized that what she was saying was helping me to expand my perception of the world we lived in. I continued to listen as she went on.

"What we see on display is a result of negative forces that seem to take over the lives of most of us human beings. In some of us, we have not yet learned how to control these negative forces; therefore, the forces take over our lives and manifest the chaos and confusion that we see around us. In some of us, we may have learned how to manage the negative forces and we strive to live a life of balance. But you also have to realize that even when we manage to find balance in our own lives, we still live in a world where a lot of people have not yet learned how to manage the negative forces that live inside them. And those people may attack us in one form or another."

"That is very deep, *Mbuya*," I couldn't help saying.

Grandma slowly turned her head, looking directly at me as she continued to speak. "You may want to live your life in peace, but you find yourself a victim of a violent crime. Your possessions might be taken away from you by force, you may be raped, or your family may be harmed in some way. You or your family members may be victims of any number of cruel or violent acts at the hands of your fellow human beings. The negative energies—or you may call them bad spirits—that cause people to harm others possess us when we don't learn how to maintain a sense of connection to Source. It happens when we forget that we originate from Source and are here in this world as part of Source. We forget that at our core, we are still love. In that forgetting, each of us seeks the meaning of life outside of Source. We seek the meaning of our lives in the things of the world, separate from Source."

Grandma's eyes stared into mine as she said, "Therein lies the cause of the suffering that we human beings inflict on ourselves, on each other, and on nature." I held her gaze as the words she spoke sank in. Then she broke the gaze, once again turning back to stare at the valley as she continued on.

"We seek meaning in things that we accumulate. In the olden days, it was about the number of cows and goats that a man owned, the size of the land that he had, or the number of wives and children he had. In these modern times, people seek meaning in many countless things that I do not even understand." Grandma cast her gaze to the ground, shaking her head. She was quiet for a moment.

I was fascinated by what I was hearing. This concept that we as human beings lose our way and seek an identity outside of Source was new to me. Of course, in hindsight I could clearly see that this is what I and many others do. In my case, and I am sure in the case of many others, this is done out of ignorance. Now that my grandmother had planted this thought in my mind, it was as if my mind opened up and I could clearly see the endless list of things we identify with: our family names and fortunes; the churches, groups, or clubs we belong to; who we are married to; who we associate with; the level of our education; the positions we hold in our professions; the level of income we earn; the size of our bank accounts; the properties we accumulate; the fancy clothes we buy; and the big houses we live in—the list goes on and on.

Grandma continued to speak, her eyes still downcast. "What is even worse is that we start separating ourselves into different groups based on these false measures. In the old days, we separated ourselves on tribal lines, and we also separated ourselves into those with wealth and those without it."

Lifting her head and gazing into the distance, she said, "With the coming of *varungu*, they taught us that we all should follow their religion and become Christians. This created a division of those who joined the Christian religion and those who followed our traditional ways of worshiping Source. But it goes further than that. Even for the Christians, there seems to be different kinds that do not mix. You are told you are either a Catholic, an Anglican, a Methodist, a Lutheran, a Seventh-Day Adventist, an Apostolic Faith, or this or the other. Each group has its own set of beliefs and rules, and these groups do not agree with each other on many issues of how to live a life that is rooted in Source. The Christians said they were bringing the truth to us, but they, among themselves, could not even agree on what that truth was." Grandma went quiet again, lost in thought.

My grandmother had touched on a subject I had always found to be a bit confusing: organized religion. My experience with most religious organizations and groups—whether they were churches, factions, or sects—was that they tended to focus on differences between groups of people, thereby promoting fragmentation rather than focusing on similarities to promote unity. Most religious organizations also seemed to be formed around one or a few power-hungry individuals who somehow managed to command unquestioned influence over their followers. Even if the groups were initially founded on admirable principles, something tended to happen along the way, and, before long, the power and control issues came into play.

The other thing I had noticed as well was the inconsistencies in what people who belonged to religious groups professed to believe as part of their religious faith and what they practiced in their real lives—when they took away the robes and left the pulpits, when they left the houses of worship, when they were behind closed doors. As a child, I used to find it confusing when church leaders and elders would preach on morals and values in church, and then would do things that were contrary to what they were preaching. As a youngster, it was hard enough trying to learn right from wrong and to grasp what was acceptable and unacceptable behavior within a society. Adding layers of inconsistencies was just, well, adding more confusion—at least that was my experience.

Unfortunately, as an adult I still witnessed these inconsistencies in what people preached and what they practiced. And this is not just in religious groups, but in different settings—government, schools, corporations, communities, and even within families and among friends.

I noticed that I was getting lost in my thoughts, so I took a deep breath and focused my attention back on what my grandmother was saying as she resumed her teaching.

"If you look at every level of human society, you will see divisions based on one measure or another. And with those false divisions comes the notion that I am better than you. With those false divisions comes the notion that we are better than them."

Grandma closed her eyes and took a few deep breaths. When she reopened them, she looked directly at me. I held her gaze. I knew this was one of her ways of conveying to me that she was about to share something of great importance, so I was alert.

"I have spoken to you about how we human beings lose our sense of connection to Source, and that most times we don't know how to regain that sense of connection. When we lose our sense of connection to Source, we forget that we ourselves are co-creators with Source and we forget that we have the ability to create any experience that we want in our lives. We forget that we can create good health. We forget that we can create wealth. We forget that we can create the resources we need to live our lives. Most important of all, we forget that we are one with other human beings and with nature." Grandma coughed softly, clearing her throat. Her gaze shifted to the distant horizon as she continued to speak.

"This is when the fighting begins. We begin to fight among each other for control of what we see as the limited resources available in the visible world. We forget that there are more resources available in a form that is not visible to us. We forget that, through our powers of co-creation with Source, we have the ability to bring the invisible resources into visible forms." Grandma paused to catch her breath, her gaze still on the horizon.

"In our limited perception, we fear that the limited resources we see and perceive with our physical senses will run out, and therefore we want to claim them for ourselves before someone else does. We begin to think in terms of shortages and we start gathering everything we can lay our hands on for ourselves. That is when you see a brother killing a brother over cattle; that is when you see one tribe killing another tribe to take their land, women, and children." Grandma cleared her throat again before continuing.

"Once the fighting starts, there is no end to it. If I kill you and take what is yours, then your children will kill me and take what they think I took from you. And my children will kill your children, and the vicious cycle continues." A long pause followed.

"Life is meant to be very simple," Grandma eventually said. "When I see myself in you, then I cannot hurt you. That is because in hurting you, I will be hurting myself. When you see yourself in me, then you cannot hurt me—again because in hurting me, you will be hurting yourself. If we see each other in this way, then we can see how as the human race we are all one. And in our oneness, we go back to our original selves and see ourselves as part of Source that we are. We rise up to the level where we no longer see the lines of separation between one human being and the next, and we regain all that we lost at the point of separation. We regain our humanity, and with that we regain our inheritance of living in love, peace, and joy with each other. In that state, we intuitively know that we are co-creators with Source, and we summon our creative powers and create that which we need. When we begin living in this way, the perception of shortages disappears."

My back was feeling stiff from sitting on the ground for a long time. I shifted slightly, finding a more comfortable sitting position. And I continued to listen to my grandmother.

"With the perception of shortages gone," Grandma continued, "there is no need to hoard resources. There is no need to pile mountains of possessions while others go without. There is no need to hoard cattle, money, food, or any other forms of possessions. With the perception of shortages gone, there is no need to forcibly take away resources from others because you think the resources may run out someday in the future. Eventually, this way of living will make violence and wars unnecessary. For if tribes or nations stop fighting over resources and possessions, there is nothing left to fight for."

Grandma appeared to be running out of breath, but she continued talking, her eyes now sparkling with excitement.

"Once we as the human race see ourselves as the same as nature—the birds, the fishes, the animals, the trees, the forests, the rivers, the valleys, and the mountains—then we see our oneness with nature, and we go back into our true selves and regain all that we lost at the point of separation. Collectively as the human race, we treat nature with respect, and we go back to living in harmony with nature."

Continuing on, Grandma said, "Without this simple return to the wisdom of knowing ourselves as beings connected to Source, we will continue to generate the kind of world that we live in today. We will continue to see the cruelty and violence that we see today. You do not have to look very far to see the evidence of destruction that has already started, from the individual level through families and communities. For us to go back to living in harmony, we need to let go of the negativity and return to love."

Grandma turned to look at me, a smile on her face. "I have spoken many words to you," she said, "and I want you to reflect on these words for yourself."

She got up and walked into the surrounding bushes. I remained seated, lost in my thoughts. When I finally got up, I saw that Grandma had already tied her firewood bundle. Piled beside her firewood bundle were some logs she had collected for me. I thanked my grandmother and tied the logs in a bundle, and we started downhill, heading home.

When we got to the foot of the hill, I spotted a group of children in the distance. There were about twelve to fifteen of them, ranging from about six to fourteen years of age. They were dressed in school uniforms, the girls in blue dresses and the boys in blue shirts and blue shorts. They were heading to the primary school across the river. The school was built before I was born. It had been recently renovated, the walls plastered and painted a pale yellow and the roofs covered in shiny zinc metal sheeting. This was part of the development programs that the government was implementing in rural areas. I really commended the government's efforts focused on improving education standards for children in rural areas across the country.

I thought of the opportunities that lay ahead for these children, if they worked hard in school. Then I thought of the life lessons my grandmother was teaching me. And something rose in my mind. What if, in addition to learning to read and write, these children were also taught life lessons similar to the life lessons my grandmother was teaching me? What if they also learned about Source and co-creating with it? I thought of the opportunities that could open for children who received a Western education together with traditional knowledge such as the teachings that my grandmother was passing on to me. The possibilities would be endless.

Unconditional Love

Divine Presence
I thank you for the blessing of the realization of who I am
Beyond name and form; beyond birth and death
I embrace the true nature of that which I am
As spirit connected to you, the Infinite Intelligence
As unconditional love expressing in human form
I take control of my thoughts, my words, and my actions
My thoughts are full of insights, revelations, and activating power
My words are full of wisdom that encourages, inspires, empowers, and heals
My actions reveal your love for your creation
I am a channel for you, Divine Energy
To flow from the invisible into the visible world
I am a channel for you, Eternal Presence
To bring a message of love into the world
This is how I honor you, Divine Love
In this day and in all the days that I will walk in this world
Living my life here on earth as it is in heaven
In you, I rest for always
Until the day I return home into you
Amen

FORGIVENESS IS THE KEY TO A
LIFE OF PEACE AND ABUNDANCE

On waking up the next morning, I quickly dressed and went outside, ready for my walk with my grandmother and for the day's teaching. When I didn't see Grandma out in the yard, I got a little concerned. I walked over to her hut and found her inside, searching for something. I bid her good morning and she answered my greeting distractedly, continuing to sift through her belongings. She picked a blanket, gave it a vigorous shake, and then put it down. She picked another blanket, shook it, and piled it on top of the first blanket. She lifted her *mutsago* and put it down. With a heavy sigh, she picked the blankets again and gave them another shake, now muttering under her breath.

"What are you looking for, *Mbuya*?" I finally asked.

"I lost my *nguwani*," Grandma replied. Lifting her hands in the air in a gesture of resignation, she said, "I can't find it anywhere."

Grandma went back to riffling through her things as she continued to speak. "I had it with me when I went to sleep last night. I do not know what happened to it after that. I know we have big rats here, but even the rats would just gnaw holes into my *nguwani*. I do not think they would carry it back to their hiding place."

Laughter was bubbling inside my chest as I listened to my grandmother, but I tried to hold it in. Finally, I couldn't hold it any longer and I burst into a loud laugh.

Startled, Grandma looked at me sharply. Watching her face, I saw the surprised look slowly morphing into confusion, the confusion dissolving into a soft smile, and then the smile blossoming into a wide grin.

"My *nguwani* is on my head, isn't it?" she asked rhetorically, lifting her right hand to touch her head, confirming her suspicion.

"*Maiweee! Inga kuchembera hufa chokwadi* (Mother! Getting old is like dying)," Grandma said, the grin still on her face. "If you had not been here, I would have spent the whole day searching for my *nguwani*. I cannot go anywhere without protection on my head."

I stopped laughing and simply gazed at my grandmother in admiration. I hoped I would be as wise and as strong as she was when I got to be her age.

We finally walked up to our sitting area on the hillside. We settled in for our silent communion with Source, with our eyes closed.

When I opened my eyes, Grandma was looking at me, a serene expression on her face.

"Do you have any specific questions today?" she asked.

"Yes," I responded. "Yesterday, you talked about the need for human beings to let go of negativity and return to love." Grandma nodded, still looking at me. "How do we do that?" I asked.

Grandma continued to nod and said, "That is a good question. We will make it the lesson of the day."

Grandma gathered her shawl around her shoulders, closed her eyes and took several deep breaths. She remained silent for a while and I sat quietly, watching her.

Grandma finally opened her eyes and looked at me. "The sun was created by Source, and it fulfills its purpose from one moment to the next in silence," she said. "You now understand me when I speak of this, don't you?" Grandma asked. I nodded at her. Shifting her gaze to the horizon, she said, "As the sun shines, it releases energy that sustains all living things. We all need the sun to survive. The sun shines on all of creation with equal favor, without any withholding of its energy," she paused for a moment.

"We as human beings are meant to live our lives the same way as the sun. The only problem is that we have forgotten how to do that," she added.

Grandma stopped to cough, and then took a few more deep breaths. "Can you imagine if the sun was a human being and behaved like a human being? Imagine if one day the sun said, 'I am mad at the world and will not shine and release my energy for the next two months.' What do you think would happen then?"

"Living things would die," I responded.

"Yes! All life in this world would freeze and die. Without the sun, the world would be a cold and barren place. There would be no life."

Continuing on, with her gaze still on the horizon, Grandma said, "Or suppose the sun said, 'I am mad at these few people over here and will not shine on them for the next two weeks.' What do you think would happen?"

Not bothering to wait for my answer, as she was sure I got the point, Grandma continued. "You see, it is not in the sun's nature to do that. The sun, as an extension of Source, shines on everyone and on everything and allows everyone and everything to flourish." A brief pause followed.

"So too should we," Grandma continued. "As human beings, we should allow energy from Source to flow through us every single moment to express in the world. We should shine our rays on the world as the sun shines its rays on the world. Do you know why?" Grandma turned to look at me, displaying the familiar twinkle in her eyes. I shook my head, knowing I was about to learn something of profound importance.

"There is a simple answer to this question," Grandma said, her gaze settling on the valley below us. "What we don't see with our human eyes is that the way the sun sustains life in the world by providing a continuous source of energy is the same way that we human beings sustain the life of our hopes, our dreams, and our desires. For our hopes, dreams, and desires to flourish and come to fruition, we have to find a way to continuously shine our rays of attention on them." She paused, letting that important point sink into my mind.

"The people around us also need us to shine our rays of attention on them," she continued. "They need us to pay attention to them so that they can strive, flourish, and reach their full potential and express their gifts in the world."

Turning to look at me, Grandma said, "Think about how a mother focuses her energy and attention on her newborn baby." Returning her gaze to the valley, she continued, "This is because the mother knows that without that attention, the baby will wither and die." She paused again, taking a deep breath.

"The need to have the attention of others focused on us does not end when we become adults," Grandma continued. "It just changes in form and nature. As babies, we need someone to feed us, clean us, and teach us how to do basic things. As adults, we need others to notice us, appreciate us, encourage us, inspire us, cheer us on, or just simply acknowledge our existence. Human beings need other human beings to survive and thrive."

Grandma coughed, clearing her throat. "So you see, how we use our attention is very important not only for our lives but also for the lives of those around us, and, if you think about it, for the lives of those around them and then for the world as a whole. We have to guard our attention and use it wisely. Every day and every moment, we have to check how we are using our attention. In this way, we can look at our attention as a powerful tool that can be used to change lives and eventually change the world." Another short pause followed.

"If you were to closely watch yourself or any one of us, you would be surprised at how easy it is to put our attention on things that do not matter," Grandma continued. "We spend our time thinking about things that went wrong in the past, even though we know there is nothing we can do to change the past. We spend our time thinking about how someone did something that hurt us, and we hold a grudge against them. We make a vow that we will not speak to them or to anyone in their family again. This can go on for years and decades. What we do not know is that when we focus on negative things that happened in the past, we no longer shine our rays to give energy to the things that are important in our lives and in the lives of others." I could feel the resonance of truth in what Grandma was saying.

"Learning to let go of the hurts and grudges that most of us carry in our hearts is key to living our lives the same way as the sun," she continued. "Let us say that something happened a long time ago. Perhaps someone did not do what they said they would do; perhaps someone cheated you; or perhaps someone mistreated you in some way. You were hurt because of the action of that someone, and you carry this hurt in you. What you carry within you are the thoughts that someone hurt you, and each time you replay those thoughts in your mind, you feel the negative emotions associated with that incident rise up in you."

Grandma's gaze lifted. She looked at me briefly, to see if I was paying attention. I nodded, letting her know that I was listening. Then her gaze settled back on the valley, as she continued to speak.

"When you choose to replay the hurtful incident in your mind, you are doing yourself damage on several levels. You are choosing to flood your system with negative emotions that hinder your access to Source. You are choosing to limit the flow of energy from Source through you to express in the world. You are choosing to take time away from co-creating with Source; instead, you are spending your time perpetuating negative emotions. You are choosing to block the flow of life energy through you, which is needed to allow the flourishing and fruition of your hopes, dreams, and desires. You are choosing to limit your growth and perhaps the growth of those around you who need your attention."

Grandma paused for a long moment. I remained silent, waiting to hear what she had to say next. Then she finally said, "It is no longer about the person who did what they did to you. It is now about how you are choosing to let the incident take away your joy and your creativity. It is now about how you are choosing to withhold your attention from your hopes, your dreams, and your desires. It is now about how you are choosing to withhold your attention from others who need it. Once this becomes clear to you, it may dawn on you that practicing forgiveness in your life is a key element in living a life of peace and abundance."

Returning her gaze to me, she said, "Why peace and abundance, you may ask."

I nodded, letting her know that was a question I had. She smiled, nodding back at me.

"Well, let me speak about that now," she said, her gaze shifting back to the valley.

Grandma cleared her throat and then started speaking again. "Once you forgive events, then you stop replaying them in your mind and generating negative emotions in you. When you no longer generate negative emotions, what you are left with is a peaceful mind. With a peaceful mind, you access your heart and you access Source, which is the well of love, joy, and creativity. You start living your life in Source. You start co-creating with Source. Anything created in cooperation with Source yields abundant results. You start seeing abundance flow effortlessly to you in all areas of your life. You experience more love, more peace, more joy, and even more material things, if that is what you want. With that small adjustment, you live a life of peace and abundance. You live your life like the sun. You now shine your rays on your hopes, dreams, and desires and you shine your rays on those around you. As a result, you flourish and those around you also flourish."

I could see that Grandma was getting tired, her voice was growing hoarse. "Life is really very simple, my child. It is just that we human beings, in the ignorance of our true nature, make it seem as if life is complicated. We generate complicated situations, and then we get lost in those complicated situations and cannot find our way back."

Grandma reached for her walking stick as she continued to speak.

"There are very few things you need to know to live a blessed life."

Using the straight end of her walking stick, she drew a short line in the ground.

"The first is that you are an extension of Source appearing in this world in visible form, and that by maintaining your sense of connection to Source, your life will be a guided journey every step of the way. You are never alone at any moment of your life. Source is always with you. Source speaks to you through your heart and through your mind. You only need to listen and follow that guidance."

Grandma drew another short line in the ground, parallel to the first one.

"The second is that you are a co-creator with Source, and you gain this ability to co-create when you focus on love and on being of service to others as the motivation behind everything you do. In any situation that you find yourself, you need to ask yourself some questions. What do I need to do to show care and concern for those around me? Am I expressing appreciation? Am I being kind? Am I being respectful to this person or in this situation? Am I displaying a spirit of generosity? How can I be of service?" She paused briefly before continuing.

"These questions are a reminder to keep love flowing."

She paused again, drawing another short line in the ground.

"The third is to learn to forgive and let go of the past so that old mistakes and hurts do not steal your joy and fulfillment in the moment."

Turning her gaze to look directly into my eyes, she said, "If you live your life following these simple practices, you will be living your life like the sun."

Then she closed her eyes and slowly raised her right hand to rub her wrinkled forehead.

When she opened her eyes again, her gaze focused on the distant horizon, her hand settling in her lap. "So you see, my child, the lessons I have learned in my life that I want to pass on to you are very simple. I am not here to teach you which herbs and roots to burn so that you can keep bad spirits away. I do not believe there are bad spirits that lurk in the dark waiting to possess us. What I know is that the so-called bad spirits are negative energies that we let fester within our minds when we no longer sense our connection to Source. I am also not here to teach you which herbs and roots to use to treat ailments of the body. As you know, that was your grandfather's gift, and he was very good at it. I never learned his ways because that was not my gift."

Shifting her gaze back to me, she continued.

"What I have learned about life that is worth knowing I am passing on to you. My child, our elders used to say, '*Chapinda munzeve chawaridza bonde.*'" Grandma was quoting a Shona proverb that literally translates to "What has entered the ear has spread a mat." I knew she meant to convey her hope that what she was sharing with me would take root, and that I would heed and practice the teachings she was passing on to me.

"All you need in life is to maintain your sense of connection to Source at all times," she added.

With that, Grandma said she was going to rest for a while. She spread her shawl on the ground, lay down, placed her hand under her head as a pillow, checked her head to make sure her *nguwani* was in place, and then closed her eyes. I gazed at her face as she dozed off. She looked peaceful.

I was both astonished and amazed at the knowledge my grandmother was sharing with me. The wisdom she was imparting seemed to deepen and broaden with each single day.

I had known my grandmother all my life, but I now realized that what I had known was just the exterior part of her. I had never seen the dimension of the being that I was now witnessing. I had no idea of the existence of the mystical person who was introduced to me as she shared her teachings with me.

Grandma and I spent a few more days together. On each of those days, we went to the hillside, spent time in silence, and then she went into the lesson of the day. She shared her wisdom on many aspects of life including marriage, raising children, keeping family ties, honoring parents, living a life of service to others, making offerings to ancestral spirits, and living in harmony with nature. And she shared her wisdom on death and the afterlife.

Grandma reiterated what she had said before: that she knew she was teaching me the old ways our ancestors had followed and that not everything was relevant in the modern world I was heading toward. However, she urged me to give consideration to the ancient practices that I might be able to adapt in my modern life.

I have to admit that as my grandmother was sharing her profound wisdom with me, I didn't quite comprehend the true significance of everything she said—but I listened. Something deep inside of me heard the words she spoke and knew them to be the truth. But on the level of my reasoning mind, I didn't quite grasp all the deeper meanings. It has taken me years of life experience to fully appreciate the significance of my grandmother's lessons.

The day before I left Zimbabwe to fly to San Francisco, members of my family gathered at the homestead again, as they had promised. We spent the day and night eating, dancing, celebrating, and saying our goodbyes. It was a flurry of activities all over again.

On the day of my departure, I went into Grandma's hut to bid her farewell. We gently stared deep into each other's eyes for a moment. No words were spoken; none were necessary. It seemed all that needed to be said had been said. We hugged, and I left her sitting on the very same spot she had been sitting on when I arrived, the very same spot she had been sitting on the last time I bade her farewell to go overseas.

A few months after I left home, I received the sad news that my grandmother had passed away in her sleep. My family relayed words of comfort. They said Grandma had left this world with a peaceful smile on her face, and that her body was laid down in her grave with that smile still on her face. I asked if she had left word for me. I was told Grandma had not left any word for anyone. I was told that Grandma had died in silence, the same way she had lived in silence. I was told many came from near and far to mourn and lay her to rest. I was told most people remarked at how Grandma had lived her life with quiet dignity. I was told that others remarked that it was a shame that no one really got to know her in the time that she had been here in this world.

I got to know her, and beyond that I got to know why she came on her journey to this earth. She had come to be a daughter, a wife, a mother, a grandmother, a great-grandmother, and above all a messenger. Grandma was a messenger who came to deliver a message from Source. When she knew in her heart that the time had come to deliver the message, she had delivered her message to me. I knew her,

I knew who she was, and I knew that she had done her part to fulfill her purpose. And now I knew she was at peace, resting in Source. I knew she was home, our true home.

I shed tears of farewell for my grandmother, but for the most part I gave gratitude because I had been allowed to know her.

Blessing of Forgiveness

Divine Love, my redeemer and savior
I am grateful for the blessing of forgiveness
For in it is the opportunity to let go of the past
And all the mistakes and misgivings that it carries
I am grateful for the blessing of forgiveness
For in it is the opportunity to let go of the future
And all the fears and worries that it promises

Divine Love, my redeemer and savior
With this new understanding of forgiveness
I forgive all the disappointing experiences in my past
I forgive myself and others for the disappointing experiences
I let the past pass away
I lay it to rest, never to haunt me again
And I am free of the burden of the past

Divine Love, my redeemer and savior
With this new understanding of forgiveness
I release the projected disappointing events in my future
I release the fear, worry, and doubt for what is to come
I let them dissolve and disintegrate
Never to come to pass in my life
And I am free of the burden of the future

Divine Love, my redeemer and savior
With complete forgiveness in my life

I am no longer troubled by the past
I am no longer burdened by the future
I am a free spirit resting in the flow of life
Ready to co-create with you
And be a channel for your manifestation

Divine Love, my redeemer and savior
With forgiveness in my life
Show me how I am to serve others here on earth
For it is in serving others that I serve you
It is in serving others that I serve myself
With you flowing through me and manifesting in the world
I finally live my life here on earth as it is in heaven
Amen

Living the American Dream

The lessons I learned from my grandmother stayed with me until I arrived in San Francisco. In what I can only describe as an unfortunate lack of foresight on my part, I put the knowledge and wisdom that my grandmother had shared with me on hold. Instead, I focused on the hustle and bustle of starting a new life, in a new culture, in a new city, in a new country. I convinced myself that my priority was to get established in my new environment and career first. I thought I would work on the spiritual aspects of my life later, when I had more time. I know, I know! You are probably saying that is backward thinking, and I agree with you. It was backward thinking.

But you have to understand my state of awareness—or lack thereof—at that time. Despite what I had clearly heard my grandmother say about our oneness with Source, I still focused on the God that had been introduced to me by the missionaries. Instead of seeking ways to connect to Source as my grandmother had taught me, I still focused on what my young and impressionable mind had taken away—and retained—from what the missionaries had taught me about Christianity.

Whenever I tried to think deeply about God, my mind would get lost in all that I grew up hearing. I would remember the myths of Satan and his band of followers, the notions of the devil and his fork, the unleashing of the wrath of God on those who disobeyed him, and the promise of burning in hell until eternity. I often got overwhelmed and gave up any attempt to reconcile the notion of the God I had been taught about in my early childhood with the true nature of God as the loving, nurturing, caring, and forgiving Source. I had not yet incorporated my grandmother's lessons into practices that would guide my life. I had not yet integrated the wisdom she had shared with me.

At the time of my arrival in San Francisco, my focus was on something else. It was on something that had driven me since I was a little girl growing up in the rural areas of Zimbabwe. I wanted to make a positive difference in the world. I remember having dreams of grandeur. I would spend hours dreaming about how I was going to be this powerful and successful person who would bring positive change to my community and to the world. And it seemed that everyone else—my parents, my siblings, my teachers—had similar expectations for my life.

My parents had done an excellent job providing for me and my siblings as we were growing up—by village standards at that time. They had ensured that the family had enough to eat, and that each of us received a set of new clothes at least once a year—usually at Christmas. Most importantly, my parents had impressed on me and my siblings the importance of an education, and they had provided each of us an opportunity to receive a good education. They had constantly reminded us that a good education was the ticket out of the hardships of rural life and into the endless opportunities that lay ahead in the world.

As a young person, I had looked at my rural environment and decided I wanted to live a better life than what I was seeing. And I wanted a better life for everyone else around me. I saw people spending all their time working hard to eke out a living from the land. But despite all the hard work, sometimes they came out empty handed. The crops sometimes failed for one reason or another—there wasn't enough rain, there was too much rain, the rain came too early in the season, the rain came too late in the season, the rain stopped too early into the season, the rain continued for too long into the season. I saw bright boys and girls denied an education because their parents couldn't afford to send them to school. I saw young girls married off at tender ages because the *roora*—money and other items a man pays to his in-laws in a traditional marriage—was needed to sustain the girls' families. I saw infants die due to lack of adequate healthcare in the rural areas. I saw the poverty around me and the daily struggles to survive. I saw all this and I was motivated to find a way to get out and make my fortune. I wanted to return and bring relief to ease some of the burdens endured by the people of my community. Finding a way to make my fortune became my dream.

Getting a good education was no hardship for me. I loved studying. I loved learning new things. And I loved learning about modern life in faraway countries. I set my heart on getting the best education I could get, which led to a graduate degree in a science discipline. Then I set my sights on my next adventure, which was to pursue a career as a research scientist in America. America is where I was going to find my dream.

America is where I found my dream. And America is where I lost my dream.

I will tell you what happened.

I came to America as a research fellow at a university in San Francisco. My advisor was a famous professor whose cutting-edge research in cancer biology was widely known. We had communicated, of course, before I came to San Francisco. He had asked for my travel itinerary and I had provided that to him, not thinking much of it. I was a little surprised when he offered to pick me up from the airport. In his communications, he had told me not to worry about immediate accommodation as this was being arranged for me. With everything taken care of, so to speak, I had flown from Harare to London, caught a connecting flight to Boston, and then caught another flight from Boston to San Francisco, to complete the last leg of my journey into a new adventure.

The plane landed at San Francisco International Airport at about half-past eight in the evening. I went through immigration, collected my baggage, and sailed through customs with no problems. With my carry-on bag slung over my shoulder and pulling my two suitcases behind me, I walked out of the customs area into the arrivals lounge.

I stopped for a minute, taking in the scene in front of me. People milled about, waiting to welcome passengers disembarking from planes. Men in suits and caps held placards with nametags. I guessed they were chauffeurs waiting to receive important guests. Children dashed into the open arms of their parents—a mother or a father, perhaps coming back from a business trip. Lovers rushed to embrace each other, kissing passionately, not seeming to give a thought to the presence of an audience.

Then I started to worry. What if my advisor wasn't able to make it to the airport? What would I do then? I didn't quite know where to go. I would be stranded at the airport.

Then another thought popped into my head. I remembered the incident of my first meeting with my graduate advisor in England. That got me worrying about a different matter altogether. I started worrying about the proper protocol for introducing myself to my advisor—if he did show up.

As the worry thoughts churned in my head, I saw a large man approaching me. He was over six feet tall, had the muscular body of an athlete, and appeared to be in his early fifties. To my surprise, the man grabbed me in a bear hug, picking me up clear off the floor.

"You must be *Ye-e-e-e-ka*!" the man shouted in a booming voice, mangling the pronunciation of my name. "Welcome to America!"

Then as suddenly as he had picked me up, the man dropped me. My legs must have been as stunned as the rest of my body, because they gave out and I landed on the floor, on my bottom. The man gave a bellowing laugh, loudly clapping his hands. Looking down at me and shaking his head, he held out his hand to help me up. When I took his hand, he yanked me to my feet, almost pulling my right arm out of its socket.

"Thank you," I piped tentatively, lifting my left hand and rubbing my throbbing right shoulder. I proceeded to straighten my clothes, giving myself time to regain my composure—well, the little of it that was left. Then I stuck out my right hand to introduce myself. I thought this was as good a time as any to do so.

"Hello, I am Yeukai Mandizvidza," I squeaked.

"You can call me Yeu," I offered.

The man gave my hand a vigorous shake, introducing himself as Bill and then introducing his wife, Rose. I hadn't even noticed the dark-haired matronly looking woman who was standing by, watching quietly. She appeared to be in her late-forties. On her face was an expression that seemed to be a cross between a sympathetic smile and a chuckle.

"Hello, Yeu," Rose said as she stepped forward, engulfing me in a warm embrace and planting a soft kiss on my right cheek.

"Don't worry, my dear," she whispered in my right ear. "You will get used to Bill. My husband thinks everyone is a football player."

Of course that didn't make much sense to me. I knew nothing about American football at that time—I grew up with soccer.

My advisor and his wife, Bill and Rose, took me to their home that night and gave me dinner and a place to stay. Their house, which was located in an affluent neighborhood of San Francisco, had a self-contained studio apartment in the basement. Bill and Rose said they offered the basement apartment as temporary accommodations to foreigners who visited their laboratory. It turned out that Rose was the office manager of the lab. They said I could stay in the apartment for up to two months as they were not expecting the next visitor till then.

The next day, Rose drove me to the university and introduced me to the other members of the lab—graduate students, research fellows, and visiting professors. She showed me my assigned space, a corner desk and an adjoining lab bench that already had the equipment I needed to get started on my research projects. Then Rose helped me with the administrative paperwork I was required to complete to start my new job. Over the next several weeks and months, I got to know the other people in the lab and in the department, and I threw myself into my research projects. I rented an apartment two blocks away from the lab and moved in one month after my arrival in San Francisco. I thought I had made a good start on my life in America.

After a couple of years pursuing a career in academia, I realized that academic research wasn't going to get me to where I needed to go. I realized that it wasn't exactly the ticket to the wealth I was after. The work was exciting, but the pay was low. So I jumped ship and joined the biotech industry. I was sad to leave the people who had welcomed me with open arms, but I felt I needed to follow my dream of building my fortune.

In the mid-1990s, the biotech industry was experiencing an economic boom. Savvy researchers and their visionary colleagues in the business world were starting companies that applied the new science of genetic engineering to develop practical products and services. Joining forces, the scientists and their business colleagues were turning research findings from academic institutions into new human medicines and agricultural products. Enthusiastic investors poured money into the biotech sector, looking to turn lucrative profits from the startup companies.

With investment dollars pouring into the sector like rain during a tropical storm, startup biotech companies mushroomed left, right, and center. I was told that all one had to do to get startup funding for a biotech company was mention a few buzz words to investors, words such as "genome," "protein," "genomics," "proteomics," "innovative research," "informatics," "structure-based drug design," and "breakthrough drug." Better still, I was further told one could be smart and incorporate some of these words or partial words in the name of a company for recognition. Many companies were formed around what later came to be known as biotech hubs—Biotech Bay in Northern California, Biotech Beach in Southern California, and Genetown in the Massachusetts area are a few examples.

I joined a small biotech startup near San Diego. I was one of its first few employees. The company had sophisticated technology for automating compound design to generate target-specific drug candidates that could potentially be developed into medicines for treating human diseases. The technology promised to slash, by more than half, the time it took to move from initiation of compound search to identifying a drug candidate—a winning pitch to potential investors. I was fascinated by the science and technology and enticed by the company's prospects for success.

Right from the start, my job was fast-paced. There was something exhilarating about working in a new and highly competitive industry, with colleagues who were some of the best in that industry. I found it all very exciting—the research, the conferences to deliver research findings and learn about new technologies from competitors, and the animated discussions on what could be the next frontier in the field.

And there was always the ultimate reward—the promise of participating in the process of bringing a new and lifesaving medicine to the market. There was the promise of being involved in discovering and developing a drug that could treat, cure, or otherwise mitigate human disease. It was intoxicating.

Just like everyone around me, my days were very busy with activities. I worked hard and did the best job I could.

The industry job came with grueling work hours, but it also came with a pretty good paycheck. As I started to make more money, something in me changed. My focus changed. My focus became about building my fortune to live the American dream life. I set my sights on climbing the proverbial corporate ladder so that I could enjoy the creature comforts that America had to offer. Somewhere along the line, my dream of making my fortune so I could bring relief to those I had left behind seemed to have fallen by the wayside.

I took to the American lifestyle like a duck takes to water. I found it very easy to live life focusing on the physical world that I could experience with my five physical senses. And there was a lot to experience.

Here in America, everything was done in a grand way—bigger equaled better, louder equaled wiser, faster equaled livelier. And, outrageousness seemed to be regarded as creativity. At least that's how it appeared to me.

Talk of living in excess!

People worked hard to earn money and shopped hard to spend the money they earned. There seemed to be no rest in between.

It didn't matter how much money you earned. Whether you had a small or big paycheck, you spent it fast. If you had a small paycheck, you spent it on small things—gadgets, trinkets, and knickknacks. If you had a big paycheck, you spent it on big things—designer clothes, fancy cars, impressive McMansions, fast boats, luxurious planes, and exotic islands. The focus was on accumulating material things.

I soon joined the national pastime of "shopping till you drop."

The shopping malls were everywhere, and they were huge. No matter where you went, the malls seemed to be packed with merchandise and people. There seemed to be some sort of excitement in going out to the malls and coming back with huge shopping bags filled to overflowing with stuff.

I clearly remember my reaction the first time I visited one of the so-called big-box discount stores. The store was housed in a building that could easily hold two soccer fields. As I entered through the automatic sliding double doors and caught my first glimpse of the inside, I was awed. I stood to attention.

What a sight!

In all directions, as far as my eyes could see, I saw rows upon rows of shelves packed high to the ceiling with items of all kinds. There were toys, TV sets, stereo systems, computers, carpets, doors, bicycles, car tires, car repair kits, clothes, cleaning supplies, fruits, vegetables, breads, cheeses, meats, and on and on. I had never seen so much stuff housed in a single room like this before in my life. Surely this was a sign of living in a country of wealth and abundance, I thought.

From where I stood, I could see big bold signs meant to lure the shopper. "The Cheapest Prices in Town Are Here!" and "Reduced to Half-Price!" the banners read.

And the store was packed to overflowing with people. Most were pushing huge shopping carts piled high with boxes and packages. I could be one of those people too, I thought. With the great bargains I was seeing, I could afford to buy as much as everyone else. As that thought ran through my mind, a store attendant approached with a shopping cart that he quietly handed to me. He must have recognized the look of exhilaration on my face and pegged me as a prospective high spender. I thanked him and, grabbing the shopping cart, started my stroll along the aisles. I could feel the energy building. My heart was racing and my palms were sweating. The excitement was palpable.

A banner advertising toilet paper caught my eye. "60% Off Original Price!" it read. That seemed like a good deal to me—never mind what the original price was, it was sixty percent less than that now, wasn't it? I grabbed the package, plopping it in my shopping cart. There must have been seventy or more rolls of toilet paper in the package. I didn't bother to count. A faint thought rose at the back of my mind—*I would need to have diarrhea every other day to use this much toilet paper.* But I didn't pay much attention to that thought. I had to focus on the killer deals in front of me.

In addition to the toilet paper, I bought a humongous jar of pickles, an eight-pound jar of peanut butter, a six-pound can of tomato sauce, a four-pound jar of mayonnaise, and the list went on and on. I came back for more the next week and the week after that.

I discovered more shopping malls and more stores. Shopping became my favorite way to pass the time, whenever I wasn't working. Before each trip to the stores, I would tell myself that I was just going to scope out the deals. But each time I came home with a load of stuff. I bought electronics, furniture, bicycle parts, luggage, books, sports equipment, clothes, shoes, cleaning solutions, jars of condiments. I was amazed, and thrilled, that I could afford to buy all these things.

God bless America, I thought.

With time, I met people who liked shopping as much as I did. Among these were Louise from Michigan and Joyce from Ghana, who quickly became my very close friends for many years. Louise and Joyce worked for one of the big management consulting firms in downtown San Diego. Their jobs came with huge paychecks, and they knew how to spend their money. I tagged along when they went on shopping sprees for designer clothes, fashionable shoes, stylish fur coats, high-end furniture, and top-of-the-line electronics.

I met some of Louise's and Joyce's friends and acquaintances, high spenders like them, and got invited to some of the high-society parties. I liked one of the men I met at such a party and went out with him for a while. His passion was fast cars, so I joined that club for the couple of years that we dated. After that relationship ended, I met another man who had a passion for boats, and I joined that club for the one year that we dated. A couple more relationships came and went, following the same pattern. I noticed that the relationship with each of these men seemed to fizzle out after the realization—on both parties—that there was no common bond beyond working hard and accumulating things, and then bragging about those possessions.

It didn't take long to accumulate a lot of stuff I didn't really need. I moved apartments several times, each time moving into a bigger space to accommodate the stuff I was buying. Then I bought a humongous house, which came with a humongous mortgage. My friends—more accurately the group of people I had surrounded myself with—were buying huge houses that were beyond their means and needs, so I bought a huge house that was beyond my means and needs. The theme was luxurious living, so the house came with all the works, whatever was the rage at that time. I had to have the granite kitchen countertops, kitchen island, stainless steel appliances, maple cabinetry, hardwood flooring, raised-panel interior doors, cathedral ceilings, sunken tubs in en-suite bathrooms, grand bonus room pre-wired for home theater entertainment, swimming pool, and outdoor kitchen area. The furnishings had to be elegant, of course.

Oh! I forgot to mention that I lived alone in the huge house.

The house came with what I was told and came to view as a hidden benefit: access to another source of money. A source that kept on giving—so I was made to believe. This was the art of refinancing. House prices were skyrocketing like the price of oranges in a drought year. The demand for housing was high. The price of my house doubled in less than four years. And the offers to access credit through refinancing poured in. The eligibility criteria for accessing the credit seemed to get lower and lower with each offer. Everyone I knew was refinancing their houses. Refinance rates became the new talk at parties, with people referring each other to the financial houses that had the lowest requirements for accessing home equity. So I kept refinancing my house. When I needed money to upgrade my kitchen cabinetry, I refinanced. When I needed money to add a gazebo to the pool area, I refinanced. When I needed money to pay for a trip to Europe, I refinanced. It was like getting money for free—getting money that didn't need to be repaid.

Except, the money had to be repaid by someone at some point in time. And the financial houses racked profits in fees and interest payments.

Then there was the exotic travel. That seemed to be another upcoming trend. And being the follower that I was, I joined in. I thought it was important that I hold my own when it came to the social gatherings that seemed to be forums for comparing notes on the recent trips to whatever exotic destination was in vogue at that time. The destination could be Las Vegas, Aspen, Anchorage, St. Thomas, Bali, Barbados, Bora Bora, Hong Kong, or the numerous European destinations. The destinations were endless—they were advertised on TV, on the Internet, on billboards. Each was billed as the "destination of a lifetime." Whose lifetime? I never really knew, and I never really bothered to ask.

There was another exciting aspect to traveling: racking up frequent flier miles. It became the buzz for a while. And I took as many trips as I could afford. Most of the time joining Louise and Joyce and their friends on their exotic trips. And I made sure to let it be known where I had been and how many frequent flier miles I had accumulated.

I have to say that I did enjoy traveling and meeting people from other cultures. Each time I visited a new country, I made sure to go beyond the tourist destinations to meet the "real people" and learn as much of the local cultures as I could. While my traveling companions spent time lounging at the pools, gambling in high-stakes casinos, or rubbing shoulders with the high-and-mighty, I would often take buses to the markets and gathering places to meet the ordinary people in the countries we visited. It was fun and it also saved me some money. I was doing fine moneywise, but I wasn't exactly loaded like my travel companions. I went along on most things, but I had to draw the line for myself at some of the frivolous spending.

I don't actually remember anyone telling me that I had to do what other people were doing, that I had to spend money on what other people were spending money on. I just assumed it was expected. If this was what everyone else around me was doing, then it must be what living was about, and I got on with it.

There was also one more unspoken aspect to all this. There was some kind of competition going on. One was expected to compare themselves with their peers and strive to ensure that they owned more things than their peers, wore more expensive clothes, drove better cars, lived in more exclusive neighborhoods, took more exotic vacations, and so on. This seemed especially true in the workplace where these measures determined whether one was accepted in the so-called inner circles, particularly when it came to promotions within the organizations. I often heard that you had to dress the part of a successful person, which meant wearing designer clothes. I heard that you had to drive the cars that successful people drove, which meant driving Mercedes Benzes and BMWs. I heard that you had to travel to exotic destinations that successful people visited, which meant whatever destination the company's upper management was vacationing in that year. So I joined in the race.

Mind you, I don't actually remember sitting down with myself, or with anyone else for that matter, to evaluate the validity of the assumptions I was making and the actions I was taking. I didn't stop to ask myself the question: What is the endgame for all this? Not during those years anyway.

The thing is, I didn't think any of us had the time to sit around and ponder philosophical questions like that. I know I didn't. I had to focus on the race at hand, working hard to earn the money I needed to finance my shopping and travels. And, of course, I had to spend hours on end strategizing how to make more money so that I could stay ahead of the game. I had no time to spend on impractical philosophical reflections, so I thought.

Over a decade and a half, I lived in what some would consider exciting cities, traveled to many exotic destinations, and met interesting people. However, a time came when all this began to seem meaningless. The thrill of purchasing things lessened considerably, and I also noticed that the thrill didn't last as long. The excitement of visiting new places diminished. And meeting new people lost its novelty. I started to feel a little removed from the life I was living. It was as though I was watching all this happening to someone else.

I brushed aside the uneasy feelings of discontent many times. My focus was on making money and spending money. To me, that seemed to be the measure of a successful life, and I wanted, so terribly, to portray the image of someone living a successful life.

People around me said that I should be excited. They said that I should be happy. They said that I should enjoy what I had.

Oh, yes! I pretended to be excited. I pretended to be happy. I pretended to enjoy what I had.

But deep down, I was terribly unhappy. I felt empty. I felt lonely. I felt disconnected.

I was working hard to earn money that I so desperately needed to maintain the lifestyle I thought I had to have. But the things I was accumulating didn't give me a sense of joy. The trips I was taking didn't give me a sense of fulfillment. The relationships I had with the people I knew didn't give me a sense of community and belonging.

In reality, I was lost.

I didn't know what to do, so for a long while I covered the sense of emptiness by working harder and spending more money.

But, as I discovered for myself, one can put off experiencing an existential crisis only for so long. One day, it came crashing down on me.

It was during the week of the Fourth of July holiday in 2007. I had taken the week off from work in anticipation of joining my friends for our annual week-long pilgrimage to Las Vegas to party. But at the last minute, I had changed my mind and decided to stay at home, which was odd. I had never turned down an invitation to go partying before, especially if it was partying in Las Vegas. But for some reason, I chose to stay behind.

I spent the week at home alone.

On the Friday of that week, the second day after the holiday, I spent the day doing mundane chores around the house. I had a quiet dinner and then sat on the couch in my living room to watch TV. I surfed the channels for a while but nothing caught my attention, so I switched the TV off. I remained seated on the couch, in the dark, not bothering to turn on the lights. I sat in silence and let my thoughts drift.

I needed to find new ways to bring back some fun into my life, I thought. I needed to find ways to bring back the fun in purchasing new things, traveling to new destinations, and meeting new people. After all, I had done very well in my career and was earning a good salary, so I had more money to spend. I just needed to work at bringing the thrill back. The ramblings along those lines continued for a while.

Then, from nowhere, a thought crystallized in my mind: *Wait a minute. Just hold on. Am I seriously trying to find strategies for bringing excitement back into mindless shopping, aimless traveling, and meaningless relationships?*

That thought caught me off guard. A jolt ran through my body.

And the questions poured in, one after the other. Is this what my life was about? Was I here in this world to accumulate material things, to travel to exotic destinations, and to engage in meaningless relationships? Yes, everyone else around me was doing the same, but what was the meaning of it all? What was my life plan for the next two, five, ten years? What did I want to leave behind in the world when I was gone? What would be my legacy?

Those questions triggered memories of my grandmother's lessons. I started remembering my grandmother's enthusiasm when she talked about meeting Source when her days here in this world were over. She had said that she was eager to return to Source knowing that she had completed the assignments she came to do. I thought of the example of the seed she had shared with me those many years ago. She had said that a seed becomes a plant that provides food and shelter, and eventually the plant flowers and produces more seeds to continue its cycle of life. Like my grandmother, the seed returns to Source with a sense of having fulfilled its purpose here on earth.

What about me? I asked myself. What will I have to say when my time here on earth is over? What is it that I am creating? What new ideas am I bringing into the world? What difference am I making in the world? Who am I serving?

I had no husband, no children, and no pets. I had no passionate causes that could be remotely considered as working for the good of humanity and the world. I was living a meaningless life. If my life were to end right now, I thought, there would be nothing left behind to mark my passage through this world. It would be as if I never existed.

Needless to say, those were very uncomfortable and sobering thoughts for me. But there was more.

It seemed as if asking these existential questions opened a floodgate, which let out long suppressed emotions, each seeking to be acknowledged and heard. I had no control over what was coming out. All I could do was sit still and let the emotions pour out. It seemed as if my life was being displayed in front of me and I was seeing it with clarity for the first time—seeing my life with no blinders to cover up any parts that I didn't want to face.

What I saw didn't paint a pretty picture.

For the first time, I saw that the moments of my life were filled with repetitive thoughts of self-judgment, self-condemnation, and self-punishment. The incessant thoughts that played in my mind were a variation of the same things. I am not good enough. I am not smart enough. I am not pretty enough. I am not worthy. I have no power. I don't have the right connections. I can't do the things that I really want to do. I have made so many mistakes in my life that I cannot recover from.

I recognized a pattern in the way the thoughts seemed to play out in my mind. A particular thought would rise up in my mind, say about a wrong decision I had made a long time ago, unkind words I had said to someone, or unkind actions I had taken against someone—anything that had a heavy negative tone to it. Then the thought would play round and round like a broken record, taunting my mind. Sometimes the taunting went on for a few minutes, sometimes an hour, sometimes several hours, sometimes several days. Then the thought would subside and I would regain control of my mind again, but only for a while. With time, another thought would rise up and take over my mind and continue the taunting. And I never ran out of negative thoughts to use in tormenting my mind. I had a huge store of those, it seemed, and I could access any one of them at any time.

I would play out thoughts of events from the past that triggered feelings of guilt, regret, or shame about things that I had done that I wasn't supposed to do. I would play out thoughts of events from the past that triggered feelings of blame, anger, or resentment about things that I felt others did to me that they shouldn't have done. I would play out thoughts about projected events in the future that triggered feelings of fear, worry, or doubt.

I recognized the pattern of mental suffering that I subjected myself to every single day.

It became clear to me that I lived my life with a constant feeling of discomfort, unease, or outright dread in most situations. My mind was so full of negative fragmented thoughts that sometimes I found it hard to stop the racing thoughts long enough to make a simple decision such as what to make for dinner or what to wear to work. My decisions, even the mundane ones, were riddled with doubt. I often struggled with the same questions in many situations. Am I making the right choice if I do this, or should I be doing that instead? What if I am wrong? Will this decision come back to torment me in the future? What if I am wasting my time? What if I am wasting everyone's time? Does it even matter what I do or don't do? Do I even have to be here? Would it be better for everyone if I wasn't here?

I realized that I had nothing tangible to hold onto as a way of guiding my life and grounding my decisions. Each time I made a decision, it was as though I was rolling the dice. And, of course, if things didn't turn out the way I had hoped they would, the blame kicked in right away, followed by the guilt, regret, and shame.

I don't remember how much time passed that Friday evening as I sat on the couch. Eventually, I went to bed in the early hours, overwhelming thoughts still on my mind.

I woke up after what felt like only a few winks of sleep. It was as if something had woken me up. Even though my body was tired, my mind was awake. And a thought came in. It suddenly became clear why I kept myself so busy. I came to the realization that I kept my days full of activities—running around doing this, doing that, or doing the other—so that I could avoid moments of self-reflection that showed me the emptiness and pointlessness of my life. I kept myself busy by working very hard, earning money, and then spending the money on things that had no real value to me or to anyone else. That seemed to be the price I had to pay to avoid facing myself.

Then the recollections of my grandmother's lessons that had come to me the night before returned. I knew that I had been shown the path of light in my life, in the lessons that my grandmother had taught me. But in my humanity, I had chosen not to take the path of light. I had followed a different path that had led me to where I was now, living my life in quiet despair.

I didn't want to live a meaningless life anymore. I wanted my life to stand for something in this world.

I knew I had to change the direction of my life. I knew I had to go back to the wisdom of my grandmother.

But my grandmother was no longer there to provide answers for me, and I didn't know any wise people I could go to for guidance. I didn't know what to do next. Yet I knew I had to do something different from what I had been doing all these years.

With that clarity in my mind, I drifted back to sleep.

And a dream came to me. The strange thing was that when I woke up later that morning, I could only remember a fragment of the dream. In the fragment of the dream that I remembered, I had had the sensation that my grandmother was around. I hadn't seen her with my eyes in the dream, but I had distinctly heard her voice whisper to me, "Go back to your roots!" It was just that one whisper—ever so soft, ever so gentle, but distinctly real.

I got out of bed and went on with my day. But that dream was not far away from my mind for the rest of the day, and for many days and weeks after that.

At first, I tried to dismiss the dream, thinking it probably was a figment of my confused state of mind. But I couldn't let go of the words from the dream. Many thoughts kept running in my mind. What if those words were some kind of message? What if those words were some type of guidance? What if I was being shown what I needed to do next to seek the answers to the questions I had for my life? Wasn't the remote possibility of a hidden message in the dream enough for me to do something, anything?

With that in mind, I took three months' leave of absence from work and headed back to Zimbabwe. I began to think that perhaps in my home country there were others who, like my grandmother, were knowledgeable in important matters of life. And that perhaps I could find one or more of these people, and they could be my guides as I searched for the answers to the questions of my life. And that perhaps just being among the people of my community, going back to my roots, would give me a sense of whatever it was that I felt was missing in my life.

Lost in the Wilderness

I have wandered the globe
Traveling far and wide
In search of my identity and my center
Thinking what I am may be found in the world
Many a time I have gotten lost

In the valleys and canyons of time
But the search has been in vain
For my identity and my center
Are not to be found in the things of this world

In those I met along the way
Many a time I caught a glimpse
A glimmer in the eyes of one
A radiance in the smile of another
A loving kindness in the touch of yet another
Each time I stayed a while
But these would fade with time, as they often do
For my identity and my center
Are not to be found in the people of this world

In many a place I searched
In high places and in low places
In blue skies and in deep oceans
On mountain tops and in river valleys
On rainbow colors and in tunnel ends
In hallways and on byways
In no place did I find what I am
For my identity and my center
Are not to be found in the places of this world

With the passing of the years, weariness sets in my heart
I am exhausted and I am spent
I am lost and I cannot go on
Though I still hunger and thirst
To know that which I am
I must rest my mind and my body
I must give up the worldly search
For my identity and my center
Are not to be found in the things of this world

GONE ARE THE WISE

Wat I experienced when I returned to Zimbabwe after being away for so long—a decade and a half—was more than a reverse culture shock. In hindsight, I realized that going through that experience, going through that shock, jogged my system and gave me the impetus to start turning things around in my life.

I arrived at Harare International Airport around midafternoon on a scorching September day in 2007. I had left San Diego International Airport about thirty-two hours earlier on a five-hour flight to John F. Kennedy Airport in New York City. There I had caught an eighteen-hour non-stop flight to O. R. Tambo International Airport in Johannesburg. After a short layover in Johannesburg, I finally boarded a South African Airways jet for the approximately two-hour flight to Harare.

I went through immigration, collected my baggage, and went through customs without incident. The immigration and customs officers were polite and efficient, but I sensed a lethargy and resignation in the way they conducted themselves. I didn't know what to make of this, so I put it out of my mind as I proceeded to the arrivals hall. There I found a handful of family members waiting to welcome me home—my parents, my elder brother Martin, my elder sister Mary, and my younger sister Mugu.

I was glad to see my family members, and I hugged each of them in turn. My parents seemed to have aged a little since the last time I had seen them, which was two years earlier. We had met in England to attend the graduation ceremony of my brother Mark, who had completed a degree in medicine and was now doing his residency at one of the London hospitals. Before that, my parents had visited me a few times in California over the years. As I looked at them, I could see they were both smiling but I sensed a bit of weariness behind the smiles.

I hadn't seen *Mukoma* Martin, Sis Mary, or Mugu since the time I left Zimbabwe. *Mukoma* Martin appeared older than I would expect for a man in his mid-forties. I had expected a few gray hairs and perhaps a slight potbelly, but what I saw was an ashen-faced skinny man with a full head of gray hair. He stood as if he was carrying the weight of the world on his shoulders. Sis Mary looked no different. Of the three girls in our family, Sis Mary had always been the heavyset one, with the figure of a bustling matron. But all that was gone. She looked skinnier than I was, but it wasn't the healthy kind of slimness one would desire. And there was a general lassitude about her.

Mugu was the only one who was full of life, both figuratively and literally. From our regular communications by email and phone calls, I knew that she was pregnant with her first child, going on seven months now. Looking at the way her belly protruded in front of her, it seemed the baby was ready to pop out at any moment. She herself looked radiant, cheerful, and energetic, and she was the one taking charge and directing everyone else.

We piled into *Mukoma* Martin's car—a midsized sedan that had seen many years—and started the drive to his home. He and his wife still lived in the same house they had bought years ago.

As we drove from the airport, I was shocked at the poor state of the roads. What used to be well-maintained thoroughfares bordered by rows of vibrant trees, stretches of manicured lawns, and masses of colorful flowering shrubs were now rutted bumpy lanes bordered by dirt.

Traffic crawled, the drivers of the vehicles concentrating on avoiding the numerous potholes that littered the roads. My brother was doing his best to negotiate the obstacle course, but his car was no match for the poor state of the roads. The car—and we, the passengers—bobbed up and down and leaned from side to side as we went on our way.

My brother gave me a quick rundown of what to expect as we approached his home. There was no running water in the house, he told me. Water for all bathroom and cooking needs was fetched by buckets from the outside reservoir. Electricity supply to the neighborhood was erratic, with a total of two hours' supply in any given day. People relied on firewood or paraffin stoves to cook and on candles and flashlights for light at night. Garbage was burned in a pit behind the house; there had been no garbage service collection in the city neighborhoods for years. Then he casually added that the government and the utility companies were broke and could not afford to maintain the services.

Mukoma Martin turned the car into the driveway leading to his home, driving through the familiar wrought-iron gates. I noticed the absence of cheerful flowerbeds along the driveway; I remembered those from my last visit. The front yard that used to be covered by a lush lawn was now mostly dusty earth with scanty patches of brown grass.

My brother stopped the car in front of the main house. As we were climbing out of the car, *Mukoma* Martin's wife, *Maiguru* Sara, came out of the front doors. She was still quick on her feet, as I had known her to be, but she too appeared older than her age. She rushed over to give me a bear hug. She apologized for not meeting me at the airport, explaining that she had stayed behind to prepare my favorite dishes. I knew I could count on my sister-in-law to make me feel special. She was one of those people with a unique knack for making everyone feel important and appreciated.

We walked through the front doors of the house and entered the living room. The room was neat, but had a slightly shabby appearance. The leather on the couch set was peeling and ripped in a few places. Old curtains hung on the windows. Faded paint covered the walls. The only items brightening the space were the dozens of framed photographs on the walls. Most were of my brother's three boys, now dashing young men.

We sat down to ask after each other's well-being. When I asked after the well-being of my parents, *Mukoma* Martin, and Sis Mary, they all said that they were fine. But I could tell that none of them were fine. Gone was the jubilation of past homecomings. I could tell there was something that no one wished to discuss at that time. I decided not to press for details right away. There was plenty of time for that.

After we completed the greeting ritual, *Maiguru* Sara suggested I freshen up. She said a bucket of warm water was waiting for me in the bathroom. She walked me to one of the guest bedrooms where I found my luggage neatly piled in one corner. She said the meal would be served shortly. I thanked her as she left the room.

I washed and changed into fresh clothes and then joined the others, who were now seated at the dining room table.

Two more people had arrived—Sis Mary's husband Jonah and Mugu's husband Noah. I hadn't met Noah in person, but I had seen photographs of him, and we had talked on the phone many times. We exchanged greetings, both men apologizing for not meeting me at the airport due to work. Jonah was a professor at the local university and Noah was a teacher at a high school in Harare.

Maiguru Sara served a delicious meal of *sadza*, beef stew, pumpkin leaves in peanut butter sauce, and boiled okra. As we ate, we caught up on news of my siblings who were not present. In addition to my brother Mark, who now lived in England, my five other brothers had emigrated from Zimbabwe. Maurice, Melvine, and Marshall and their families now lived in South Africa. Matthew and his family now lived in Botswana, and Maxwell and his family had moved to New Zealand. All of them, like a lot of young professionals in Zimbabwe, had escaped the economic hardships in the country in search of greener pastures.

Mukoma Martin's three boys were attending college in South Africa. Sis Mary's children were in Botswana—the boy was in college and the girl was in high school. The standard of education in Zimbabwe had declined considerably over the years. For those who could afford it, sending their children to be educated in foreign countries was no longer a luxury, it was a necessity. I knew my parents missed having all their children and grandchildren around them, but that was just a sign of the times.

After we finished lunch, *Maiguru* Sara ushered everyone back into the living room. This was when my family started recounting the things that had happened in Zimbabwe while I was away. What I came to know that day, and in the days that followed, was that not having running water, electricity, and garbage collection services was nothing compared to the real challenges that people faced on a daily basis in my country. The lethargic appearance and haunted looks on the faces of so many people were an aftermath of living through severe hardships caused by the ravages of the HIV/AIDS epidemic, a near collapse of the country's economy, and the day-to-day struggles of trying to support families on inadequate resources.

Of course, I had kept up to date on the news in my country by emails and phone calls to my family members, and by reading online newspapers over the years. So I was aware of the hardships that people were experiencing in my country. I had done my part to help my family members by sending them money for basic necessities. But that evening I discovered that what I had been aware of was only a very small part of what had transpired in my country.

My family recounted the events for hours, and I listened.

My sisters and their husbands eventually left for their homes around ten p.m. Feeling weary from my journey, I excused myself to retire for the night.

"*Ave mangwana!*" I said, rising to my feet.

"*Ave mangwana!*" my mother, my father, *Mukoma* Martin, and *Maiguru* Sara responded in chorus.

I exited the living room and walked along the short hallway to the guest bedroom. Once in the bedroom, I collapsed on the bed, lying on my back, staring at the ceiling. Even though my body was tired, my mind was wide awake.

What my family had recounted to me that day played back in my mind. With their stories in the background, I recalled the optimism I had felt about the direction of progress in my country fifteen years earlier, when I left to go to America. Back then, I had thought the black-majority government running the country was making significant progress to honor the promises it had made when it took over power from the white-minority government at independence. Zimbabwe's economy was in a position of strength then. Living conditions for all its citizens, especially for its poorest people living in rural areas, had shown visible signs of improvement. Schools were being built to educate the children of the country. Hospitals and clinics were being established to provide basic medical care for all, even to those living in the most remote areas of the country. Conveniences like electricity, running water, and telephone services were being brought to shopping centers designated as growth points within rural communities.

I had expected this progress to continue. And I had expected a narrowing of the gap between the living conditions of the rich citizens and the poor citizens of my country.

In reality, over the course of the last fifteen years, the living conditions of most people in my country appear to have declined to levels below what they were during white rule. And the gap between the minority rich and majority poor had widened to unprecedented levels.

I have never been good at understanding factors that drive the economies of countries, and I am not any better at understanding government administration and social welfare systems either. But I found myself reflecting on some of the factors that I thought had contributed to the sorry state of affairs in my country.

My understanding—mind you, at the level of an average citizen—was that the HIV/AIDS epidemic, misguided government policies, endemic corruption, and the successive years of drought that the country had experienced were high on the list of factors that had led to the hardships most people were experiencing.

I started thinking about the HIV/AIDS epidemic, the AIDS crisis.

AIDS severely impacted many countries in Africa, and Zimbabwe is one of them. I remembered the first AIDS case in Zimbabwe had been reported in the mid-1980s. At that time, not a lot of information on the disease was available, not just in Zimbabwe, but in most countries—including developed countries. In fact, I remember people denying that such a disease existed. As a result, many people hadn't taken measures to protect themselves and others from contracting the virus and developing the disease.

The AIDS infection rate in my country had risen through the 1990s. By the time programs to combat the spread of AIDS were implemented, a lot of people had already been infected by the virus. In 2005, I remember reading official reports estimating that close to a quarter of the adult population of Zimbabwe was infected with the AIDS virus. And I knew by that time many people had already died and many more were continuing to die of the disease.

In Zimbabwe, as in most African countries impacted by AIDS, the disease was mostly killing people in their prime years of productivity—that is, people between the ages of twenty to fifty years old—the so-called "breadwinners" of society. Those who died left young children to grow up as orphans.

I pondered on the reasons why the AIDS epidemic had happened or why it had been allowed to spread and take such a devastating toll on the human race, especially on the people in Africa. I really didn't have any answers.

I turned over on the bed, lying on my left side, facing the bedroom window. Soft moonlight streamed into the room. My mind drifted away from the AIDS crisis, focusing on some of the government policies I thought had contributed to the decline of the Zimbabwean economy.

The land redistribution program that was implemented in 2000—seven years before my visit—was, in my mind, the single government policy that had dealt the worst blow to the economy of my country. Zimbabwe's disastrous land redistribution program and its aftermath had been widely documented and publicized. I had read some of the news articles and even read some of the so-called expert reports.

Most people had agreed that the land issue in Zimbabwe needed to be addressed—that land needed to be equitably redistributed among the country's population. I had been one of those people. At the time that Zimbabwe gained independence in 1980 and for a decade or two after that, the majority of the black people—who for the most part depended on subsistence farming for their livelihood—were still eking a living from tracks of unproductive barren land in what had been referred to as native reserves during colonial times. Most of the fertile agricultural land was still held by very few white commercial farmers. By some estimates, in the year 2000, whites constituted less than one percent of Zimbabwe's population but still held nearly half of the country's land. These were lands that the European white settlers had forcibly taken away from the tribal people. I still remembered the stories that my grandmother used to tell about how tribes were forced from their settlements in the lush valleys and chased into the hills.

From my understanding, the land redistribution policy, at its core, was meant to be a progressive program to benefit all the people of Zimbabwe, especially the poor black population. The first step would have been for the government to buy back some of the land from the white commercial farmers. The next step would have been to redistribute the acquired land to the many poor blacks who wished to become small-scale commercial farmers. This would have enabled the poor black farmers to work the land and raise their standard of living, while contributing to the country's economy. The whites who wished to continue farming would have retained enough land to continue with their trade and to keep contributing to the country's economy.

In reality, what happened was that the government, or people acting on behalf of the government, had forcibly taken land from white commercial farmers.

Groups of thugs armed with clubs, picks, axes, hoes, shovels, and knives—most calling themselves war veterans from the liberation struggle—had systematically invaded and illegally occupied white commercial farms, forcing the owners to leave, in some cases with no time to gather their possessions. The white farmers who resisted the occupation were brutally attacked. In some incidents, the white farmers were murdered in cold blood. The stories of brutal attacks and killings of white landowners made it into the local and international news circuits, but nothing was done to stop the land grabs and killings by what at that time appeared to be groups of unruly law-breaking thugs.

However, there was a hint of a coordinated force behind the land grabs, especially when one looked at who benefited the most from the land confiscated from white farmers. It soon became apparent that the wealthy and well-connected high-society members of the black ruling class of Zimbabwe were the ones who benefited the most from the land grabs. Most of the fertile, productive, and developed tracts of land acquired through the seemingly chaotic land grabs perpetrated by lawless thugs ended up being officially allocated to those in power and to members of their families and their friends. The productive parcels of land were distributed to people who had no interest in farming and contributing to the country's economy, but rather just wanted the land as status symbols. Instead of farming to produce food to feed the masses and for export to earn foreign currency for the country—as had been the role of the white farmers—most of the new landowners let the arable land lie fallow.

My body was beginning to ache from lying still on one side, so I turned over to lie on my right side, facing the doorway. And my mind shifted to the aftermath of the land redistribution program, which again was public knowledge.

Within a year or two of the implementation of the land redistribution program, Zimbabwe became a net importer of agricultural products. For many decades before the land grabs, Zimbabwe produced sufficient food to feed its people and had a huge surplus to export to other countries and earn foreign currency. In fact, before the land grabs, Zimbabwe used to be called the breadbasket of Southern Africa.

But with the farms now in the hands of people not interested in farming, Zimbabwe no longer had enough food reserves and had to import food to feed its starving masses. Instead of exporting excess corn to neighboring countries,

Zimbabwe had to import corn from Malawi, Zambia, and as far as the United States. There were hordes of poor black farmers who, if given productive land, were eager to farm the land to feed their families and feed the nation. These black farmers were ready to produce surplus agricultural products for export to earn foreign currency and thereby positively contribute to the country's economy. But the reality was that these aspiring small-scale farmers were still farming the barren plots they had farmed under white colonial rule. They were still breaking their backs on unproductive plots of land and coming out with meager harvests that could not sustain their families through the year, let alone earn income to pay for their children's education. They were still disenfranchised.

In the meantime, Zimbabwe's economy was crumbling. A significant part of the country's manufacturing industry was related to agriculture, such as production of chemicals used in farming and processing of agricultural produce. These agriculture-related manufacturing industries were some of the first to fail immediately following the land grabs. But even more devastating to the economy was the loss of foreign currency earnings from agricultural exports. Within a short time, it increasingly became difficult for the country to import basic resources required to run the manufacturing industry. There was limited foreign currency to import oil, machinery, transport equipment, and chemicals for industrial use. As a result, the manufacturing industry collapsed, taking its jobs with it. And things just kept sliding downhill from there.

I reached out and turned on the switch for the bedside lamp, but nothing happened. Then I remembered that there was no electricity. Fumbling in the dark with my hand, I located a candle and box of matches on the bedside table. I got out of bed and lit the candle, and then carried it to the bathroom down the hall. After I finished using the bathroom, I walked back to the room. I blew out the candle and lay back on the bed, settling into a comfortable position. I knew I wasn't going to fall asleep for quite a while.

My mind turned to the devaluation of my country's currency, the Zimbabwean dollar (Z$), which was one of the most visible indicators of the country's economic decline. At the time of Zimbabwe's independence in 1980, the Z$ was worth roughly the same as the British Pound Sterling (£), and it was worth more than the United States dollar (US$). Fast forward to my visit in 2007—twenty-seven years after independence—and the value of the Z$ had plummeted, and was continuing to hemorrhage against other major currencies.

Over the years, I had heard about the prevailing hyperinflationary climate in my country, with increasing inflation rates being quoted as 1000 percent, then 10,000 percent, then 100,000 percent, and then all the way up to and exceeding 1 billion percent. The fact that the government kept printing paper money not backed by hard assets didn't help the situation. At the same time, the Z$ kept being redenominated, with zeroes "chopped off" the currency denominations in an attempt to manage the monetary situation.

It was challenging to keep track of the value of the Z$ against other currencies. At the time Zimbabwe gained independence, the exchange rate for US$1 was approximately Z$0.50—that is, US$2 for Z$1. Not very long following the land grabs, the value of the Z$ began declining. At one point the exchange rate for US$1 was Z$300, then it went to Z$3000, then Z$30,000, then Z$300,000, then I lost track. To add to the complication, there was the official bank exchange rate and also the unofficial black market rate—which was just as important as the official market rate in terms of driving the country's economy.

It was dizzying to try and keep track of all the fast-moving parts. It wasn't so much the numbers but the practical implications of these numbers that affected the average person on the street. In practical terms, that meant that one needed to carry a large wad of money to buy a loaf of bread. And it also meant that the price of that loaf of bread was likely to increase several times in the course of the day. Families found themselves in positions where they could afford bread one day and not afford it the next, because the price of that bread had skyrocketed overnight. The not-so-funny joke that started making the rounds was that Zimbabwe was full of millionaires who couldn't afford to buy a loaf of bread. One could have Z$5 million that was worth less than US$0.50.

Most people had witnessed the value of their savings evaporate while sitting in bank accounts. The most affected were the retirees. Most of these retirees, not being savvy investors, may not have known about asset diversification. They had worked hard all their lives to build nest eggs of cash reserves in savings accounts, only to see those nest eggs disappear, with zeroes systematically lopped off their fortunes as if devoured by marauding ants.

I thought about the hordes of people who had fled Zimbabwe to escape the harsh economic conditions. Most had gone to neighboring countries—South Africa, Botswana, Zambia. A significant proportion had gone abroad—to England, the United States, Australia, and New Zealand. Young professionals—doctors, nurses, teachers, lawyers, engineers, architects—left the country to seek opportunities elsewhere, creating a brain drain. Even those with no formal skills left to seek employment in other countries as domestic workers and farm laborers, or to perform any other menial jobs. People who went to other countries sent money back home to their parents, their children, and their relatives. More often than not, it was the money from the diaspora that was keeping food on the table for most families in Zimbabwe.

I shifted my position on the bed again, stretching to release the tension in my body. I settled back, and my mind drifted to how the decline of my country's economy had affected members of my own family.

The only members of my family doing well were my brothers and some of my cousins who had left Zimbabwe to live in other countries. Those still in Zimbabwe were experiencing the hardships faced by others in the country. My parents were among the retirees who had seen their fortunes perish. Their savings had evaporated through hyperinflation and dollar redenomination and their pensions were lost as the government was broke and could not afford to pay pensions. On top of that, they were witnessing their adult children struggling to support families, and they couldn't help. They too needed to be supported.

Mukoma Martin and his wife had seen the middle-class lifestyle they had worked hard to build for themselves evaporate. His law firm, which had a team of over ten lawyers the last time I was home, was now reduced to just him, a paralegal, and a secretary. Instead of providing legal counsel to multimillion-dollar corporate deals, he was now helping clients who were trying to protect their properties from being confiscated by greedy and vindictive politicians. He said that in most cases this was a losing battle as the laws to protect property rights were no longer respected. He was just "keeping the lights on," he told me, waiting for the time when the political and economic conditions changed and he could rebuild his firm to what it used to be before. His wife had not fared any better. The bank she worked for had been one of the first to collapse, and she had not been able to find a job in years. She was contributing to the family upkeep by helping clients with tax filings during tax season. This didn't bring in much income as most people had no income to speak of, and most businesses had failed. Whatever money my brother and his wife earned went to pay for the education of their boys.

Sis Mary and her husband were just about managing to make ends meet. Jonah's salary as a professor at the local university was not much. He too said that he was just holding on, waiting for the change that would turn the tide. My sister, a social worker by training, had finally left her low-paid government job and established a business sourcing groceries and household items from neighboring countries for resale in Zimbabwe. That business was what was mostly supporting the family. That was how she and her husband could afford to send their children to be educated out of the country. Just like *Mukoma* Martin and his wife, they too had given up on luxuries like new clothes and such, because all the money they earned went to their children's education.

Mugu and Noah were struggling to make it on Noah's salary as a high school teacher. Mugu had graduated from a local university with a Bachelor of Arts degree a few years earlier, but couldn't find a job. They were concerned about money, with a new baby on the way. My aunts, uncles, cousins, and their families were in more or less similar situations; they too were struggling to make ends meet.

My mind continued to wander from one subject to the next, but I must have dozed off at some point because I was woken up by a gentle knock on the bedroom door. My mother walked in and sat on the edge of the bed. We exchanged morning greetings and then talked for about an hour, mostly about things in general, but also about personal issues that could not be discussed in front of others. When my mother left the room, I washed up, got dressed, and then joined my family for breakfast.

By about nine o'clock, *Mukoma* Martin said he was ready to drive me around Harare to pay my respects to some of my relatives—aunts, uncles, and cousins. I needed to pay respects to the relatives who were still living as well as those who had died while I was away. Unfortunately, a lot of the relatives I had left behind had passed away, mostly from AIDS-related complications.

Even though my family had shared stories of the hardships in Zimbabwe and I had spent the night reflecting on the situation in my country, what I hadn't done was to adequately prepare myself for seeing, in person, the effects of the devastation in people's lives. Being a witness to the suffering of others can be very hard to take in. That was the experience in store for me, starting that day.

We started by visiting relatives who lived in the southern part of the city, in high-density neighborhoods heavily populated by low-income families. In one neighborhood, I noticed streams flowing along the streets, even though this was the middle of the dry season. My brother must have spotted the puzzled expression on my face, because he quickly explained that I was looking at the overflow from the sewage system. He added that the sewage systems in most high-density neighborhoods had collapsed. As I looked around, people went about their way, deftly sidestepping what I had just been told were streams of raw sewage.

During conversations with my relatives, I learned that people were going for days without food in these neighborhoods, and I could see it in some people's faces. Most adults had no jobs as most companies had closed due to the collapsed economy. They could not earn money as street vendors either, as the government had dismantled that informal sector. And they could not leave the country to seek employment in neighboring countries due to lack of money to obtain the required travel documents and pay for the long journeys. They were basically stuck in the miserable lives that had become their existence.

Things were no better for those who still had jobs. What they earned was not enough to support families. Monthly salaries for civil servants—teachers, nurses, doctors, administration workers, office clerks—were not enough to cover the cost of transportation to work, let alone buy groceries or pay rent. Even for those who were fortunate to have sufficient money, mostly remittances sent by relatives working in other countries, there were no goods to buy in the shops. The supply chain had come to a complete grinding halt. Most stores didn't have basic items like sugar, salt, flour, cornmeal, cooking oil. Families relied on going to neighboring countries—South Africa, Mozambique, Zambia—to shop for groceries, or they bought groceries from the brave traders who had established cross-border businesses to import the needed supplies.

The collapse of the healthcare system was another major challenge, especially given the widespread illness and deaths from complications related to AIDS. I knew that government hospitals and clinics had no medicines or supplies. People were dying from opportunistic infections that could be treated if the medications were available. To make matters worse, many healthcare professionals had fled Zimbabwe to find gainful employment in other countries.

We visited a sick aunt who had been admitted at a government hospital. In my university days, this hospital used to be a premier institution that housed a world-acclaimed medical school. Those glory days were long gone, I found out.

The sight that greeted us at the hospital was horrible. The hallways were littered with people in various stages of deterioration. Skeletal forms lay on the floors, covered with blankets. Each was surrounded by relatives who sat waiting for the inevitable death of their loved one. In the ward where my aunt was, patients lay on the few hospital beds, covered with ragged-looking bedclothes.

My aunt was happy to see us. She was weak, suffering from advanced tuberculosis. She told us that even though she was in the hospital, she wasn't receiving any medication and her condition wasn't improving.

The situation was even worse in rural areas. When I visited my village, a lot of the people my age had died from AIDS, leaving children behind. This was the case in most villages across the country, I was told. At some homesteads, one saw a higher number of graves in the graveyards than the number of people living in the huts. Children, most below the age of ten, told stories of burying one parent one month and then burying the other parent the following month. A few fortunate children were taken in and cared for by a kind aunt, uncle, or cousin. Most of the orphaned children, though, lived with elderly grandparents. These grandparents had no means of supporting the children, outside of the little infertile plots of land they farmed to get food. The grandparents had no money to buy groceries and clothes, let alone pay tuition and buy uniforms so that the children could attend school. Other children found themselves alone, with no one to take care of them. The older siblings had to find ways to support their younger siblings. They did whatever they needed to do to earn money to survive.

As tragic as all this was, there was an even darker side to the AIDS story in Zimbabwe. This was the myth that men with AIDS could be cured of the disease by engaging in sex with a virgin. Only this wasn't a myth anymore in some households, but was being practiced behind closed doors. Some men were raping young girls. They were raping their daughters, nieces, daughters of their servants, daughters of their next-door neighbors, orphans left in their care—any little girl they had access to. And some men just indulged their fetishes for having sex with young girls, often raping victims multiple times. In addition to the trauma of being raped and the possibility of getting pregnant, some of these girls ended up being infected with the AIDS virus and contracting the disease.

Each time I met a young girl, I found myself wondering if they had been violated. And sometimes that unspoken question was answered by the tears that welled in the young girls' eyes when our gazes met and held. It was as if their eyes wanted to tell their stories. Most girls would not openly talk about what happened to them, as it was considered taboo to talk about such shameful things. Only a few had the courage to expose the men who had attacked them. Even when some girls revealed the identity of the rapists, oftentimes no one did anything to help. So the girls bore their wounds in silence.

One particular story broke my heart. One day I accompanied my cousin Ida who volunteered her time as a rural health worker. Ida counseled AIDS patients, often providing end-of-life care. She was a registered nurse by profession and had worked in government hospitals for many years. After retiring from nursing in her early fifties, she returned to live in the village where we had both grown up. She said she felt compelled to help patients living with AIDS in the surrounding communities. I greatly admired Ida for devoting her time and offering her skills to help AIDS victims who, in most cases, were marginalized by circumstances. I looked up to Ida as a role model for what it means to selflessly give to others. On that day, Ida was visiting a twelve-year-old girl who lived with her grandmother in a nearby village. The story that girl told left an indelible mark on my mind.

The narrow track leading to the village where the girl lived was impassable, even by a four-wheel-drive vehicle. So we had to travel on foot. As we walked there, Ida reminded me that I knew the girl's grandmother, *Mbuya* Svosve, from our childhood days. I vaguely remembered the name. Ida said the girl's name was Makomborero (blessings).

When we arrived at *Mbuya* Svosve's homestead, we were greeted by a weak bark from a scrawny dog lying under the eaves of a rundown grass-thatched hut, the only standing structure on the homestead. Piles of rubble marked the remnants of other structures that had once been part of this homestead. The dog didn't even get up. It could barely raise its head. It did, however, continue to follow our movements with its eyes.

A short thin woman with a full head of white knotty hair came out of the hut, alerted by the dog's bark. She was shabbily dressed, a loose-fitting cotton dress draped on her small frame and touching her ankles. She had no shoes, her callused feet showing below the hemline of the dress. Judging by her features, she looked to be in her late sixties. As I looked at her closely, I recognized the face that went with the name. I remembered *Mbuya* Svosve from my childhood. She used to live quite comfortably and had several well-educated children. Taking in the state of her homestead, I wondered what had happened to reduce her life to such abject poverty. I knew there was a story behind the decline of *Mbuya* Svosve's life circumstances, but whether I would come to know the story was another matter.

Mbuya Svosve greeted us warmly and ushered us into the dimly lit hut, rushing to spread a straw mat and motioning for us to sit down on the mat. As we sat, I noticed the girl we were visiting—Makomborero. She had been lying on a mat and was struggling to sit up. *Mbuya* Svosve rushed to the girl's side and gently pulled her up by the shoulders, propping her back against the walls of the hut. The girl slouched against the wall, with her eyes closed. The effort of sitting up seemed to have tired her. A threadbare cotton dress covered her thin body, a knitted woolen hat perched on her head. *Mbuya* Svosve pulled up the thin blanket covering the girls' legs, tucking it around her waist. In an attempt to straighten the girl's appearance, *Mbuya* Svosve gently wiped drool from her mouth and tugged at her hat, securing it around her head.

"If we had known visitors were coming today, Mako," *Mbuya* Svosve said, addressing the girl by her nickname, "we would have washed and changed clothes to look presentable, wouldn't we?" She continued with her attempts to spruce up the girl. "Look at us, we appear as if we are mad women, don't we? We appear like homeless people. But it's all going to be alright, my child. You wait and see, it's all going to be alright. The Almighty has not forgotten us. His mercies will shine on us in his good time."

The girl opened her eyes, a feeble smile on her face. And the grandmother smiled back and leaned in to give the girl a long hug. They seemed lost in their own little world, comforting and soothing each other. For a moment, it seemed we, the visitors, were forgotten.

"*Maiweee!*" *Mbuya* Svosve exclaimed, letting go of the girl and turning to Ida and me, visibly collecting herself. "I am losing my manners. Let me sit down so we can ask after each other's well-being." She retrieved a headscarf that had been lying on the floor and tied it securely around her head. Then she sat on the floor across the fireplace from where Ida and I sat, her legs crossed. We exchanged formal greetings, and in that process Ida introduced me to *Mbuya* Svosve and Mako.

On learning who I was, *Mbuya* Svosve looked at me and said, "I am glad that you have returned to see us. You stayed away too long. Now you find us living under these very difficult times. I never knew life could turn out this way. I never imagined that life could be this hard." I followed her gaze as it slowly swept across the interior of the hut.

"I am sorry things are hard," I said. That sounded like an inadequate response, even to my own ears. But I decided not to say anything else to try and compensate for that inadequacy. I knew that nothing I said was going to be of much use under the circumstances.

Mbuya Svosve nodded at me and then turned her attention to Ida. "The last two days have been very difficult for Mako. She has not been able to get up by herself. She is very weak. We have not had much to eat this past week. This is not good for her in her condition."

Her gaze settled on the dying embers in the fireplace as she continued to speak. "I went to get our package from the council offices this week, but came back with nothing."

I knew *Mbuya* Svosve was referring to food packages that were meant to be distributed to AIDS patients and their families in rural areas. An international donor agency provided the food packages to the government, and local councils handled the distribution of the food packages. What I was told though is that not all the food packages reached the intended beneficiaries. Some of the food packages simply disappeared, and at other times the intended beneficiaries were asked to pay for the food that was supposed to be free.

"This time," *Mbuya* Svosve continued, "the people at the council offices told us that we had to buy the food to pay for the government fuel."

Shaking her head and then shrugging her shoulders, she said, "Well, I am an old woman with no one to support me. I have no money, so I came back empty handed. I will keep going every week. I am praying for the Almighty to put someone kind in charge so that we can get the food we need."

Ida reached into an oversized tote bag she carried with her wherever she went. She pulled out a paper bag with food supplies she had brought from her home. She got up on her knees, offering the bag of food to the elderly woman.

Mbuya Svosve clapped her hands in a gesture of gratitude, and then stretched both arms over the fireplace to receive the bag. Ida handed over the bag and then sat back down on the mat.

Mbuya Svosve looked inside the bag. Then she slowly raised her gaze to Ida, tears welling in her eyes. "May the Almighty bless you, my child," she said. "May the Almighty protect you and keep you safe. May the Almighty protect all those you love and keep them safe. I thank you for your kind heart. I don't know what I would do without your help." She wiped the teardrops that had spilled onto her cheeks with the back of her hands, composing herself.

"These past few years, the Almighty has tried me," *Mbuya* Svosve continued to speak, now gazing at the fireplace again. "These have been the hardest years of my life. At the same time, the Almighty has also shown me that he is always there to provide for my needs. He has given me strength to endure the hardships. And whenever I am ready to give up, he sends someone such as you to help me. For that and for so many other blessings, I will keep praising him all the days of my life." *Mbuya* Svosve paused, her gaze still fixed on the dying fire. Silence stretched in the hut.

"Now that you have brought us food," she eventually said, looking at Ida, "I will prepare some for Mako. I know the food will help to bring some of her strength back." She turned her attention to preparing food for her granddaughter, rekindling the fire and setting a pot of water to boil.

Dipping her hand into the bag she had received from Ida, *Mbuya* Svosve brought out a packet of Cerelac porridge mix, a packet of dried beans, a small bag of cornmeal, a small bag of dried vegetables, a packet of salt, and a small bottle of vegetable cooking oil.

As *Mbuya* Svosve was preparing the food, Ida told Mako that I was visiting to hear her story. Mako's gaze turned to me, her dull brown eyes looking directly into mine. I held her gaze. After a moment, she nodded weakly. Then she slowly shifted her gaze to look at the flames that were now dancing in the fireplace. In a tremulous voice, she recounted what had happened to her.

Mako said she had watched her parents fall ill and then die of AIDS within a few months of each other—her father first, and then her mother. Her aunt, her mother's sister, had taken Mako and her two younger brothers to her home in a nearby town. Mako said that she had been grateful to her aunt and her family for offering them a home. But then the aunt's husband started raping her within days of their moving into the house. This was about five years earlier, when she was only seven. The uncle had told Mako that she needed to repay him for taking care of her and her brothers, and that he would throw them out on the street if she didn't do what he wanted.

Fearful that she and her brothers might be left homeless, Mako said she had kept quiet about what was happening. Two years back, she had developed a persistent heavy cough that wouldn't clear up, and her aunt had taken her to the clinic for treatment. As part of routine testing, the clinic had performed an HIV test, and the results had shown that Mako was HIV-positive. On hearing this, the aunt had asked Mako to pack her few belongings and leave the house. This was when Mako had gotten on a bus to come and live with her grandmother in the village. She said she knew she had AIDS. She said she knew she was dying. And she said she knew it was going to be a slow and painful death, just like the deaths of her parents.

Mako's gaze shifted from the fire, her brown eyes meeting mine again. "I am glad about one thing," she said, her voice now steady. "I am glad that my brothers still have a safe home."

A heavy lump had lodged in my chest, making it difficult to breathe. I didn't know what to say to Mako, so I just stared back at her through the haze of tears that had welled in my eyes. Rather than offer some inept platitude, I felt it was best to maintain a moment of silence.

Mako broke the gaze, turning to her grandmother who had brought her a plate of steaming porridge. She ate a few spoonfuls and then thanked her grandmother and Ida for the food and said she wanted to rest for a while.

"Remember, *Mbuya*, what you promised me," Mako said to her grandmother. "Please remember that after I die, I want you to tell my uncle that I forgave him. Tell him that I want him to be one of the people who carry my casket to the graveyard. I want him to know that he is forgiven." With that, she slowly lowered herself onto the mat and lay down, closing her eyes. Tears tumbled down my cheeks. Ida was openly sobbing beside me.

"I remember, my child. I remember. I will do as you wish," the grandmother promised, her voice quivering. She pulled up the blanket and tucked it around Mako, gently running her right hand down the girl's left cheek. "You go to sleep now, my child. You go to sleep. It's all going to be alright. The Almighty is watching over us. It's all going to be alright."

Opening her eyes again and extending a weak arm, Mako grabbed her grandmother's hand, clasping it to her chest. "You have been very good to me, *Mbuya*," she said. "I am so sorry that I have been so much trouble to you. I don't mean to be. Please forgive me."

"Hush, child," the grandmother said, tears rolling down her cheeks. "There is nothing to forgive. The Almighty has already given me my blessings in you. Makomborero means blessings, doesn't it? Besides, when the Almighty gives us heavy loads to carry, he also gives us strong backs to carry those loads."

Mako weakly nodded to her grandmother, releasing her hand. The grandmother continued to stroke the girl's cheek, soothing her. "Go to sleep, my child. Go to sleep."

Once again, the grandmother and her grandchild seemed lost in their own world, comforting one another.

Mako finally released a soft sigh and closed her eyes. *Mbuya* Svosve sat beside her grandchild until the girl fell asleep. Then she suggested that we go outside for fresh air, leading us through the narrow doorway of the hut. As we sat down in the shade under the eaves of the hut, my eyes glanced at the graveyard a few feet from the edge of the cleared yard. Several graves stood silent in the afternoon sun.

Ida and I visited for a little while longer with *Mbuya* Svosve. Our conversation turned to lighter subjects. At one point *Mbuya* Svosve asked about my life in America and I told her a few stories. As we were leaving, I retrieved some money from my bag and handed it to *Mbuya* Svosve. I knew the money wouldn't make a dent in the challenges that this woman and her grandchild were facing. But I didn't know what else to do at that time. *Mbuya* Svosve thanked me and wished me well in my travels.

Over the next two days, I heard more stories of pain and suffering as I accompanied Ida on her visits to see patients.

But, amid all that, people got on with their lives. They stopped long enough to tell their stories, if you asked them. And then they got back to doing what they needed to do to survive and to take care of their families. The resilience I saw in people was something to be admired. I could not imagine myself enduring hardships such as I was witnessing and then waking up each morning to do what needed to be done. It just seemed a bit too much for me.

There was a different story to be told, though.

This was the story of the minority rich and well connected of the black Zimbabwean society. These were the people in high positions in the government, the army, the police force, and the intelligence agencies. It also included prominent business tycoons, renowned property owners, and influential church leaders. These were the so-called *chefs*—a term used in my country to refer to the elite class or people with power. These people and their families lived lives of excessive luxury and indulgence. They were the ones with million-dollar mansions, in US$ currency. And they drove top-of-the-line Mercedes Benzes, BMWs, or Hummers; often having ten or more cars in their multi-door residential garages. Most in this group did their monthly grocery shopping in South Africa, Dubai, and Hong Kong and bought designer clothes in Milan and on Fifth Avenue in New York. They, of course, dropped this information in casual conversations so that you would be aware of their wealth, just in case you somehow missed it after seeing their mansions, cars, and clothes.

In my mind, these people in the rich upper class had contributed the most to the collapse of the Zimbabwean economy. This was through misguided government policies, rampant corruption, unchecked greediness, and excessive pursuit of self-interest.

I am not saying that every rich black person in Zimbabwe was involved in corruption or shady deals of some kind, because then I would be misrepresenting the facts. There were a few wealthy Zimbabweans who had built their business empires by honest and admirable means—true shining examples of economic success coming from hard work and smart business sense. More often than not, one would find that these were the folks who donated some of their wealth to help the poor. They built schools and hospitals to serve poor communities, they set up scholarship funds to educate bright students from poor families, and they dug wells to provide clean water for people living in rural areas. I have nothing but respect and admiration for people who perform such selfless acts. Unfortunately, such selfless people represented only a tiny minority of those with wealth in Zimbabwe.

The people in the rich upper class I am talking about were those out to enrich themselves, their families, and their friends by any means, with no care or concern for others outside their inner circles. Most of these people owned several farms that had been confiscated from white farmers during the land redistribution fiasco. The stories I heard about the deterioration of the agricultural sector of Zimbabwe were sobering.

According to these stories, the "cell phone farmers"—the popular term used to refer to the new land barons—had sold the equipment they had found on the confiscated farms. They had sold trucks, tractors, tillers, combine harvesters, threshers, and irrigation equipment to make a quick buck. Each year, I was told, these land barons received free farm inputs—such as fertilizer, seeds, and agricultural chemicals—from the government. These farm inputs were meant to stimulate agricultural production. But the new land barons sold the supplies on the black market—the parallel market—to make a quick return. They did not use the free farm inputs to grow food to feed the nation or to produce cash crops that could earn foreign currency for the country. Instead, they sold the free supplies to finance their high-flying lifestyles.

The wide expanses of green pastureland with herds of fat cattle that one used to see when driving along the Harare-to-Mutare highway were now gone. In their place were stretches of dusty barren fields, with the occasional piece of abandoned farm equipment rusting in the elements. In the meantime, a large proportion of the country's population was going to sleep on empty stomachs.

It was disconcerting to witness the arrogant display of excessive wealth, mindless consumerism, and blatant corruption of the elite class of my country superimposed on the extreme poverty and hopelessness that the majority of the people were living under. This juxtaposition grated on the nerves. This hardening of hearts to the suffering of others was difficult to comprehend.

The irony that I myself had lived a consumer-centered life in America was not lost on me. I shuddered with embarrassment as I recalled the lifestyle I had been living for many years. To soothe myself, I told myself that at least in my case I had worked hard to earn the money I had spent on a consumer lifestyle. I also told myself that my consumer spending had been limited to what I legitimately earned, and that I hadn't enriched myself through corrupt practices. I did, however, become more sensitized to the plight of the poor people who had to witness the gluttonous lifestyles of the rich while they watched their own children starving.

There was something else that I found unsettling about the situation in my country.

It seemed that watching the wealthy, well-connected, and powerful members of society blatantly abuse their positions and power was encouraging a culture of corruption on all levels of society. You had to bribe your way through layers of bureaucracy to get anything done. That seemed to be the new norm, and you either played the game or you did not get what you needed.

Of course, corruption had existed when I was growing up, but this appeared to be corruption taken to a whole different level. Perhaps I was naive then, but when I was growing up, it seemed those involved in corrupt practices went to great lengths to hide their shady activities, as it was frowned upon in decent society. Integrity and keeping one's family name clean were of paramount importance then, as I remembered. Not so anymore. People were now very blatant about corruption; in fact, most boasted about it, as if it was a status symbol. More often than not, people were now asking for bribes for providing services that they were employed to provide. I was told that with very little earnings, ordinary people with any position of authority had to charge corruptly for their services to make ends meet. You were expected to pay a bribe to the teacher to teach your child, to the school administrator to admit your child to his school, to the hospital staffer to ensure that you received the medications you needed, to the local politician to get a permit to establish programs to help poor people in the area he or she represented, and the list went on and on.

Officials stole food supplies that were meant to be distributed to starving people in rural areas whose crops had failed, not through their fault, but because of poor rains. These officials then sold the food supplies and lined their pockets, with no concern for the children of the poor who were going to bed hungry on many nights.

According to reliable sources, most of the money donated by other countries and international donor agencies for various development and social programs meant to benefit the poor never made it to the intended beneficiaries. That money disappeared within official corridors, so to speak. All this was happening in broad daylight, and there seemed to be nothing much anyone could do to stop this theft. The police and legal systems were no help, as most in those institutions were also involved in corrupt practices. This was very close to a social breakdown, I thought to myself.

Over the last few years, I had heard from some academic corners that Zimbabwe would make a perfect case study on how to destroy a country's economy in a matter of a few years. As I witnessed the sorry state of affairs in my country, I had to agree with that assessment. In 1980, when Zimbabwe gained independence, the incoming black government was handed over a country that had a robust infrastructure, a self-sustaining economy, and one of the best education systems in the world. Fast forward twenty-seven years and all that had been destroyed, and the country reduced to its knees. It was hard to believe this had happened in a country that had shown so much promise to deliver for its people. And it was painful to witness.

There was something else that I noticed in the attitude of some of the people that I encountered during my stay in Zimbabwe.

Some people would size you up as quickly as they could after meeting you—to determine if it was worth their time to get to know you. People asked you pointed questions to determine your economic status so they could see if you could be of any value to them. They asked very specific questions. Which suburb do you live in—high-density, low-density, or exclusive enclave? What type of house do you live in? How many properties do you own? What type of car do you drive? Where do you send your children to school? It seemed there was a standard set of questions used to size people up.

On hearing that I had lived in America for many years, some people had an initial false impression of what knowing me could do for them and their families in terms of economic gain. Understandably, they often assumed that I was one of the *chefs* coming from abroad, and that getting to know me might benefit them in some way. I noticed that people initially approached me with an engaging and charming attitude. But this almost invariably faded into indifference and even outright rudeness when they found out that I wasn't one of the *chefs* bringing back lots of money to shower on everyone, or that I wasn't going to entertain them with outrageous accounts of my high-flying lifestyle.

That I, in fact, was a lost traveler on a quest to find my identity was of no interest to people. No one had the time and energy for that; all the time and energy had to be spent trying to find out how to make a quick dollar. For the less fortunate, it was to make a dollar so they could feed and shelter their families. For the well connected, it was to make a dollar so they could finance their outrageously extravagant lifestyles. And the rich made their dollar either by asking you to invest in their latest ventures—some genuine and some not so genuine—or by asking you for bribes and favors outright.

Even the youngsters wanted to know what you could do for them or what they could get out of you. It was all about the deal. Education was of secondary importance. Talking to them about the importance of a good education was a waste of their time. They wanted to know how to get to the next deal that would make them fast money. It seemed all their efforts were focused on chasing money and chasing material things.

After a month of being in Zimbabwe, it became clear to me that my country was facing serious challenges that had no quick and easy solutions. It became clear to me that I didn't know how to help the people of my country. I didn't have the technical skills, the political connections, the social platforms, or access to the vast amounts of money required to begin addressing the many challenges I saw in every facet of life. It also became clear to me that the answers I was seeking for my own life were not to be found here. There were no wise people who could be my spiritual guides here.

With a heavy sense of disappointment, I made the decision to return to California.

I knew that returning to California was the right decision for my life, but a part of me felt that I, once again, was abandoning people who needed my help. I felt that I was abandoning my family. I felt that I was abandoning people like Mako, the girl dying of AIDS in a small dilapidated hut. I felt that I was abandoning people like Mako's grandmother, *Mbuya* Svosve, whose devotion to her grandchild could only be matched by her faith in the Almighty and her resilience to endure extreme hardships.

But I also knew the reality of the state I was in. I was lost. I didn't see myself playing much of a positive role in turning things around for my family, or for people like Mako and *Mbuya* Svosve. I felt I wasn't much use to anyone until I found myself first. And I promised myself that I would revisit this decision once I found my feet again. That promise seemed to abate some of the angst surrounding my decision to leave my country. So I made arrangements for my departure.

Our Beloved Land

Divine Presence, the origin of all that is seen and unseen
I call on your love to break the dawn
On the deep and pervasive darkness that shrouds our beloved land
Lost and confused, the people no longer know which way to turn
To seek deliverance from the scourges they face every day
The despair, powerlessness, and hopelessness
The hunger, poverty, and destitution
The suffering, sickness, and death

Divine Presence, the creator of the heavens and the earth
I call on the spirits of our ancestors who roamed this land before us
Those who trusted the land to provide for all their needs
Wisdom and guidance from you, the Creator within
Peace and stillness from the hills and the mountains
Shade and shelter from the forests and the valleys
Food and nourishment from the fruits and the flowers
Healing and anointment from the leaves and the roots
If only we can remember what our ancestors knew and practiced then
All this could be ours again one day

Divine Presence, the eternal home of our spirits
I call on each and every one of us
To trust in the land to provide for all our needs again
And to turn to our neighbors and tell them what we know
About the wisdom and guidance of you, the Creator within
About the peace and stillness of the hills and the mountains
About the shade and shelter of the forests and the valleys
About the food and nourishment of the fruits and the flowers
About the healing and anointment of the leaves and the roots
Let your word spread like wildfire across dry savannah plains
A premonition of the thirst-quenching rains to come

Divine Presence, the source of the power that runs the universe
I call on all the people of our land—the young, the old, the timid, and the bold
To shake off the confusion and join hearts and minds
To hold a vision for the delivery of our beloved land that is our home
From a leadership that rules with ignorance, indifference, and callousness
To leaders who govern with wisdom, vision, and compassion
From an elite class gripped by corruption, greed, and self-importance
To humble benefactors who share their gifts with humility and kindness
From a disenfranchised mass living in fear, hopelessness, and despair
To citizens who feel heard, inspired, and empowered
We ask that you restore our beloved land to be the promised land that it once was
With opportunities for all—the young, the old, the timid, and the bold

Divine Presence, the source of the energy that sustains our lives
I call on the people to lean on your strength, the Almighty One
And access the energy that you are
As that energy is alive and well within each of us
Waiting for us to tap into it again
To deliver us from the oppressions of the day
Let this energy fuel each one of us
With strength to endure what we have to endure
With courage to rise up and do what we have to do
With compassion, kindness, and tenderness toward one another
For this is what will keep us going
Until the time when love returns
To break the dawn over our beloved land

REMEMBERING THE HEART

Before I flew back to California, I had one more visit to make. I needed to visit my grandmother's grave again. I had visited Grandma's grave for the first time within a few days of my arrival in Zimbabwe. That first visit had been to pay my respects. This next visit was not to pay my respects; this was a different kind of visit.

The day before I was due to fly out, the Thursday of the last week of October, I drove to our village by myself. I left Harare early in the morning and arrived at our homestead by midafternoon. The place was deserted. My parents, now both retired from teaching, were staying with Mugu and her husband in Harare, waiting for the birth of the new baby. I was going to meet my parents and a few other family members the next evening at Mugu's house for our farewells.

I drove through the wooden gate, parked the car under one of the shade trees, and headed straight for the two graves lying quietly side-by-side on the *ruware* at the edge of the yard. I bowed my head slightly in the direction of my grandfather's grave in respectful acknowledgment, and then I sat down beside my grandmother's grave.

A deep fatigue weighed down on my body. I felt as if I was going to drown under its weight. I leaned my head onto the whitewashed walls of the grave, cushioning my forehead on my right forearm. I rested my left hand on my heart and I broke into uncontrollable sobs. Great, heaving bursts shook my shoulders. Tears streamed down my cheeks, falling onto the stone surface below. And then I started talking to my grandmother, words tumbling out between sobs.

"I am sorry, *Mbuya*, I let you down," I sobbed. "I am so sorry that I betrayed your trust. You trusted me with your most precious gift of wisdom, and I have not lived the wisdom you taught me. I have not lived my life with a sense of connection to Source as you taught me. I have not shared your wisdom with my brothers and sisters, so that they too can live their lives with a sense of connection to Source. I have not shared your wisdom with those I have met in my life, to spread the knowledge."

The words poured out of my mouth as if they had a life of their own. "*Mbuya*, in my ignorance, I rejected your wisdom to pursue what I thought was a better and more modern way of life in faraway lands. I pursued a life focused on accumulating material things and chasing worldly pleasures. I thought these would bring me a sense of security, a sense of power, a sense of peace, a sense of who I am. But who I am got lost somewhere along the way."

A deep ache throbbed in my heart and a huge lump lodged in my throat as the next words spilled out of my mouth. "I ask for forgiveness from you and from Source. I was overcome by my human weakness. I now know that I have been pursuing delusions all these years. My identity is not in the things I own. My identity is not in the knowledge I find in books. My identity is not in the people I know." The stream of words continued to pour out.

"You taught me long ago that who I am is in Source, and why I am here is to co-create with Source and to love and serve others. I know that now, *Mbuya*," I sobbed. "Please help me to get back on my feet again. I am so lost. I am so confused. And I am so afraid. Please help me find my way back to Source. I don't know who else to turn to. I don't know what else to do. Please help me, *Mbuya*," I pleaded. Then I let the tears pour out in silence.

Eventually, the sobs died down and the gush of tears subsided to sporadic trickles rolling down my cheeks. I continued to sit quietly with my body still leaning against my grandmother's grave, my eyes closed. Then I became aware of a silence surrounding me. I kept my attention on that silence for a while. Of its own accord, my attention shifted from the silence surrounding me to a stillness in my heart space, in the middle of my chest. I don't remember ever reaching this place of deep stillness within me before. I noticed that the fatigue that I had felt earlier had subsided and was replaced by a sense of peace. As I continued to put my attention within, a vision came to me.

In my vision, my grandmother was sitting beside me, as she had done all those years ago, and she was counseling me, just as she had done then. I was fully aware that I was imagining seeing my grandmother, and that I was imagining hearing her voice counsel me. I knew that what I was hearing were the thoughts in my own head. Nevertheless, I sat very still, not wanting to break the connection to the voice that was whispering soothing words of comfort to my soul.

"Yeukai, my grandchild, our elders used to say that a child who does not cry for help will die in the cradle." My grandmother spoke in a soft and gentle voice. "It makes me glad to hear your cry for help. Because a cry for help summons that help to you. That is the way it is. That is the way it has always been. That is the way it will always be."

My grandmother's voice continued, "Let the tears you cry be tears of cleansing, not of sorrow. Let the tears you cry wash away the burdens that you carry on your shoulders. Let the tears wash away the confusion, doubt, and fear that cloud your mind. And let the tears wash away the sadness, grief, and despair that weigh down your heart. When all these negative energies are released and washed away, a space is created inside of you. And it is only then that the love from Source can flow into you and fill this space." A hiccup rattled through my chest, but I let my attention settle back to the stillness in my heart space and continued to listen to my grandmother's beautiful, soothing words.

"Once the cleansing is complete and the love from Source fills you up, my child, there is nothing to apologize for, and nothing to be forgiven. You did nothing wrong. And nothing is lost. All is well just as it is." The voice paused. I kept my attention trained on the silence it left behind.

"You can turn your life around and follow the path of your heart in any moment," the voice continued, a beautiful song to my ears. "All you need is willingness, and I see there is willingness in your heart." A shudder ran through my body.

"You do not need to go anywhere special. You do not need to seek anyone special. You do not need to look for any kind of magic. All you need is to remember your heart and to go into it. For it is through your heart that you will rediscover the love, light, and radiance that is your spirit, the essence of who you are. Your spirit always has been and always will be forever rooted in Source. You are in Source right where you are." Another pause followed, but I kept listening. And the soft voice returned.

"Listen to your heart and follow its guidance from this very moment. Do not wait for tomorrow to come. Do not wait until you receive a sign. Do not wait until something that you think ought to happen has happened. The time to start changing your life by following your heart is now, not later." I noticed the image of my grandmother gently undulating in rhythm to the words she was speaking.

"I am here to help you on this journey. All I ask is that you listen to my voice and follow what I speak. Are you willing to do that, my child?" I nodded my head and continued to listen. "Take a deep breath and continue to focus on your heart as you are doing right now." I took a deep breath in and slowly released it, keeping my eyes closed and my attention in my heart space. I could still see my grandmother's image in my mind's eye, and I could still hear her gentle voice as she continued to speak.

"Feel the gentle beating of your heart. Let your heart be the only point of focus for you right now and sit with it for a while." A long silence followed. I kept my focus on my heart in that silence, and I could feel gentle wave-like sensations rising from within my heart space and spreading throughout my body.

"Right here, right now, you are spirit rooted in Source," the voice continued. "You have reached the dwelling place of Source. You are one with the energy that runs all that is seen and unseen in creation. In this moment, as you feel this sense of connection, know that you are whole, you are complete, you are safe, you are protected, you are cared for, and you are loved. In this moment, you have come back to your eternal home, the origin of all your power." The voice was like a gentle wave washing all the dirt and grit from my being.

"As you are connected to Source in this moment, bring your concerns to your mind and surrender them to Source. Surrender everything to Source. For in Source, your confusion is lifted and you are left with clarity of mind. Your doubts are cleared and you are left with a deep faith in life. The fears that grip you and seem so real are exposed as nothing more than a collection of thoughts with no real substance. In Source, you discover that what appeared to be real and threatening is a false appearance." A gentle breeze wafted through, caressing my skin.

"Start living your life in this new way of being. Start asking questions that you may have from this place of clarity. And each time you ask a question, return to your heart and to the stillness and wait for the answers to come. The wisdom that you seek is already here within you; it rises and reveals itself to you when you put your attention on your heart and reach the stillness within. The answers that you seek will rise from your heart." My grandmother's voice was almost a whisper now, but she continued to speak.

"This is the place where you come to release your burdens, your doubts, your fears, your worries, your anxieties, your anger, your grief. This is the place where you come to be encouraged, uplifted, inspired, and empowered. This is the place where you come to receive guidance for your life. This is the place where you come to imagine the experiences that you desire for your life. This is the place where you come to be reminded of the purpose of your life in the world." I sensed a shift deep in my heart space as I listened to the words.

"You are not here in this world to accumulate possessions. You are not here in this world to compete with others. You are not here in this world to take away from others. The urge to do all those things was coming from the fear you carried inside." Another pause followed, the moment of silence stretching.

"You are here to receive what you ask for." The voice eventually returned. "You are here to share with others that which is freely given to you. You are here to be the one who encourages, uplifts, inspires, and empowers others. You are here to learn from the experiences of your life. You are here to learn from the people you meet along the way. Your heart will know when you meet the teachers who have something to teach you about living your life rooted in Source. Learn what the teachers have to teach you." I had to strain to hear the voice as it was starting to fade away.

"You have to remember one thing, Yeukai, my child. For the blessings to come to you, for your visions to come to fruition in your life, you have to follow the guidance that you receive in your heart. You have to do what your heart tells you. If you do not follow your heart, then nothing will change for you. But if you follow your heart, your life will be guided by the energy from Source that will carry you for the rest of your days here on earth." Another short pause followed.

"Anytime you feel lost or overwhelmed, just close your eyes and focus on your heart and reach the stillness within. This stillness is your spirit that is rooted in Source. Then surrender to Source whatever it is that burdens your heart. It is in this surrender that you will receive the guidance for your life. It is in this surrender that what you need finds its way to you. This is the way to live your life rooted in Source. This is the way it is. This is the way it has always been. This is the way it will always be."

With those parting words, the voice ceased to speak and the vision of my grandmother vanished from my mind's eye.

As I continued to sit with my eyes closed and my attention on my heart space, I felt a sense of being forgiven. I felt as if all the negativity in me was suddenly dissolved and washed away. And what was left was a deep sense of peace.

I continued to sit by my grandmother's grave, holding on to the sense of peace. It was only after I started feeling hunger pangs that I remembered I hadn't eaten all day. I said a silent prayer and then stood up from the graveside and walked to my parents' cooking house to prepare a meal.

I knew where my mother kept the food supplies, so I quickly found the ingredients to throw a meal together. I found pieces of dried meat in one of the decorative clay pots on the *huva* at the front of the cooking house, a bottle of cooking oil and a packet of salt in the wooden cupboard beside the *huva*, and a tin of cornmeal by the fireside. I fetched water from the borehole and picked onions and tomatoes from the vegetable garden adjacent to the borehole. Back at the cooking house, I started a fire and prepared a meal of *sadza* and a stew of dried meat with onion and tomatoes. I ate the simple meal sitting under the cool shade of the *muonde* tree—the same tree that used to be my grandmother's favorite spot for her midday naps. By the time I finished eating and washing the dishes, it was late afternoon. I decided to spend the night, opting to drive back to Harare in the morning. I knew I had plenty of time as my flight was not until midnight the next day.

I woke up around four o'clock the next morning and got out of bed. As I dressed, I had a distinct inclination to visit the prayer spot by the hillside where my grandmother and I used to sit. I trekked up the path to the hillside. The spot was gone, of course, the area now covered with brush. I found a flat stone close by and sat on it, facing east. As I watched the sunrise, it felt like I was transported back to the days when I sat on this hillside with my grandmother.

The sky was covered by a thin layer of pale gray clouds. The sun, peeking from behind the clouds, first appeared over the valley in the east as a white globe with a faint yellowish halo. As it continued to climb out of the valley, the sun slowly dissipated the thin layer of clouds—revealing a clear blue sky.

Closing my eyes, I became aware of a sense of peace surrounding me. This was similar to the sense of peace I had experienced the day before. I felt a sense of being accepted just as I was, a sense of being appreciated just as I was, a sense of being in harmony with whatever was transpiring at that moment. This feeling was in striking contrast to the usual sense of rejection, dread, resistance, fear, anxiety, doubt, and confusion that had been a part of my life for a very long time now.

I sat on the hillside for about an hour, not thinking of anything in particular, not worrying about anything, not planning any next moves, and not even pondering the great questions of life. I just gave myself the opportunity to be with the peaceful feeling for as long as I could hold onto it. I didn't receive any words of wisdom or revealing answers—just the sense of peace made that time feel very special to me. It felt as if a deep wound around my heart had been cleaned with balming salts and was finally starting to heal.

Eventually I got up and went back to the homestead, packed my things, and drove back to Harare. I arrived at Mugu's house late in the afternoon. I spent some quiet time with Mugu and my parents. Mugu's husband came back from work in the evening. Sis Mary and her husband and *Mukoma* Martin and his wife arrived just as we were getting ready to sit down for dinner.

We had a quiet and uneventful dinner, and then around nine-thirty p.m. my family took me to the airport to catch the last plane out to Johannesburg, where I would catch my connecting flight to New York City and then another flight back to San Diego.

Remembering the Heart

Divine Presence, as I meet you in my heart
I thank you for the images I see in my dreams
Showing me what my life can be

If only I could believe the possibilities they foretell
My life would be the same as the sun in the eastern horizon
That, with ease and grace, paints a poignant sunrise in the sky

Divine Presence, as I meet you in my heart
I thank you for the melodies I hear in the songs
That you whisper softly to me
If only I could discern the messages they bring
My life would be the same as the waves of the ocean
That, with ease and grace, undulate in a rhythmic dance of the ages

Divine Presence, as I meet you in my heart
I thank you for the roses and the sweet scent they give
Reminding me of the sweetness of life
If only I could breathe in the scent they bring
My life would be the same as the gentle breeze across the plains
That, with ease and grace, delights as it wafts away to distant terrains

Divine Presence, as I meet you in my heart
I thank you for the food that I taste
Nourishing and sustaining my mind and body
If only I could receive the goodness it brings
My life would be the same as the rain that falls from the sky
That, with ease and grace, nurtures and livens the earth

Divine Presence, as I meet you in my heart
I thank you for the touch of your hand
Guiding my life at every turn
If only I could follow the guidance of your hand
My life would be the same as the waters of the rivers
That, with ease and grace, flow on their way home to the ocean

FACING AND RELEASING
THE FALSE SELF

O n my return to California, I went back to work and settled into my old life. On the surface, it seemed as if everything was the same as before. But something had changed; something had shifted at the level of my heart.

On reflection, I realized that my trip to Zimbabwe hadn't been so much about finding wise teachers as I had interpreted the dream that sent me packing my bags and flying across continents. With the benefit of hindsight and a lot of time spent in contemplation, I began to catch glimpses that hinted at a larger meaning behind the trip that I had taken.

When I was in Zimbabwe, I had seen what happens when human beings are overtaken by negative energies that drive greed, corruption, and selfishness. I had seen what happens when human beings worship power, money, and possessions above all else. I had seen what happens when human beings lose the ability to feel compassion for other human beings. The poor in my country were facing hunger, sickness, despair, and death. But those in power were turning a blind eye to the suffering of their fellow citizens. In fact, those in power—in their insatiable pursuit of more power, more money, more possessions—were actually causing the worsening of living conditions for the poor.

Beyond that though, I realized that the most valuable lessons I had learned came from witnessing the poor as they moved through the challenges they faced on a daily basis. I had witnessed the resilience of the human spirit that kept pushing on under the most difficult of circumstances. And I had witnessed the power of faith and forgiveness. In people like *Mbuya* Svosve, I saw how, with tenacity and a strong faith, one could find the resilience to face hardships with dignity. In people like Mako, I saw forgiveness in practice; she had forgiven her uncle for raping her and sentencing her to a slow death by AIDS. I had witnessed the sharing and caring among people with very little.

In my heart, I knew that the events I had witnessed were related to my quest to know the truth and to understand the purpose of my life. In the weeks and months that followed, I sensed a quickening of pace in my search for answers. And in this way, I allowed myself to become a student of life.

I have often heard the saying that when the student is ready, the teacher will appear. My teachers appeared to me in many different forms—some in recognizable forms, others in not so obvious forms. I kept an open mind about who my teachers were. I kept my grandmother's counseling by her graveside in my mind. I knew that those who showed up in my life did so, at the particular time they showed up, because I needed to learn what they had to teach me.

I learned from teachers with religious affiliations and from teachers with no religious affiliations. I learned from teachers with several academic degrees and from teachers with no formal education to speak of. I learned from celebrity leaders who commanded large followings and from lone figures who talked to flocks of pigeons on city sidewalks. And I learned from senior citizens with heads full of gray hair and from children with milk on their noses.

Even though I had struggled with organized religion growing up, I still listened and learned from what I thought were some of the most profound teachings—whether from the Christian, Judaic, or Muslim faiths. What I listened for, and gravitated toward, were messages that resonated with me. I did not judge or reject a message because of the messenger—I did not "shoot the message" because of the messenger who delivered it to me.

I was led to books that shared the teachings of enlightened beings—those who had not only awakened to their true nature as extensions of Source but were also liberated from selfish desires and tendencies and were the embodiment of humility in action. Some of the teachers I read are long gone, and others are still with us in the world of the living. I read *Be As You Are: The Teachings of Sri Ramana Maharshi*[2] by David Godman; *The Art of Life*[3] by Ernest Holmes; *The Power of Now*[4] and *A New Earth*[5] by Eckhart Tolle; *The Celestine Prophecy*[6] and *The Secret of Shambhala*[7] by James Redfield; *The Presence Process*[8] and *Alchemy of the Heart*[9] by Michael Brown; *The Book of Secrets*[10] and *The Path to Love*[11] by Deepak Chopra; *Spiritual Liberation*[12] by Michael Bernard Beckwith; *The Four Agreements*[13] by Don Miguel Ruiz; and *The Healing Wisdom of Africa*[14] by Malidoma Patrice Somé. I even read books on modern psychology and leadership—*Emotional Intelligence*[15] by Daniel Goleman, *Success Intelligence*[16] by Robert Holden, *The Leader Who Had No Title*[17] by Robin Sharma, and many other titles by many other authors. I listened to self-help audio programs, including *Ask and It Is Given (Part I and Part II)*[18] and *The Teachings of Abraham: The Master Course Audio*[19] by Esther and Jerry Hicks.

I was also led to seminars, retreats, and congregations that taught the principle of oneness of all people—with no divisions across race, religion, nationality, class, or social status. I discovered and took classes on prayer as a way to come into and sustain a conversation with Source and the ancient ritual of meditation. With meditation, I learned the many ways to clear the mind of incessant negative thoughts that can easily take over one's life. I was led to small remote villages in the jungles of the world to learn the practices of tribal people who lived their lives rooted in Source.

With an openness to the messages that I received, I was amazed and thankful to discover how much information was available to those seeking the truth and seeking to understand the purpose of their lives. I started receiving answers to the questions I had from many different sources.

Some of the most powerful teachings I received came from wise teachers I met through synchronistic events. One such event was my meeting with Monica Michaels, who became a dear friend.

About a year after my return from Zimbabwe, I met Monica at a dinner party thrown by a mutual friend. Finding ourselves sitting next to each other at the dinner table, Monica and I had struck an easy conversation, and before too long the conversation had turned to the subject of seeking the truth about life. That is when Monica had invited me to attend monthly spiritual meetings that she hosted at her house, and our friendship had grown from there.

Monica was a petite woman in her early fifties and had a vivacious, infectious personality. When she eventually shared her story with me, I learned that she grew up in Arizona where her parents still lived. She and her husband had moved to California two decades earlier and raised two boys who were now adults. One of the boys had moved back to Arizona where he taught high school, and the other worked in New York. Unfortunately, Monica's husband had passed away five years earlier, following a long battle with lung cancer. Even though years had passed and Monica now had a boyfriend, Nathan, she said she still missed her husband.

Monica told me it was during her husband's illness that she had turned to spirituality in search for answers to questions she had about matters of life and death, having failed to find satisfactory answers in organized religion. She said she had started hosting the monthly meetings because she wanted her husband to feel the support of others during his time of transition. Following her husband's passing, Monica said she had continued to host the meetings because she strongly felt there was a need to bring people together to discuss topics on spiritual matters, outside of religious dogma. She said she enjoyed playing host and I knew that this role suited her personality well.

The group that met at Monica's house was composed of people from different religious backgrounds and traditions—Christianity, Judaism, Islam, Buddhism, Hinduism, African traditions, and Native American traditions. The group had grown and continued to grow organically, with each of the group members inviting people whom they thought could add interesting perspectives to the discussions. The group now had about fifteen regular members. The common bond among the group members was the search for a path that allows one to live a life more aligned with a higher power that each of us sensed was real.

One of the things we did in our meetings was to share our various cultural beliefs, traditions, and practices for maintaining contact with that higher power. I found it both fascinating and eye-opening to learn the meaning behind some of the elaborate ceremonies and practices from other cultures. I also eagerly shared the traditions of the Shona-speaking people for making offerings to the ancestors and for worshiping Source.

I very much enjoyed attending the meetings at Monica's house. I found it comforting to be around other people who were on a similar path in life and accepted the mysterious nature of the journey. There was no need for explanations or justifications. I found that openly discussing spiritual issues with other likeminded people helped to clarify my thinking, enhance my learning, and accelerate my assimilation and practice of the new information I was acquiring. After each session with our small group, I walked away feeling energized and optimistic about my journey into something deeper than what appeared on the surface of my life. I was very grateful that I had met Monica and that she had invited me to join the group.

Monica was also instrumental in recruiting David Hall, the elderly white gentleman who led our group. When I first joined the group, I had learned that David had been leading small spiritual groups like ours since the sixties. Even though he was in his early eighties, he was still in good health and mobile, and had a razor-sharp mind. All of us in the group were grateful for his willingness to share his time and knowledge with us.

What I loved about David was his vast knowledge on what he called the Presence, which is how he referred to God or Source. He talked about the visible part of the Presence that we encounter in our daily lives and then the invisible part that we are immersed in, but are unaware of. I especially loved the manner in which he recounted stories about his encounters with this invisible world. He said that those who could perceive the invisible world accessed creative powers not known to other human beings. I found that by listening to his stories, I too was beginning to encounter glimpses of this invisible world in my everyday life.

What attracted me the most about the invisible world, as described in David's stories, was its focus on what he called the jewels of life: unconditional love, infinite beauty, and healing power. He said the most common expressions among the beings of that world were gratitude, appreciation, and compassion. He said the focus of the beings there was on cooperation and on empowering one another so that everyone could reach their highest potential. I found this focus to be completely different from the focus of the physical world we lived in, where hatred, anger, revenge, and domination were rampant.

And what I loved even more about David was his ability to explain esoteric concepts in simple terms that others could relate to their own lives. Whenever we had a meeting with him, I got very excited because I knew I would have the opportunity to learn a powerful life lesson.

We had our meetings on the first Sunday of each month. Monica loved to cook for the group so the meetings sort of became our Sunday dinner-and-a-lesson combination. Monica usually cooked the main meal and everyone else brought a side dish, dessert, or drinks. We would sit at the dining table for the meal and chat as we ate. This was a good time to catch up on what had happened in our lives since the last meeting. Then we would gather in Monica's living room or sit out in her garden for the day's discussion. Usually David asked the group to pick a topic that we wanted him to focus on for each meeting, or we would just ask him questions and he would provide answers based on his experience and knowledge.

At the end of one meeting, I had asked David if he could talk about the ego in one of our future meetings. I had been reading about the ego and was struggling to get a good grip on the concept and how to attenuate it in my life. David had agreed to focus our next meeting on the topic of the ego.

On the Sunday of our next scheduled meeting, we had our meal and then sat in Monica's garden to enjoy the late afternoon sun of a lovely spring day. David settled into a lawn chair at the front and we gathered around him, some people sitting on chairs, some on decorative stones scattered around the sitting area, and some on the grass. I sat cross-legged on the grass, leaning my back against a stone.

My gaze went to David, comfortably seated in his chair. He was dressed in a flannel shirt and a pair of khaki trousers, the clothes hanging loose on his thin frame. His gnarled hands rested on his knees. Thin wisps of white hair were neatly brushed back on his head and sharp eyes peered from his wrinkled face.

Then my gaze shifted to the surroundings. The canna lilies in the bed by the wooden fence along the south side of the garden were in bloom, brilliant red spikes rising from dark green foliage. My gaze followed the lawn-covered slope on the western side of the garden, stopping at the wooden fence at the back. An apple tree stood in the middle of the gentle incline, covered in clusters of pink and white blossoms perched at the ends of bare branches. A waterfall, placed to the right of the apple tree, cascaded down a stone waterway, emptying into a shallow pool just to the right of the area where we were sitting. The waterfall was a beautiful feature in the garden and also served to buffer the noise of the traffic from the busy freeway about three blocks from Monica's house.

My attention came back to the group as David started to speak.

"As you all know, today's discussion will focus on the ego," he said. "This is one of my favorite topics," he added.

"The reason I like to talk about the ego is because I see a huge potential for people awakening to their true nature once they realize what the ego is, or rather what the ego is not. Actually, it is more important to realize what the ego is not. The ego is not the individual; the individual is not the ego." He paused, looking around the group.

"The term ego itself came from Sigmund Freud, who, as most of you know, is the father of modern psychology. Ego was one of the three constructs of Freud's structural model of the human psyche. Today, I want us to examine the ego in a way that is relevant to our everyday lives." Lifting his right hand and using his fingers to count, he asked, "How might the ego show up in our lives? What does it feel like to be in the grip of the ego? What sort of behaviors might one display in the grip of the ego?" He put his hand down, resting it on his right thigh.

"In its simplest form," he continued, "the ego is the false sense that says 'I am a separate entity apart from everything else.'" He paused briefly, and then continued to speak. "Most of us feel this illusory sense that we, as individuals, are separate from other individuals and from everything else in creation. This feeling of being separate causes fear to arise in us. This fear causes us to feel that we are vulnerable to attack by forces that want to take our life from us. As a result, we feel the need to defend ourselves in order to continue existing. We start perceiving things around us as threats and we start building our defenses. Other human beings are seen as threats to us and we don't let them near us. To maintain this stance, we find ways to magnify the separateness. We judge others, we condemn others, and we punish others—oftentimes just in our thoughts but other times in our actions as well. Sometimes we even seek power so that we can control and dominate others. The ego feels an illusory sense of security by having control over others; but this, of course, is a false sense of security."

As I listened to David, I noticed patterns in my own behavior that were similar to what he was describing. I listened intently as he continued to speak.

"There is also another aspect of the ego that is important to point out. Because of the illusory sense of separateness the ego creates for us, we feel alone and isolated, we feel disconnected from everything else. A sense of incompleteness or lack arises. Then we start identifying with things that we think will give us the feeling of completeness or wholeness. We grasp for and cling to things like power, money, and possessions. Or we go after social status, education, or experiences. As we gain these things, we begin to mistake them for who we are; we begin to take these things as our identities. This is all an attempt to bolster that false self-image." He paused before continuing to speak.

"However, gaining those things and identifying with them doesn't give us the sense of completeness or wholeness that we seek. As a result, the wanting intensifies and we go after more things—be it power, money, social status, houses, cars, clothes, farms, sexual relationships, or even the achievements of our children. This is when the ego takes over and the grasping, clinging, wanting, and accumulating more becomes our way of life."

It seemed as if David was describing my life, describing the lives of many people I knew. And I realized that what he was saying was similar to what my grandmother had said many years ago.

"We develop appetites that cannot be satisfied, and we come to the point where we don't care who gets hurt or disadvantaged as long as we can keep feeding the wants of our egos." David continued to speak. "The messages we get from this ego entity that we become are mostly delivered in the form of our own thoughts. But sometimes the messages come through people close to us, such as our parents, husbands, wives, children, friends, or coworkers. For the most part, the messages sound so normal and part of our everyday life that we don't recognize them as coming from the ego. They are delivered in subtle and clever ways, disguised as concern for our welfare. Let's use a hypothetical person to illustrate this point, shall we?" David said.

"A person may have a thought that goes like this, 'So my friend got an advanced degree and goes around boasting about it. I can do it too. I can even get a degree in something harder and see what she will say about that.'" David leaned forward in his seat, his elbows resting on his thighs.

"This might come from the person's wife or husband: 'Look at the neighbors. They bought the latest BMW model. We can buy a far more expensive car than that. And we can install a swimming pool in our backyard, while we are at it. I am willing to bet they will not beat that. We can get the bank to loan us the money. Money is no problem.'"

He paused briefly, and then asked, "You see how ordinary this sounds. This sounds like normal conversation that you may hear at a family dinner." He leaned back into the chair, settling more comfortably in his seat.

"Or perhaps it's the person's mother who might say: 'You know what John's mother told me the other day? She said that John is now a doctor and he is married to a doctor as well. She said John and his wife just bought a mansion in an exclusive neighborhood of town. Well, I didn't have anything to say to respond to that. Why can't you be more like John? You and John were very close when you were children. What happened to you? I feel so ashamed.'" David looked around, smiling. "Anyone heard something like that from their mother?"

A few people in the group chuckled, but nobody said anything. David arched his eyebrows in amusement, but continued to speak.

"Or perhaps the person might have political ambitions and the message comes as, 'You need to seek high political office and be the one with power. Once you get the power, you have it made. You can get the money, the cars, the clothes, and the women. With power, you can do whatever you want and you can make people do whatever you want them to do.'" He paused briefly, taking a deep a breath.

"I could give you hundreds of examples, but I think you are beginning to see the point that I am making," David continued. I looked around the group and saw heads nodding. "And it goes on and on. When we take the time to listen carefully to the voice of the ego, we notice that there is a heavy dose of judgment or a heavy helping of guilt in its messages. There is a hint of 'you are not enough the way you are.' There is a 'you need to be better than someone else to feel complete.' There is a 'you need to be something that you are not right now to feel worthy.' Notice that it's about what you need to do 'to be better than,' 'to look better than,' 'to have more than.' It's not about what you can do to create in the world. It's not about what you can do to be of service to others. It's not about what you can do to inspire others to rise up to their highest potential." He paused again, clearing his throat.

"A person will continue to chase after the latest 'this' and the latest 'that' as the voice of the ego directs them," he said, "until one day it dawns on them that after doing all those things they thought they had to do and those things that other people said they should do, they still don't feel connected, they still don't feel complete, they still don't feel worthy. They are unhappy, they are lonely, and they live life in quiet despair. And they still don't know what to do to turn things around in order to live a life that is worthy."

He paused, and then asked, "You now see what happens when the ego takes over control of our lives?" We all nodded our heads.

Monica asked, "David, are you saying that people should not follow their dreams? What if someone wants to obtain an advanced degree, buy the expensive car, or acquire the huge house? Is that necessarily something bad?"

"No, no, no," David quickly responded, shaking his head. "I'm not saying people shouldn't follow their dreams to obtain the advanced degree, buy the expensive car, or acquire the huge house. Not at all! If that is what brings them joy, and they have the financial means to get the things they enjoy, then they should go for it. All I'm saying is that they have to know that getting the degree, the car, the house, or whatever form "it" is for them, is not going to bring the sense of wholeness they may be seeking. The source of wholeness is not found in what one owns, what one does, or who one knows. The wholeness arises from within and originates from a felt sense of connection to the Presence. This comes from knowing that they are a part of the whole already as they are and that they are secure and protected." I was engrossed in what David was saying.

"With an awareness that wholeness and security are found in a sense of connection to the Presence, a person can go out and get that degree, car, or house. What may become apparent is that the motivations behind the person's actions may shift. A person may pursue that degree because it will bring knowledge that can be used to bring manifestations that help others. Perhaps the person acquires the credentials and skills that can be used to build businesses that develop technologies to move the world forward. Perhaps the person acquires credentials and skills that can be used to attract resources needed to bring development to underdeveloped parts of the world. Or the person may seek political office because they genuinely believe they are the best candidate with the ideas that will positively transform the lives of other people in the community they wish to serve. In this way, the person is now doing what they enjoy and at the same time serving others and serving the world. It's no longer just about what's in it for them on a personal level. It's no longer about the ego seeking to enhance its false self-image by having more than, becoming more than, or having control over."

Another silence followed, and then David asked, "Do you see the difference here?" I saw heads nodding in agreement as I looked around.

Monica chimed in, "Thank you, David, for clarifying that for us. This is very interesting, and we would like to hear more." David smiled and continued to speak.

"But there is yet another aspect to the ego that we have not covered. This is the aspect not so much related to wanting or accumulating or security, but more of a resistance to the flow of life. This is when the ego takes the form of heavy negative energies. These negative energies are sometimes experienced as avoiding or pushing away life, some type of contraction into a shell. Sometimes it's quite the opposite. Sometimes the negative energies are experienced as openly attacking others mentally, emotionally, or physically. In either case, a person may start living in a way that causes pain in his or her life, and in the lives of others."

David retrieved a handkerchief from his pants pocket and wiped his brow.

"Please bear with me as I share some hypothetical scenarios that illustrate the subtle workings of the ego in this respect." He placed the handkerchief back in his pocket and continued on.

"In one scenario, say we have a man, and let's call him James, which is a common enough name. Let's say James suffered repeated abuse as a young child, and he was emotionally wounded at an early age. He had no one to teach him how to process the negative emotions and heal the emotional wounds, so the wounds festered. As an adult, James is an angry person. He constantly complains about everything, he finds fault in almost every little thing, and he has the need to assign blame to someone for anything that does not go well in his life. He becomes a mean person, and, worse still, he takes that meanness out on his family. He feels pain and that pain wants to cause pain in others, so he behaves in ways that inflict pain on those around him. He mentally, emotionally, and physically abuses his wife and children. He hurts them. And they too develop wounds that go unhealed."

David sighed, sadness enveloping his wrinkled face and creeping into his voice as he continued to speak.

"The most affected is James's eldest son. Let's call the son John. By nature, John is a sensitive boy." I sensed a deepening of the sadness in David's voice as he continued.

"In addition to the physical beating of his son John, James also verbally abuses him, especially making fun of his sensitive nature. James mocks everything that John tries to do. He tells John that he is no good and will never amount to anything in life. He criticizes and belittles John in front of other children." David paused, licking his dry lips.

"John becomes an adult and leaves home, but he can never escape his father's derisive voice. He has dreams to create a better life for himself, but whenever he tries to pursue any of his dreams his father's voice comes back to mock him. John loses confidence in himself and stops even trying. As a result, none of John's dreams come to pass." I noticed a slight quiver on David's lips, but his voice remained steady.

"John sees himself as a failure, and the guilt and shame of that failure are his constant companions. His mind torments him. His days are filled with self-judgment, self-loathing, and feelings of unworthiness. He has a hard time sleeping. He sees others who succeeded at what he wanted to do and is filled with so much jealousy that he can hardly breathe." Tears were welling in David's eyes, but his voice remained strong as he continued to speak.

"Finally, John discovers that he can escape the harsh judgment in his mind and escape the guilt and shame of his failure by drinking alcohol. He starts by drinking two beers one night and notices that the alcohol quiets his mind and he is able to sleep, so he keeps drinking every night to get a good night's sleep. After a while, the two drinks don't provide the relief he needs so he starts downing four, five, ten beers every night before bed. Then a time comes when it's not only at night that he needs to drink—now he needs to chug five beers in the morning to function during the day. And he starts drinking hard liquor to supplement the beer. Before long he needs to drink pretty much the whole day to face the world. He has become an alcoholic. He now has the stigma of being an alcoholic in addition to the guilt and shame of being a failure that started him on this downward spiral. Now he has fresh behavior that the ego uses to judge him. And the vicious cycle continues."

Silent tears trickled down David's wrinkled cheeks, but he continued to speak, his voice still steady. I continued to listen, a burning wetness invading my eyes and a stifling tightness lodging in my chest.

"In this story, the hypothetical man I called James is my father and the hypothetical son I called John is me. I just told you the story of the early years of my life," David said, revealing what I thought most of us had probably guessed by now.

There was a long silence; none of us moved.

Tears spilled from my eyes and flowed down my cheeks. I swiped at them with my hand. This was the first time I had heard this side of David's story. I looked around and saw tears in the eyes of the people sitting next to me.

Then I noticed Monica coming back with a basket of face towels. I hadn't noticed her leave to go into the house. I must have been engrossed in the story. Monica passed out towels to David and to each member of the group. She then dropped to her knees beside her boyfriend, Nathan, who was visibly sobbing. She wrapped her arms around his shoulders, gently rocking his big frame. Nathan turned into Monica's embrace, enveloping her in his arms and burying his face in her neck. His sobbing intensified.

It seemed David's story had touched wounds in many of us.

"As you know, my story has a happy ending because I am sitting here in front of you," David finally spoke. "I can see that right here there are some among us with stories to tell. Many have stories like mine, but perhaps with no happy endings yet," he continued, wiping his face with the towel that Monica had handed to him. I wiped my face too, the moist towel feeling good against my skin.

"Let the tears fall, sob if you have to," David said. "Releasing tears is one of the body's many ways of letting go of the pain that it is holding inside. Even after these many years, tears still fall from my eyes, and I let them. I understand why the tears fall. I know the body still needs to release residues of pain that linger inside. There is no shame in letting the tears fall. It is a necessary part of the process of letting go of negative energies within. It is a natural part of the process of healing." Another long silence followed, punctuated by muffled sobs from the group.

"Events similar to what I have just described are realities to more people than you can imagine," David finally resumed speaking. "We have communities of people walking around with emotional wounds they don't know how to heal, except by going out and inflicting pain on others, in whatever form. You hear about angry and confused youngsters obtaining guns and shooting fellow students in schools. You hear about young men gang-raping young girls. You hear about disgruntled workers slaying their coworkers with machine guns. You hear about all sorts of torture and horrors that human beings inflict on other human beings. These are expressions of negative energies that live within and among us, even though we may not acknowledge the existence of these negative energies or discuss them in polite conversations. It is only after we are exposed to horrible events—either through the media, through our own unfortunate experiences, or through the unfortunate experiences of those we know—that we acknowledge the existence of these negative energies." David's tears had dried. He continued to speak, a pensive expression settling on his face.

"We may refer to these negative energies as evil spirits, demons, the devil, Satan—or some other ominous-sounding name—as if they are tangible things that swoop in to wreak havoc in our lives and in the world. These are not tangible things. They are intangible forms of energy that start at the individual level, but can also spread to a group of people or a whole nation—leading to the atrocities that we sometimes see in the world." He put the towel on the ground and sat with his back straight in the chair, his hands clasped in his lap.

"Now let's look at the effect of the ego in a group dynamic," David said. "Here the collective ego of the group most often manifests in the form of power and control over others. There is the need to demonstrate superiority over those seen as less than the people in the select group—in one way, shape, or form. Usually, there tends to be one person in the group with the strongest ego who is the leader. For whatever reason, the other members of the group follow the directions of the leader, regardless of whether what they are being asked to do makes sense or not, hurts others or not. You have heard about one group of people saying to another group, 'Our race is superior to your race; therefore, you will be our slaves.' We have seen the wounds that were caused by that kind of mass thinking and behavior. Even to this day, we as a human race are still processing the negative emotional impact that resulted from the practice of enslaving other human beings." He swallowed.

"Or we still hear, 'Our religion is superior to your religion; therefore, you either convert to our religion, or we will kill all of you until there is only our religion in the world.'" He paused, sweeping his gaze across the group.

"Ring any bells?" he asked. "We have seen the wars resulting from religious extremism throughout the history of human beings to the present day," he added.

"And there is the 'We want control over the world.' We have seen the many atrocities committed from that need to dominate the world—from the wars of antiquity, through Hitler's atrocities, to modern-day wars." David took a deep breath before continuing.

"With each atrocious act, the ego gains power over humanity. With each violent act, the ego gathers fuel to feed on. With each horrendous act, the ego expands and spreads to even more humans. The atrocious acts breed fear, hatred, revenge, viciousness, cruelty, and ultimately lead to what we may call inhumane behavior." David took another deep breath, closing his eyes. He was quiet for a long moment. He slowly rubbed his forehead with his fingers a few times, then he finally opened his eyes and continued to speak.

"We have seen how the effects of the ego can be traced to our behavior as individuals. At the level of the individual, we fail to find healing for the emotional wounds that we carry. We seek some type of relief by inflicting pain on others. Then the victims wounded by our behavior may seek relief by inflicting pain on others, and the vicious cycle continues until we have horrible acts such as the mass murder of school children by a lone gunman, the attempted extermination of a whole group of people such as what happened with Hitler and the Nazi regime, and the acts of genocide, the so called ethnic cleansings, such as what happened in places like Rwanda and Burundi."

Nancy, a regular attendee, asked, "David, what do you think needs to happen so that human beings can turn the condition of the world around from the acts of violence such as you are describing and the many other horrific events that have occurred and are still occurring in the world? It seems in recent years there has been a rise in the level of violence being inflicted by human beings on other human beings, on the animals, on the plants, and even on the earth itself. What can stop this?"

David acknowledged Nancy's question with a quiet nod, and then shifted his gaze to the ground in front of him. He was silent for a while, thinking. Then he raised his gaze to focus on Nancy and said, "Well, you are asking a very pertinent question that most of us wrestle with every day, Nancy." He paused again, as if ordering his thoughts before continuing. "The way I see it, a profound shift has to happen at the level of our human consciousness. Our collective consciousness has to shift into the realization of our unity in the Presence and the realization that we are expressions of that one Presence in our diverse forms. With that realization, we can transcend the current conditioning of the collective human mind that leads us to think that we are isolated beings separate from everything else and that causes the ego to arise as it tries to protect that separate self-image and bolster it in the ways we have discussed today." He cast his gaze to the ground again as he continued speaking.

"I think this kind of mass shift in consciousness would have to be an act of grace from the Presence." Another pause followed, and David kept his gaze downcast.

"Will this kind of shift happen? Will it happen in our lifetime?" he asked. "These are questions that none of us knows the answers to." He raised his gaze from the ground to look at the group as he continued to speak.

"What I do know is that this shift can happen at the level of the individual human being at any time. In fact, these shifts at the individual level are happening all the time. And it seems more and more people are going through these shifts in consciousness and then living their lives with the knowledge that they exist as a part of the Presence expressing in human form. Because of the shift, the actions of these people are no longer controlled by the ego; their actions are more oriented toward love and compassion. These shifts are happening at the personal level, but I think it will take a very long time to trickle down to all beings on this earth."

Nathan, who seemed to have recovered from his sobbing and now looked somewhat composed, asked, "So, David, you seem to be saying that it is possible to make the shift in consciousness at the individual level. What are some of the things that an individual can do to allow for this shift in consciousness to take place? What steps can one take to overcome the ego? What can one do to avoid the patterns of negative behavior that seem to be driven by the ego?" I could still detect a slight shakiness in Nathan's voice. His arms were still wrapped around Monica.

"I'm glad you are asking these questions, Nathan," David said, looking directly at Nathan. "This is really what we need to be focusing on as human beings—how to transcend the ego in our individual lives," he added.

"There are many practices in different traditions that can be used to attenuate the ego," David said, as he started his response to Nathan's questions. "The practices that might be familiar to most people, or certainly that are more popular in today's culture, are rituals such as meditation, prayer, martial arts, and so forth. Taking up any one of these and making it a daily practice in one's life goes a long way in overcoming the influence of the ego and the negative behaviors that it drives," he continued.

"In addition to these popular practices, many indigenous tribes of the planet follow specific practices within the context of their tribal lives. These indigenous practices are often viewed as ways to promote harmonious living among human beings and between human beings and nature. I have spent some time with native tribes across Australia, Africa, and Central and South America, learning the ways they live within their communities. I was particularly interested in learning some of the indigenous practices used to attenuate the ego." He paused for a moment, looking into the distance, a thoughtful expression on his face. "Perhaps, at a future meeting, I can share some of the indigenous practices that I found to be helpful in attenuating the ego. Would that be of interest to some of you?" he asked, his gaze returning to the group. I saw heads nodding as I looked around.

"I will be sure to schedule that as a future topic," Monica chimed in. David nodded, smiling at Monica.

"I believe that most of the practices that people use to transcend the ego have value if one is genuinely seeking to experience the shift in consciousness," he continued, his gaze sweeping across the group. "The trick is to find the practice that works for you. And sometimes one has to try a few practices to find what works the best for his or her individual situation and life," he added, then paused for a moment, looking into the distance.

"It is important to set an intention for the shift in consciousness to happen and to be aware of the progress as it happens." He continued to speak. "In some people, the shift may occur in one big swoop; whereas in others the shift is a gradual increment of awareness until a day comes that one realizes they are no longer driven by the ego, but are living life from a different point, so to speak." David paused again, his gaze returning to the group.

"By setting the intention for the shift to realize one's true nature and by following an effective practice, does that guarantee a shift?" David asked, shrugging his thin shoulders.

"Not necessarily, no?" He answered his own question. "What guarantees a shift? I don't really know. I don't know if anyone knows the answer to that question. But at the very least, by setting the intention to know one's true nature and by following an effective practice, chances are that one will notice improvements in the way they relate to life."

David paused, asking if anyone had any follow-up questions. The group remained quiet.

"There is something I would like to discuss that I think some of you might find helpful in the process of attenuating the ego," David said, shifting in his chair. "And that is the practice of forgiveness in our lives. There is tremendous power in forgiveness."

I wondered what David would say about forgiveness. I listened as he continued to speak.

"For those of us with traumatic pasts that left deep wounds, these wounds need to be faced and healed, otherwise they block our efforts to release the ego and find the unity with the Presence that we seek. Emotional wounds are like pockets of negative energy within the energy systems of our bodies. We can think of these pockets of negative energy the same way we think of blood clots within our circulatory systems. Once formed, these pockets of negative energy have a tendency to grow, just like blood clots. And they have a tendency to block the free flow of energy through our systems, just like blood clots block the free flow of blood through our bodies." David rubbed the back of his neck with his left hand. Then he settled his hand back in his lap, continuing to speak.

"For the most part, when we encounter an experience that is remotely similar to what was done to hurt us, the associated negative energies stored in us are activated and start expressing as reactions to events in our lives. They may express as fear, anxiety, anger, or hatred. When the reactions happen, we are not even aware they are being driven by the negative energies within us, and it keeps worsening until the unconscious behavior takes control over our lives. We get to a point where we become dysfunctional. And this is when we may realize the need to heal the wounds we carry inside." David paused, letting his words sink in.

"Healing our wounds may require us to systematically identify the people and situations that we have not forgiven—identify the areas where we are harboring negative energies—and then go through the process of forgiving the situations one by one. In that forgiving, we release the negative energies from our bodies. As we release these energies, we may notice that the unconscious patterns of negative reactions start to disappear." David paused again, his gaze sweeping across the group.

"I have come across many teachings for practicing forgiveness of old hurts," he continued. "In my mind, there is no right or wrong way, or one that is more effective than others. The key is to pick a process that works for us and allows us to dissolve the negative energies and resentments that we carry inside."

David stared into the distance above our heads. "It wasn't until I forgave my father and forgave myself that I was able to turn my life around and move on to finally live the life that I have lived. I had to forgive my father and let go of the blame, the hurt, the resentment, the anger, and the hatred that I had held inside because of his abusive behavior when I was growing up. And I also had to forgive myself and let go of the blame that I had directed toward myself for being a big disappointment to my father. I had blamed myself for not being the son that my father seemed to think he deserved. That self-blame had turned into the deep guilt and constant shame that I carried around." His face looked serene, the sadness that had been there earlier gone.

"The forgiveness process that I picked for my own life was to surrender the situation in the unity of the Presence. Some of you may call it surrendering the situation to God. It is the same thing, in my opinion." David inhaled deeply, closing his eyes.

"I came to a point where I made a deliberate choice to let go of the mental images I had held in my mind and that I had kept replaying in my head for decades. I made a choice to let go of hearing my father's voice as he hurled cruel barbs at me. I made a choice to let go of replaying the sensations of the harsh lashings of his belt on my skin. I made a choice to let go of hearing his raised voice yelling despicable accusations at my mother. And I made a choice to let go of hearing my mother's muffled cries in the middle of the night. I stopped activating these mental images and replaying them in my head." He opened his eyes, looking at the group.

"What I like about this form of healing is that we don't even have to face the people who wronged us. When I say we need to visit the situation, I mean visiting it in our imagination, not getting on a plane to have a showdown with a family member. The forgiveness is accomplished in the privacy of our minds. The forgiveness happens within us. In the case of my father, I lost touch with him when he left the family, and I never had the opportunity to face him again. But I was able to release the negative emotions that I felt toward him and that I had held within me." His voice was steady as he continued.

"This form of forgiveness can also be used if we are the perpetrator of an event that hurt others, and we are riddled with guilt and shame about what we did. We can ask for forgiveness from the spirit of those we hurt without visiting them. We can visit them if we want, we can talk about the incident or situation that happened to cause the hurt, and we can verbally ask for forgiveness. There is absolutely nothing wrong with that, if that is what we feel moved to do. But I have learned that from a spiritual perspective, this is not necessary. The forgiving happens in our own minds. It happens when we accept responsibility for what we did and then accept the forgiveness that we offer to ourselves. The letting go of the negative energy happens within our inner selves. The negative energy formation that we experience as guilt or shame exists in our mind; therefore, the forgiveness has to be at the level of our mind. This might come as a surprise, but sometimes we will realize that no one else remembers the situation that happened twenty years ago. We will find that we are the only ones who remember the event, and we are the only ones who still harbor negative energy about the situation." A long silence followed. David reached down to retrieve the towel he had dropped to the ground and wiped his palms with it.

"The other thing I have also come to know is that this type of forgiveness works in situations where the person we wronged is no longer with us. We may harbor guilt and shame about something we did or didn't do for a loved one who is now deceased. Well, from a spiritual perspective, we still have access to that person's spirit anytime, and we can ask for their forgiveness anytime." He paused again.

"Is any of this making any sense?" David asked.

I nodded my head, and as I looked around, I saw others in the group nodding as well.

"Does anyone have any questions on this point?" he asked again.

I saw heads shaking.

"Another important aspect of forgiveness is to forgive ourselves for the hurts we have caused ourselves." David continued to speak. "We might need to forgive ourselves for some of the choices we made that led to missed opportunities; it might be forgiving ourselves for the dreams that were not realized; it might be forgiving ourselves for the failures and the shame that followed. The negative energies, if not forgiven, can lead to broken lives. These same negative energies can be dissolved by the simple act and willingness to forgive ourselves. Again, this can be achieved through recognizing what went wrong and forgiving ourselves, surrendering the situation to the Presence." David paused again, lost in thought.

"There is one last piece I want to share on forgiveness," he finally said. "Once we have gone through cleaning up the old hurts, we have to be mindful not to start accumulating another stash of things we will need to forgive later. We do this by learning the art of ongoing forgiveness of people and situations."

I wondered what David meant by the art of ongoing forgiveness of people and situations. I listened as he continued.

"We live in a world with people whose actions and behaviors are driven by their egos and we are bound to meet people and encounter situations where we get hurt. The people around us are not necessarily aware of us, our needs, or our feelings. They are out to satisfy their own egos, to fulfill its incessant demands. They will trample on our feelings without so much as a 'by your leave.' They will indulge in selfish behavior that may cause us and others pain. This might be a child who is indifferent to a parent's feelings because he or she is busy trying to fit in with the crowd at their school. This might be a coworker who takes credit for the work we did because they are so focused on getting the promotion that they feel they deserve. It might be a boss who still subscribes to the style of leading and motivating through bullying and public humiliation of his employees." David bent forward in his seat, dropping the towel to the ground and leaning his hands on his thighs, his gnarled fingers intertwined in front of him.

"In any situation," he continued speaking, "we have to learn a very simple habit of not reacting in ways that escalate the situation rather than help resolve it. In any situation, we have to be mindful of whether our actions are helping to defuse the situation or adding fuel and making things bigger than they are. We need to be constantly aware of what is going on and to constantly forgive events as they happen. Once we forgive a situation, there is no negative energy associated with that situation stored in our energy systems. Once we allow the negative emotions to flow out of our bodies, they are out of our system and will not negatively influence any decisions or actions that we take in the future. That is really a simple trick to practicing ongoing forgiveness. Easier said than done, I know," he said with a small smile, sitting back in his chair. "But if you can do this, you will avoid a lot of mental suffering in your life. And you will free yourself to really live a full life. You will live a life not limited by events that happened in the past and left negative energies inside that have not yet been forgiven." David paused, looking at the ground in front of him. He remained quiet for a moment.

The sun was beginning to set, and evening was approaching. My body ached from sitting in one position for too long. I had been so engrossed in what David was saying that I hadn't shifted my position for a while.

David finally raised his gaze from the ground and said, "Anyway, I think we have covered a lot today. I hope I have given you food for thought. I think it is important for all of us to face and heal our wounds. This will go a long way in helping us to release our egos and to open ourselves for the Presence to flow through our lives." He paused again, and then took a quick look at the watch on his wrist.

"I think I will stop here for the day," David said. Looking directly at me, he added, "Unless there are any more questions?" He knew I had asked him to talk to us about the ego and I appreciated that he was checking to see if I had questions for him. I shook my head to let him know that I didn't have any questions, and I mouthed "thank you" to him.

Monica stood up. "Thank you, David, for being so generous with your time, as always. And thank you for sharing your personal story. I think all of us realize it's not a part of your life you want to keep revisiting. But I think hearing your story benefited a lot of us here. We do appreciate your indulgence today. We thank you for your deep insights on the ego. We look forward to further exploring the topic of the ego and how we can release it in our individual lives. And I think we will probably keep talking about what can be done, if anything, to start addressing the collective ego that keeps precipitating violence and wars in our world." I saw heads nodding in agreement with what Monica was saying.

Turning to the group, Monica said, "Why don't we all give our thanks to David for his time today."

We gave David an enthusiastic round of applause as a group, and he slightly bowed his head in response.

After that, Monica brought the meeting to a close and people started getting up, some going to chat with David some more.

A few of us helped Monica with the dishes and cleaning up the kitchen. We all finally left to go back to our homes just as the sun disappeared behind the western horizon.

On the drive back to my house, I kept thinking about what David had shared. I was very grateful at how he had broken down the concept of the ego in ways that I could easily relate to in my daily life. I could clearly recall situations in which I had been blinded by my need to blame others for what I thought they had done to hurt me. I could recall situations in which I had been riddled by guilt and shame for what I had done, which had resulted in others being hurt. And I could feel the negative energies rise up in me as I recalled the situations. What David had said was that I could easily let go of these energies through the process of forgiveness.

As I played back what David had shared, I couldn't help but see how similar his teachings were to the teachings my grandmother had shared with me many years before.

Forgiveness

My spirit recognizes your spirit
For on the level of spirit we are one with Divine Love
In prayer, I forgive you for what you did
Knowing those were the acts of the negative energies in you
I offer the negative energies in you to Divine Love
And in Divine Love, may the negative energies be dissolved
May they no longer have power over your mind and your life
In Divine Love, may you find the freedom
To live your life doing what you came here to do
May you live your life in love, joy, and peace

My spirit turns within
For on the level of spirit we are one with Divine Love
In prayer, I forgive myself
For allowing your actions to activate the negative energies in me
I offer the negative energies in me to Divine Love
And in Divine Love, the negative energies are dissolved
What happened no longer has power over my mind and my life
In Divine Love, I find the freedom
To live my life doing what I came here to do
I live my life in love, joy, and peace

Our spirits commune in Divine Love
For on the level of spirit we are one with Divine Love
In prayer, we forgive ourselves
For allowing the actions of others to activate the negative energies in us
We offer the negative energies in us to Divine Love
And in Divine Love, the negative energies are dissolved
What happened no longer has power over our minds and our lives
In Divine Love, we find the freedom
To live our lives doing what we came here to do
We live our lives in love, joy, and peace

Rebuilding Character to
Be a Vessel for Source

One Sunday afternoon I arrived at Monica's house for our scheduled meeting and was delighted to find that David had brought a guest, a short, delicate-looking white woman who appeared to be in her early seventies. The woman was smartly dressed in a pink pant suit and white silk blouse, her white hair tied into a neat bun. David introduced her as Reverend Veronica Morris, the leader of a spiritual community in a nearby town. He said that she was his colleague from the sixties when they used to meet to discuss spiritual matters in a small group setting similar to ours, and that she was going to talk to us about the importance of building spiritual qualities.

"I go by Roni, which is short for Veronica," Reverend Morris said, speaking in a soft voice. "So please call me Reverend Roni," she added, moving around the room and shaking hands with each one of us in turn. I was the first to shake hands with her. She gently clasped my right hand in both her hands, her hazel eyes looking directly into mine. As we held the deep gaze for a few seconds, I felt an instant sense of connection with her. Then she broke the gaze and reached over to give me a quick hug and a soft kiss on my right cheek. That was how she greeted everyone. She took the time to look a person in the eyes, as if to let her spirit connect with the other person's spirit, and then she hugged and kissed them.

There was something about Reverend Roni that seemed familiar and comforting to me. She had a peaceful demeanor about her. And she had a cordial smile—the kind that draws people in. I felt drawn to her.

After we finished our meal, we gathered in Monica's living room, some people sitting on the couches and armchairs around the room, some sitting on the floor. Reverend Roni sat on a chair at the front of the room, next to the fireplace. Beside her was a low table with a china teacup on a saucer, a stack of writing paper, and some pencils. I saw a cushion on the floor right in front of her, and I walked over and sat down on the cushion. I noticed David sitting in one of the chairs in the right front corner of the room. He was facing the group, a serene expression on his face.

When everyone had settled down, Reverend Roni began her teaching.

"I believe all of us come into this world to be of use in one way or the other," she said. "I believe we are all part of a power that brings us into this world and that flows through our human forms and our activities." She paused, looking around the room.

"I grew up with Christianity as my religion," she continued, "so for most of my life I knew this power as God. But as we all know, this power is known by different names in different traditions. Some say this power is the Spirit or the Divine Presence or the Lord Almighty. As I started teaching, I learned very early on that most people I encountered associated God with the Christian religion, and were, therefore, likely to turn away from the message I was sharing because they had beliefs that were different from Christianity. I saw my purpose in the world as bringing people from different religions and backgrounds and traditions together, and sharing the message of our oneness. I realized that for me to succeed in my mission, I had to use language that was non-denominational, so as not to exclude a majority of the very people I was trying to reach. So in all my teachings and all my interactions with others, I now refer to God as the Mighty Power. I invite you, as I invite all the people I speak with, to substitute the Mighty Power with a name that resonates with you. Because in the end we are all talking about the same power that we come from and that we exist in."

I saw people in the room nodding their heads as Reverend Roni said this. I was pulled in by the manner in which she shared her message. She had a way of communicating in a very casual, inviting, and conversational manner. I found myself hanging on her every word, and I noticed others did as well.

"Most of us may not have lived an idyllic life," she went on. "By an idyllic life, I mean a life rich in creature comforts as well as healthy emotional nourishing. I mean a life that allows one to grow into a mentally and emotionally balanced adult with an impeccable character. From my observations of people around me, I have come to the conclusion that most of us carry childhood wounds and hurts that we don't know how to heal. These unhealed wounds are a source of fuel for the ego." She paused, her gaze sweeping across the room again.

"I know that David has talked to you at length about the ego," she continued. "I understand you are familiar with how the ego uses the pain from our wounds to generate more pain and unhappiness in our lives." She paused again.

"This is true in my life," she continued. "Due to the circumstances of my childhood and the life I lived, I harbored shadows unbeknown to me. It was only in my adult life that I started to seek ways to address and heal the wounds that I carried within. A necessary part of my healing process was to rebuild my character and cultivate what I call the essential spiritual qualities. I realized that I needed the equivalent of an internal makeover so that I could live a life of purpose."

"You are going to love this, folks!" David broke in, a jovial smile on his face. "Roni is the guru on this topic."

Glancing in David's direction and smiling sheepishly, Reverend Roni continued to speak. "When I first sensed my call to be a teacher of the word of the Mighty Power, I knew that my character had been broken by the travesties of the life I had lived. I knew that my character was in need of repair. I felt like I was a vessel with holes, and that the Mighty Power could not accomplish much through me as I was at that time. It would have been like using a sieve to bring water to people dying of thirst. No matter one's level of determination, the sieve is always empty by the time one reaches the dying people."

Holding her hands to her chest, palms pressed together in a gesture of prayer, she said, "I am eternally grateful for the guidance that came through many spiritual teachers I encountered on my journey once I set the intention to heal my wounds. This guidance enabled me to rebuild my character, and I continue to rely on this guidance as I keep refining my spiritual qualities." I felt like Reverend Roni was addressing a topic that was very close to my personal situation. I felt like she was saying exactly the words that I needed to hear at that particular juncture in my life.

Stretching her right hand in David's direction, she said, "I have had the privilege of knowing and studying with David for many years. He is one of the teachers who have been there to offer me guidance on my journey. I tell you, you are blessed to have him as your teacher as you travel on your own life journeys."

David bowed slightly in acknowledgment of the recognition, but kept quiet, the serene expression back on his face.

Reverend Roni returned the bow with a nod of her head in David's direction, and then she turned her attention to addressing the group again.

"What I love now is to sit with small groups of eager students of life like you, and share knowledge that has taken me years to accumulate. I am very encouraged by the shift I see in a lot of people as they seek to understand their true nature beyond the physical appearances. And I enjoy doing my part in assisting others as they travel on their journeys." Reverend Roni paused to take a sip from the teacup on the table, gently placing it back on the saucer.

"I emphasize teachings on spiritual qualities," she continued, "because I think they are an important foundation for what comes as one travels on the path to seek the truth. I do believe that taking steps to review your character to see if you are in a condition that is fit for the Mighty Power to flow through you and manifest in the world is a worthwhile use of your time. I think it's important to ask yourself if your character is like a sieve full of holes like mine was or if you feel that you are a well-made vessel for the Mighty Power to flow through you to manifest in the world."

I glanced around the room and saw everyone's gaze fixed on Reverend Roni.

"Only you can know that," she continued. "If you go deep into yourself and answer that question in the privacy of your own heart, you will know which of these you are—a sieve or a well-made vessel."

There was a lengthy pause as Reverend Roni took the time to connect gazes with each one of us in turn. It was as if she was asking each of us to examine our hearts at that very moment for the answer to that question.

Then she resumed her teaching, saying, "And also, only you can make the decision to rebuild your character should you find it lacking. It is only then that you can be a vessel for the Mighty Power to manifest through you."

Continuing on, she said, "Today I want us to focus on how to discover the qualities that we need to strengthen in our lives so that we can rebuild our characters to be vessels for the Mighty Power. It really is a rediscovery of the qualities that already exist in you. Because you are a manifestation of the Mighty Power, and these qualities are a part of you already. These qualities may be temporarily covered up and forgotten due to the travesties of life, but they are there." A silence followed as Reverend Roni gave us a chance to digest what she had just said.

"The need to rebuild character varies in different people depending on circumstances," she eventually continued. "This is something that most of us learn as part of our journeys on the path of seeking the truth. I can help you to initiate the process of discovering the qualities that need strengthening in your character." She paused again.

"Would that be of interest to anyone here?" she asked, her gaze moving around the room. "Please raise your hand if you think this would be something helpful to you," she said, raising her right hand in the air.

I raised my right hand, mimicking Reverend Roni. Glancing around the room, I saw people doing the same. Reverend Roni smiled.

"This is truly a precious gift you are giving yourself. Spending time developing your character is a rewarding process, and the benefits will show up in all the areas of your life."

Reverend Roni took another sip from her cup, and then continued to speak.

"However, what I didn't tell you is that for the teaching I am going to share with you to be impactful, you are going to have to do some inner work," she said, making air quotes around the words inner work.

"What I mean by inner work is that you are going to have to go into your heart and ask a lot of questions and try finding your own answers to those questions. And the answers you receive will begin to guide your life. This is because your heart already knows the answers to the questions that you may have about your life." She paused, letting her words sink in.

"How much work you put into this process of asking and answering questions about your life," she continued, "determines the quality and impact of the results you experience. If you take this process to heart and really give it the attention it calls for, you will be surprised at how easily your life will open up and expand to greater heights in every possible way you can imagine."

Reverend Roni rose from her chair and said, "Let's begin with a short exercise." Then she grabbed the wad of writing paper and stack of pencils from the table, passing them to the group.

As she walked back to the front of the room she said, "I want you to take the piece of paper you just received and write down the names of people you interact with on a regular basis. Try to write down at least ten names to start with." She turned to look at the group.

"Next to each person on your list, I want you to write down at least one quality that you admire and at least one quality that you don't admire in that person. Don't worry if nothing immediately jumps to mind for some of the people on your list; just keep moving on to the next person. I will give you about ten minutes to complete this first exercise," she said, glancing at her wristwatch.

While we worked, Reverend Roni went and sat in a chair next to David and they chatted softly.

When about ten minutes had passed, Reverend Roni stood up and said, "Now that you have your list in front of you, I want you to take a few more minutes to reflect on a number of questions." She paused, looking around the room.

"And here are some of the questions you can ask yourself," she continued. "How easy was it to come up with the qualities that you admire and those that you don't admire in the people you have on your list? Did you find that you wrote down more qualities that you admire than qualities that you don't admire for some of the people on your list? Or was it the other way around? What do you think this list says about the nature of the people you spend most of your time with?"

She sat back in the chair next to David, saying, "I will give you another ten minutes to go through this exercise."

I saw my fellow group members furiously writing on their pieces of paper, and I started doing the same.

I was so engrossed in the exercise that I was a little startled when Reverend Roni clapped her hands three times to get everyone's attention.

Rising from the chair, she said, "Now I think is a good time to take a short break. When we come back, we will discuss what the list you have says about you. Yes, this exercise is about you; it's not about the people whose names you wrote down on your list. And we will discuss why this is so after the break."

We took a ten-minute break to enjoy dessert and refreshments. When Reverend Roni clapped her hands again, we all returned to our seats and settled in as she continued with her lesson.

"Now let's talk about some of the things that this exercise is meant to help you understand, and also why the exercise is about you rather than the people whose names are on your list." Reverend Roni was slowly pacing in front of the group as she spoke.

"This exercise is somewhat a reality check for you. What most of us don't realize is that our characters tend to be heavily influenced by the people we spend most of our time with. Of course, for some of us, the people we spend most of our time with are our family members, an inbuilt support network of some sort. But beyond that, we also find ourselves around friends, colleagues, and business associates. In all these relationships, there are some people we are drawn toward much more easily than others, and we tend to spend most of our time around the people we are drawn to. For the most part, our attraction to the people we gravitate toward is unconscious, and, unless we have already done our inner work, we can't easily see that we tend to mimic the behavior of those we are most in contact with."

Reverend Roni walked over to a flipchart in the left corner of the room and picked up a permanent marker that was on the ledge of the flipchart holder.

"I want you to tell me some of the qualities you liked and those you didn't like, and I will jot them down on this flipchart for everyone to see. Just feel free to shout the words that you have on your list." As she said this, Reverend Roni made two columns on the flipchart, one titled 'Admired Qualities' and the other 'Qualities Not Admired.' And then she started filling in the columns as the participants shouted words at her. This exercise went on for ten or so minutes and, by that time, Reverend Roni had jotted over twenty words under each column heading on the flipchart.

Reverend Roni stopped writing and turned to speak to us. "Now, I want you to review the names of the people on your list and see if you can associate those people with some of the qualities that we have listed under 'Admired Qualities.' Here we have words such as courage, confidence, calm, peaceful, loving, gratitude, compassion, kind, nurturing, honest, humble, generous, trustworthy, and so on. If so, what that means is that, very likely, those qualities are rubbing off on you. Those people are your role models as you build and strengthen those qualities in yourself."

She paused for a brief moment. Then turning her attention to the other list, she said, "On the other hand, you may realize that most of the people you associate with are people with characters that you don't admire. Perhaps most of the people on your list exhibit the things that we have listed under 'Qualities Not Admired.' Here we have words such as lazy, lack ambition, coward, arrogant, dishonest, selfish, greedy, insensitive, cruel, ego-driven, and so on. On close reflection, you may find that you have on your list people who live in fear or in constant worry and anxiety. These might be people with no ambition or motivation to accomplish anything in their lives. These might be people who seem to be aimlessly floating through life. These might be people who focus on the negatives in situations and spend most of the time complaining about how bad things are. These might be people who seem to have some kind of drama in their lives all the time. If this is what you see when you study your list, then it's time to make some changes to the company you keep."

David interjected, saying, "This is a great way to review and realign your associations, folks! I suggest that you take these exercises to heart."

Reverend Roni nodded in David's direction, a gracious smile on her face.

"Now, the next step in this process," she continued, "is for you to apply the information that you gleaned from today's exercises and formulate the qualities that you think you need to build into your character. One way to do this is to start by looking at the qualities you admire in the people you wrote down on your list and see if you can identify any qualities that you need to strengthen in yourself." She paused, her gaze slowly moving across the room.

"Importantly, you also want to look at the qualities you dislike and think of the opposites of those qualities, because it is the opposite qualities that you would then wish to strengthen in yourself." She stopped to think for moment, and then said, "Let me give you an example. If laziness is one of the qualities that you strongly dislike in someone, then perhaps productivity is a quality you may think of strengthening in yourself." She paused again, a thoughtful expression on her face.

"You can even think of famous people or historical figures that you admire. Examples could be Mahatma Gandhi or Martin Luther King Jr. Think of some of the qualities you find attractive in those figures. Pick a few of those qualities and add them to your list." A smile flashed across her face.

"As you digest all this information," she continued, "you will find that you will start to get a clear picture of the qualities you need to strengthen to rebuild your character into the person that you want to be."

She reflected for a moment and then said, "Let me give you a little more information that may help you with this process."

Walking back to her chair at the front and taking a seat, she said, "Sometimes people may say, 'Oh, I am courageous. I am confident. I am productive. I am good to go! Therefore, I don't need this type of exercise.' I agree that there are people who may already exhibit all those qualities. And I do appreciate that. But what I may say to you, if you happen to be one of those people, is that perhaps you may want to consider incorporating some level of humility with that courage, confidence, and productivity. I get inspired when I see courageous, confident, productive, disciplined, and highly successful leaders who lead with humility. President Barack Obama is the example that stands out for me."

As Reverend Roni said this, I saw everyone in the room nodding in agreement. I did too. I viewed President Barack Obama as a role model for my life.

Reverend Roni took another sip of her tea. Smiling sheepishly as she moved her gaze across the room, she said, "Now we get to the real homework or rather inner work that I spoke of earlier. I suggest you commit yourself to understanding the qualities that you need to strengthen in yourself. Perhaps you want to strengthen the quality of courage. In that case, I suggest that you spend some time understanding what courage is and what courage is not. Think about the people who epitomize courage for you. What are they like? How do they talk? How do they walk? What is it that you find attractive about these people?"

She studied the group before continuing. "Think about your own life and learn from it. Recall incidents where you have shown courage. What happened? What did you do? How did you feel when you were doing what you did? Recall the rush of energy that you might have felt. Relive those moments when you were displaying courage."

Reverend Roni was talking excitedly now, her voice rising.

"Think about your situation and the life that you are living right now. Is there an area of your life where you are being called to demonstrate courage? What is it that you could do in this particular situation?"

Closing her eyes, she said, "Allow yourself to imagine what would happen if you mounted the courage and rose to the occasion and did what you know you are being called to do. Visualize yourself doing what you are being called to do, and then visualize the outcome. Allow the feelings to flood your body and your mind."

She opened her eyes and said, "In other words, I am asking you to define courage for yourself. What does courage mean to you? Then I am asking you to embody the quality of courage. And I am asking you to start living your life with courage as you have defined it for yourself." She let her gaze meet with every one of us in the room, one at a time. "See, when someone else defines a quality for you and then asks you to live by that definition, you may experience some resistance. But when you agree with yourself on a definition of a quality in the context of your life, and you make the commitment to embody this quality in your life, it can more easily become a part of you. You remove the element of unconscious resistance that may otherwise hinder your personal development." She paused to take a deep breath.

"So, define the qualities that you have identified for yourself, agree with yourself on what the qualities mean for you, and then commit to embodying those qualities," she added.

"As you can see, this is not a trivial undertaking. It took me a few months to work through this process. And now and again I still take time to polish up on some of my spiritual qualities. I consciously take time out of a busy schedule to work on my spiritual qualities." She paused again, sweeping her gaze across the room.

"I urge you to do the same, so you can receive the rewards. You will find that as you work through each quality, it becomes a part of how you live your life. You will gradually notice a positive transformation of your life. You will notice that most of the struggles in your life may begin to lessen, and your life may start to unfold effortlessly in front of you. And you will be there to witness your life unfold. You will be there to tell the story."

With that, Reverend Roni concluded her teaching and said she would be happy to visit with us again another time. She wished each one of us well on our journeys to discover our true selves. We thanked her for her time and teaching, and she left.

In the days following the meeting with Reverend Roni, I took her teachings to heart and set out to work on my character. The spiritual qualities that I had identified as needing to be strengthened in myself were courage, confidence, calmness, compassion, kindness, humility, integrity, productivity, and above all a deeper trust in Source.

I enthusiastically embraced the exercises that Reverend Roni had shared. In meditation and in contemplation, I asked to be guided in understanding and embodying the essence of the qualities I had selected. These exercises did not last a few weeks or a few months as I had initially thought. Over time, I have come to my own understanding of these select spiritual qualities and have witnessed the improvement in how I experience my life. And I review and revise these spiritual qualities as part of my annual goal-setting process at the beginning of each year. I have committed to strengthening these qualities, following the teachings and guidance from Reverend Roni and from many other teachers and role models in my life.

Strengthening My Spiritual Qualities

Divine Love, Creator of all that is seen and unseen
I am grateful for your guidance as I rebuild my character to be a vessel for your manifestation
I strengthen and reflect the quality of courage—a courage that transcends fear and connects me to the knower that is rooted in you
I strengthen and reflect the quality of confidence—a confidence to act from the knowledge that I have control and mastery over my destiny in you
I strengthen and reflect the quality of calmness—a calmness in knowing that all events in my life are coordinated, correlated, and synchronized in perfect harmony with a divine plan
I strengthen and reflect the quality of compassion—a compassion born of an awareness of my deep connection to all of creation through you
I strengthen and reflect the quality of kindness—a kindness that compels me to be generous with my time, energy, attention, and gifts
I strengthen and reflect the quality of humility—a humility that allows me to surrender my human understanding for your divine wisdom
I strengthen and reflect the quality of integrity—an integrity that imparts to me the virtues of honesty, decency, and a sense of responsibility

I strengthen and reflect the quality of productivity—a productivity that focuses on taking action to serve others and to serve you

And most of all, I strengthen my trust in you, knowing all originates from, happens in, and returns into you

As these qualities become a part of who I am, I feel an all-encompassing love

A love that includes all and is for all

And in you I remain, till the day I return home

Finding Your Passion and Making It Your Gift to the World

As time went on, I increasingly became aware of a misalignment in my life. I felt that I was making remarkable progress with regards to facing and releasing the negativity that had blocked the effortless flow of life energy throughout my life. And I felt that I was making great strides in strengthening my spiritual qualities and rebuilding my character. However, there was one area of my life that I felt was no longer aligned with the new me that was emerging. I couldn't keep ignoring the fact that perhaps my career path was no longer aligned to the person I was becoming.

This sense of a misalignment between my career path and evolving life really began to intensify around the beginning of 2012.

When I started my career in biotech in the mid-nineties, I had initially found my work to be exciting and enjoyable. I had climbed the corporate ladder as I had planned to, moving jobs and companies a few times to work for the best in the industry. I was earning a good salary, had excellent benefits, and had very good prospects for advancement in my career. On the surface, it seemed as if I was living a good life and could easily continue living the same way for the rest of my life.

But with time, I started to realize that I was no longer excited about what I was doing on a day-to-day basis or the overall trajectory of my career. At some level, there was a recognition that what had fueled me to succeed in my career was in part tied to chasing material delusions. My drive to succeed did not stem so much from wanting to serve others, but was more of a means to support the consumer life style that I had lived for many years. When the urge to chase material delusions started to fade, so did the blind ambition to keep earning more money. When I stepped back and allowed myself to see things more clearly, I started viewing the day-to-day activities that I engaged in at my job as just busyness. There were strategic plans to be crafted and implemented, goals to be met, assignments and projects to be completed, meetings to be attended—first the meetings to prepare for the meetings, then the actual meetings, then the meetings to discuss what was discussed at the meetings. You get the picture!

I could clearly see that the activities that filled my days had become mundane. In fact, most of the time was spent on activities that essentially amounted to checking boxes, without much consideration of the real impact, if any, of the checked boxes. I no longer saw the unique expression of who I was in what I was doing. I no longer felt a sense of enthusiasm for what I was doing. Tasks needed to be completed and I figured out the best way to effectively complete them. I went home at the end of each day and woke up the next morning to do it all over again.

Sometimes I would watch some of my colleagues who were passionate about their work and their projects and I yearned to find something that would ignite my passion in the same way again. I wanted to work at something I would feel excited about when I woke up early in the morning, something I was eager to do, something I was enthusiastic to get started on, something that inspired me to give all that I had to give. I felt there was so much in me that needed to be expressed, but I wasn't in the right arena to allow for that expression. I felt there was so much in me that was not being used. The pressure was building inside, and I knew things had to change.

As soon as I was honest with myself about the need to make adjustments in my career path, things began to open up in ways I couldn't have imagined. It started with an offer to attend a retreat focused on personal and spiritual growth that came from my friend Monica. The two-day retreat was scheduled to be held the Saturday and Sunday of the Labor Day weekend in September of that year—2012. Months earlier, Monica had bought tickets for her and her boyfriend Nathan to attend the retreat, but their relationship had ended and she offered me the extra ticket.

The retreat was being led by a modern-day spiritual guru who was also considered a leading expert in human psychology and personal development. I had seen this celebrity on TV and promised myself that I would someday make the effort to attend one of his live retreats that people were raving so much about. Now the opportunity to do so was handed to me.

The title of the retreat was 'Finding Your Passion and Making It Your Gift to the World.' I thought how timely that was for me. I accepted Monica's offer of the ticket and thanked her for the opportunity.

The venue of the retreat was a spiritual center located on the outskirts of a small desert town a few hours' drive from my home. The night before we were to drive to the retreat, I felt so much excitement building in me that I had trouble falling asleep. Monica picked me up at my house around four a.m., and we enjoyed a quiet drive to the center. We made one stop at a small town along the way to get gas and grab a quick breakfast. We arrived at the center in time to register and pick up the keys to our rooms well before the first session of the retreat started.

The retreat was in the format of a series of lectures and contemplative sessions. The first day began with intensive lectures, advertised as "a download of the essential knowledge to assist participants in assimilating and actualizing the teachings on finding and expressing their gifts in the world." I couldn't wait for the sessions to start.

The lectures were held in the spiritual center's sanctuary, a large hexagonal room that could easily sit a few hundred people. By my estimate, there were about fifty or so participants and a dozen or so people who were staffing the event, so it was a good crowd.

The thing that struck me the most was the setting. The leader, a medium-built black man with a clean-shaven head and a neatly trimmed gray beard, was sitting on a cushion at the front of the room with his legs crossed. He was wearing a white long-sleeved robe that covered his crossed legs to the knees, and had a pair of white baggy pants underneath the robe. Next to him was a low table with a pitcher of water, an empty glass, and a small vase with freshly cut wild flowers.

Participants were invited to sit on cushions scattered on the floor in front of the leader or to sit on chairs arranged in a half circle behind the cushions. I chose to sit on one of the cushions on the floor, stretching my legs in front of me. Monica sat on the cushion next to me, with her legs crossed. Most of the other participants sat on the floor as well, with only a few sitting on the chairs.

The setting appeared unusually casual, I thought as I glanced around the room. Because of the celebrity status of the leader, I had expected a lecture hall with a professionally-designed set and sophisticated audio-visual equipment. But here I was sitting on the floor, waiting to listen to one of the most profound thinkers of our time who was also sitting on the floor.

I recalled another time when I had sat with my legs comfortably stretched in front of me, listening to another wise person share her wisdom with me. I recalled the days I had spent with my grandmother.

The morning session began with brief introductions, followed by a short, guided meditation. After the meditation, the leader poured a glass of water and took a sip. He gently placed the glass back on the table and then dove straight into the teaching.

"Each of us emanates from Divine Love, which is the source of all life. We may call this source God, we may call it Spirit. I just call this cosmic presence Divine Love, because that is how I perceive and experience it in my life. We rise up from Divine Love and appear in this world of phenomena for two reasons. The first is to awaken to our true nature as a part of this Divine Love and to keep a conscious connection to this source as we live our lives. The second is to share the unique gifts that we bring with us from Divine Love." He spoke in a soft but clear voice.

"In the two days that we are going to be here together," he continued, "we will focus on the second point—sharing our gifts with the world. This is how we fulfill our higher purpose for passing through this physical dimension. The gifts we bring from Divine Love are expressed in many various forms, such as parenting, teaching, healing, writing, singing, inventing, farming, running businesses, and many other activities that enrich the world."

As I watched and listened to the leader, I thought I detected a pattern in the way he was moving his gaze from one person to the next around the room. It seemed as if he was holding his gaze on one person long enough to share a complete thought with that person, and then he would move his gaze to the next person and share the next complete thought with that person. I found this to be a very engaging way of communicating with an audience. I settled in to listen to what was being shared.

"What I have noticed," the leader continued, "is that only a few of us take the time to discover the unique gifts that we bring into the world. And only a handful of us actually express and share those gifts with the world. Those few individuals who discover their gifts and share them with the world are, in my mind, the enlightened beings. The presence of just one of these enlightened beings is enough to change the world." He paused for a brief moment.

"Take Jesus Christ as an example," he continued. "Jesus came into the world to teach humanity how to find God as the love in our hearts. He came to show us how to live our lives rooted in Divine Love. Jesus traveled the same journey that we travel as human beings. He was born, grew up in a family, and lived in a society. He went through the trials and tribulations of daily living as any other human being. But through it all, Jesus remembered, and proclaimed who and what he was. He kept telling everyone that he was the Son of God sent into this world to teach humanity how to find the way back into love, peace, and joy."

I noticed the leader's gaze was now focusing on the people sitting slightly to my right. "A few other human beings, like Jesus, lived their lives aware of their connection to Divine Love and aware of the gifts they brought into the world. These human beings manifested deeds that have had a lasting impact in this world. I personally consider people such as the Buddha, Galileo, Socrates, Mahatma Gandhi, Albert Einstein, Mother Teresa, and Nelson Mandela to be masters who allowed Divine Love to manifest through them to bring light into the world. These individuals, through divine means or anything else you may call it, discovered their gifts and lived their lives sharing those gifts with the world. And the world is better today because these individuals passed through it." He reached for the glass of water on the table, and took another sip.

"Most of us," he continued, placing the glass back on the table, "live our entire lives without realizing that we come into this world with gifts we are meant to share. We view the world as a place of struggle, sacrifice, and suffering. We do what the people around us tell us to do, and we hope for the best. We get married, raise a family, and pass on to our children the worldview that we know. The view that this is a world of struggle, sacrifice, and suffering. We go through old age and then finally die, still not knowing what we came here to do."

Noticing some latecomers lingering in the doorway, the leader motioned for them to come in and sit down. He reached through a side slit in his robe and retrieved a white handkerchief from his pants pocket. He covered his mouth with the handkerchief as he gently coughed, with his head bowed down. Then he took another sip of water.

When he raised his head, he looked directly at me. As I held his gaze, I could feel the warmth and kindness in his eyes.

"For some of us, we start out living our lives with no clue that we bring gifts into the world," he said. "We bounce around here and there with no clear direction. We stumble into a career and do the best we can. But deep down, we know enough to realize that there is more to life than the life we are living. We seem to intuit that there is a higher purpose for being in this world. We have a vague sense that there is a higher purpose that gives meaning to our lives. And we start to search for this higher purpose."

For a moment, I wondered how the leader knew to direct that thought to me. He seemed to have summed up my life situation quite accurately. As he continued to speak, his gaze moved on to Monica, who was sitting to my left.

"The search for meaning in our lives may be triggered by a personal traumatic event. This could be the death of a loved one, diagnosis of a life-threatening illness, end of a significant relationship. Something happens that shakes us out of our normal routine."

The leader moved his gaze to the man sitting next to Monica and continued to speak. "Or in other people, the search might be triggered by a general feeling of dissatisfaction with one's current life." He paused, letting his words sink in.

"The point is," he continued, his gaze shifting to the next person, "something inside of us tells us to search for a higher purpose for our lives beyond just working to pay the bills and accumulating things that we see everyone else around us accumulating. We start asking ourselves some tough questions." He took a deep breath, letting it out slowly.

"People search for a deeper meaning in their lives through many paths. Some people search for meaning through conventional religion, some through the ways of their ancestors, some through parenting. Some people search for meaning through the work that they do. This could be music, writing, teaching, healing, inventing, running businesses, as I said earlier. In the end, all paths lead back to Divine Love." He paused.

"There is no right or wrong way of searching for a deeper meaning in your life. There is only the way that feels right for you. And there is the willingness of the search, which eventually leads you to Divine Love." He paused again, letting the silence stretch in the sanctuary.

"And if we choose to," the leader eventually continued, "we can live the rest of our lives connected to Divine Love. We can live the rest of our lives expressing our gifts in the world until we go back home all used up, having fulfilled our purpose here on earth." His gaze drifted to the people at the back of the room.

"Let's look at other examples of people who lived their lives in this way," the leader said. And he went on to describe, at length, the lives of some of the people who had lived their lives releasing their gifts and the positive impact they had made in the world. I recognized most of the names that he mentioned.

The morning session concluded, and we broke up for lunch. Monica and I followed the crowd to a cafeteria in a building adjacent to the sanctuary, where lunch was being served. We grabbed our lunches and walked to a shady area to the east of the buildings and sat down to eat, mostly in silence. I took the time to reflect on what had just been shared that morning, and I suspected Monica was doing the same.

The afternoon session proceeded in much the same way as the morning session—starting with a short, guided meditation, followed by a lecture. The leader resumed his teaching, still sitting cross-legged on his cushion.

"Discovering your gift and expressing it to make a unique contribution to the world is the secret of living a fulfilled and meaningful life," he said. "In most cases, the gift you are meant to share is something that you are already doing or very close to something you are already doing. There are a few cases where one finds that one needs to make a radical change to live one's higher purpose. Yes, that happens. But for the most part, people find that what they are already doing in their lives, or something closely related, is actually the gift they came to share in the world."

Noticing a few latecomers by the doorway, the leader quietly motioned them to join the group. They were the same people who had arrived late for the morning session. It seemed that in any group, there usually are people who show up late all the time, I thought. Noticing that my mind was getting distracted, I shook my head and refocused my attention on what the leader was saying.

"If you find that your gift is what you are doing already, then the only shift for you may be to listen to your heart and receive guidance on the adjustments you need to make so that you can focus even more intensely on that activity and release massive amounts of energy when doing what you are already doing." He paused to cough in his handkerchief.

"Your gift might be parenting, and you may dedicate your life to providing for your children. You focus on supporting and nurturing them physically, emotionally, and mentally. You do all you can to give them the best chance to grow up into well-adjusted adults who have the potential to make positive contributions to the world. You are there when they need a shoulder to cry on. You are there to cheer them on in their efforts. And you are there to celebrate with them when they succeed. If you are already doing these things for your children, then perhaps the only adjustment you may need to make is to become more attuned to each child's unique gift and to nurture that gift in your child. This may require you to let go of what you think your child must do or what career he or she must pursue, and to let the child follow his or her own heart. Because Divine Love will speak through your child's heart."

The leader paused, sweeping his gaze across the room, a discernible glint in his eyes.

"You may be the grandparent who nurtures their grandchild and encourages them to reach for the stars. In doing so, you may raise a grandchild who becomes the first black president of the United States of America. This would be the case if your grandchild is President Barack Obama." A warm feeling ran through my body as the leader said this. Quickly scanning the room, I saw the other participants nodding their heads in agreement with what the leader was saying.

"Or you may find that the hobby that you love might actually be your gift to the world," he continued. "For you, the shift may be to find ways to turn your hobby into your main activity and to allow your creative brilliance to manifest through that activity."

A rush of energy coursed through my body as I heard these words. My mind started racing, trying to figure out if I had a hobby that could be the gift I came to share in the world. But I curbed my mind's racing and listened to what the leader was saying.

"You may ask, 'How do I discover my gift?'" A smile tugged at the leader's mouth as he said this. "Well, you have come to the right place for the answer. If you don't already know what your gift is, we will get you started on finding that out. If, on the other hand, you already know what your gift is, then we will help you with the next steps on your path to expressing that gift in the world."

Shifting into a more comfortable sitting position on his cushion, he said, "Let's start focusing on practicalities." The smile on his face widened.

"You know you have found your talent, your gift, when you love what you do and give everything of your being to that task. You find joy in the actions you take to accomplish the task. When you do what you love, you are transported to another world. You feel a lightness about you, an elation almost." He paused, the smile still on his face.

"Instead of feeling exhausted by the work," he continued, "you feel energized by it. Instead of being overwhelmed by what needs to get done, you revel in the flow of it. Instead of just focusing on the end results, you are enthusiastic about the actions you take to get to the end results. You wake up each morning eager and ready to get started on your day, and when you go to sleep at night, you dream of what is to come next." His face was now bright with excitement.

"When you do what you love, you reach a depth of your being that you may not normally reach in your routine daily activities. When you do what you love, you feel as if there is an energy flowing through you that does the work." He closed his eyes for a brief moment. Then he opened them again, his face still radiating excitement.

"And, yes, there is an energy flowing through you and taking the actions that you take. That energy is the creative force from Divine Love. That is how you discover what it is you came to share with the world. It *is* that thing that you love to do the most." His eyes sparkled.

"Have you ever wondered why a piece of literature can have the power to stir something deep within you? This could be a verse in the Bible, or a poem, or a passage in a book. There seems to be some invisible energy captured in the written words, and when you read the verse, when you read the poem, when you read the passage, that energy—that creative force—interacts with something within you, and you feel a perceptible shift in your heart."

Leaning forward slightly, he said, "The energy that causes a shift within you is from Divine Love coming through the writer as he or she sits to write that piece. That creative energy gets transferred to the words of the written piece. As you read the verse, or the poem, or the passage, you are interacting with the energy vibration that is embedded in the text. You are coming into contact with Divine Love, and the energy from it is transforming your heart. It is as if once the energy is transferred to the medium, it stays there. It doesn't fade. It doesn't diminish in strength. It doesn't lose its relevance with changing times. The energy comes alive each time a reader who is ready to receive the message it carries interacts with it."

He leaned back, sitting up straight, his clasped hands falling into his lap.

"The same is true for certain pieces of music, whether it's opera, folk music, or the greatest hits of all times. The song could be Andrea Bocelli's rendition of the sacred "Ave Maria"[20] playing in a packed opera house. It could be Harry Belafonte's "Jamaican Farewell"[21] playing softly over the radio. It could be MC Hammer's "U Can't Touch This"[22] blaring over the public-address system of a fully packed downtown baseball stadium. It could be Psy's "Gangnam Style"[23] blasting over the car's stereo speakers." The audience broke into laughter as the leader mentioned Psy, a musician from South Korea who had recently taken the world by storm with his animated song and dance routine.

"There is a particular note, a particular lyric, a particular beat, a particular rhythm that moves you as you listen to the music. You may just stop and let the note settle into you. You may feel the sting of tears in your eyes. You may find yourself swaying gently in rhythm to the music. Or you may find yourself throwing limbs in all directions in a spasmodic attempt to keep up with the fast tempo of the music."

As he was saying this, a thought crossed my mind—the song could be Kanda Bongo Man's "Zing Zong"[24] broadcasting over car speakers in a rural village in Africa, sending men, women, and children into seemingly uncontrollable body gyrations. A smile crossed my face as I tuned back to listen to the leader.

"What that feeling is—however it manifests for you—is pure joy rising and washing over you." As he said this, he closed his eyes, threw his head back, breathed in deeply, and then slowly let the breath out with a soft ahhh sound. It was as if he was feeling the joy washing over his body in that very moment. He continued to speak with his eyes closed.

"That response—the pause, the tears, the swaying, the uncontrollable urge to wiggle—is a response from your spirit acknowledging that it has received the energy transmitted by the piece of music." He opened his eyes, gently sweeping his gaze across the room.

"The artist goes into his or her deeper self, into Divine Love, to compose that piece of music. When you hear the music, it creates a channel for you to connect with your deeper self that exists in Divine Love. That connection is what you experience as the response. You may have heard other people say, or you yourself may have said, 'When I listen to this song, I am transported to another world.' That other world that you feel transported to is Divine Love; that other world is your true home." He took another deep breath and released it slowly, accompanied by another long ahhh sound.

"The artist lives his or her higher purpose by surrendering to Divine Love and creating a channel through which the creative energy flows as the song that touches me, that touches you, that touches the world—and transports us back into Divine Love. In this way, we experience the presence of Divine Love in a tangible way."

As I listened to the leader, a warm glow filled my heart. It was as if my heart was responding to the power of his words.

The leader coughed softly, holding his handkerchief to his mouth. And then he continued to speak.

"Some people are the eminent scientists like the Galileos and Albert Einsteins of the world. They sit and listen to the universe. Because they are willing to listen, the universe reveals its secrets to them. These scientists then share what the universe communicates to them in the form of theories and mathematical equations to explain the composition of our physical world. Others build on those theories, and incrementally over years and centuries, humans begin to accumulate knowledge about the physical universe, and our understanding of the physical world increases." He coughed again, reached for the glass of water on the table beside him, and took a sip.

"Some people may find that their gifts are best expressed in the context of the team dynamic, working in unison with others. As each and every team member surrenders to the cause they rally around, their energies align and form a channel that is larger than the size of the individual channels that would result from each person working alone. Ideas and breakthroughs easily flow through these channels, and the creative momentum leads to quantum results. Physical feats that may seem impossible become possible." He paused, breathing deeply.

"Think about the energies that came together for man to land on the surface of the moon. Think about the energies that came together to create what we now know as the modern-day Internet that connects the world—what was a dispersed and disconnected world has now become one global village. Think about the people who have worked together to bring mobile technology to the remote places of the earth. Today, a woman toiling in her corn patch in a remote village of Africa can call her son in Australia to let him know that the lone cow she owns just had a calf."

I smiled to myself as the leader said this. I appreciated the example he had given, as it was close to my heart. I was very grateful for mobile technology that allowed me to speak to my parents and my relatives who lived in rural villages in Zimbabwe. Once again, I was reminded that my grandmother had said something similar when she had talked about ideas that come to humans from Source.

"All this is for the purpose of improving our lives here on this earth," the leader said. I thought I detected a hoarseness in the leader's voice.

"The point is that each and every one of us has the opportunity to share his or her gift with the world," he continued. "As you share your gift, you become a conduit for unconditional love and creative energy from Divine Love to flow through you as your thoughts, as your words, and as your actions that create in the world. That is how we individually participate in the growth, expansion, and evolution of the universe, and together we co-create a future world with Divine Love. Yes, it is the flow of love and creative energy that makes the world go round."

The leader stopped talking and told us to take a ten-minute break. I grabbed a cup of herbal tea and a scone from the refreshments table, and I wandered into the garden adjacent to the sanctuary. The garden was well designed, with rock boulders placed in between clumps of fleshy desert plants and flowering shrubs. A water fountain gently bubbled in the background, lending a serenity to the surroundings. I sat on a bench beside the fountain, appreciating the beauty in front of me.

When I returned to the sanctuary, I found everyone already seated, waiting for the session to start. I quietly made my way to my cushion and sat down just as the leader started to speak.

"Now we are moving into the most important segment of our day today. This is the part where each of you has the opportunity to start reflecting on your higher purpose and the gift that you came to share with the world." He paused, looking at the audience. "This is something that you may need to contemplate for some time, but I wanted to give you some thoughts that may help you as you embark on this process." Another short pause followed.

"Of course, I am assuming that everyone in this room is interested in expressing his or her gift in the world. You have been doing what you have been doing, a little of this here and a little of that there. But at some deep level, you feel that there should be more to your life than what you are living. You feel that it's time to open your gift and share it with the world." He swallowed, and then took a deep breath.

"The trouble is, it might not be clear to you what that gift is; or, for some people, you may not think you are free to express your gift. According to society, there are certain things that a person of your age, background, and education is supposed to do by a particular time. There is a timeline that everyone is expected to follow. Perhaps that is what you have done and now you feel there is no way out."

Raising his voice slightly, he said, "I am here to tell you that there is always a way out. There is always a way to live your passion, to express your talent, to share your gift. In fact, that is the only way to live a successful life." He took another deep breath, his gaze still directed at the audience.

"Here is what I urge you to do in the next few days or so, or before too long from now," he continued. "It is important that you do what I am asking of you while the lessons from today are still fresh in your mind," he added.

"I want you to set three intentions." Raising his right hand and counting on his fingers, he said, "One, set the intention for your gift to be revealed to you. Two, set the intention to commit to following through with developing the skills that you need to share your gift. And three, set the intention to share your gift with the world." He lowered his hand back onto his lap.

"You can use any free time that you have to ask your heart what that gift is," he continued. "Remember, we said that your gift is something that you love to do and that is of service to others. Your heart—or we can say the knower inside of you—already knows what the gift is. So your quest, really, is for the gift to be revealed to your conscious mind. You will find that once the gift is revealed, you will also be shown how to pursue it; and, more importantly, it will be clear to you how that gift benefits others and the world. You won't even have to wonder if what you are doing is of value to others. You won't have any doubt as to whether or not you are co-creating with Divine Love to serve others and to fulfill your purpose for passing through the world." He stopped briefly, letting his words settle.

"I urge you to set aside specific times where you sit in silence," he eventually said, "and put your attention on your heart and ask it to reveal the gift that you came to express in the world, and then go into meditation. To the extent that you can, stay aware of any ideas that may arise as you are in meditation. Just notice the ideas as they rise and fall as part of the thoughts, do not get involved by starting to think or analyze the ideas. Just watch them pass through. These ideas might come at any time—as you are starting your meditation, in the middle of it, or as you are coming out." He paused.

"When you come out of meditation," he continued, "immediately go into contemplation. The contemplation periods are where you are now thinking through and analyzing the ideas that arose during meditation. You may want to ask questions such as: Did something specific come up that is asking to be expressed through me? Is my heart pointing me in a certain direction?" He paused again, his gaze cast down, thinking.

When he raised his gaze to the audience, he said, "Let's take singing as something that floated into your mind during your meditation. Perhaps singing is something that seems very close to your heart. When you go into contemplation, think about what it is you like about singing and ask yourself some questions around that. Have you been in a choir before? Have you been part of a band? How did you feel when you were performing? Did you feel excited and enthusiastic? Did you feel alive? Did you feel a sense of being uplifted and carried away to a magical place? What is it about music that uplifts you?" he paused briefly before continuing. "And then set the intention to let the answers to the questions come to you as you go about your day." He swallowed.

"As you are going through this process, don't let your reasoning mind rush to give you what it considers reasonable answers or allow it to judge the answers that rise from your heart. Don't let what you think other people may say limit you. Really go into your heart and let it reveal its yearnings to you." A brief pause followed.

When he resumed talking, the leader said, "Sometimes, it happens that you have buried what you desire to express very deep within you, because you just couldn't see how this could come to fruition. Perhaps you thought sharing your gift with the world was not practical. Rather than live with the pain of the constant yearning for what you couldn't do or couldn't have, you may have suppressed your gift deep in your mind." He coughed softly into his handkerchief.

"For you, what may be required is some deep digging within to retrieve your gift buried under layers of resistance and denial," he continued. "In some cases, it might even be helpful to remember what you loved to do when you were a child. Take the time to ask your heart if that childhood dream might still be the thing that you love to do. How is that related to what you are actually doing today? If not related, how do you still feel about doing what you said you wanted to do as a child? Does it still excite you when you think about it? If it does, you may want to schedule some time to research the feasibility of going back to your childhood dream. Evaluate the pros and cons. From a practical point of view, what would be required? What would you have to give up? Are you prepared to give that up?"

With his gaze slowly traveling across the room and his voice carrying a pleading quality, he said, "At the very least, ask the questions. Don't just dismiss the idea as impractical—because by dismissing the idea, you might be dismissing your destiny." Another brief pause followed.

"You need to remember something else," he continued. "You need to keep this conversation between you and your heart. If you feel the need to speak with others, be careful in selecting the people you share your heart's desires with. It may not be a good idea to speak to people who have a tendency for being negative and judgmental. That is not the influence you need at this delicate phase when you are rekindling your passion in your life. This is a time when kindness and tenderness might be needed for your heart to reveal the gift that it yearns to express."

He reached for the pitcher of water and refilled his glass and took a sip.

"As you can see, there is a lot that you will need to process, but remember that the time you put into these exercises is worthwhile. You want your mind to be clear as to what your heart yearns to share with the world."

The leader opened the floor to the audience and a robust exchange followed as he answered questions from participants. I listened intently. After about fifteen minutes, the leader closed the session and told us to use the evening to reflect on what had been shared. He also urged us to start the exercises of meditation and contemplation and to listen to our hearts with the sincere intention of perceiving the gifts that were trying to emerge.

I invited Monica to join me for dinner that evening. Buying her dinner was my way of thanking her for offering me a ticket to a gathering that was opening my mind. I also knew that she was having a hard time with the recent breakup with her boyfriend, Nathan. I imagined this trip was particularly difficult for her as she had planned it as something special that she and Nathan would share—a present for both of them. I knew Monica was strong mentally and emotionally, but I also sensed that the breakup had shaken her. She had not confided the circumstances of the breakup and, out of respect for her privacy, I hadn't asked.

We had a quiet dinner at a restaurant in the small town close to the retreat. Then Monica and I bade each other goodnight and went to our separate rooms. Back in my room, I took a shower, and then sat on the bed and allowed myself to relax and go into a contemplative state.

My mind started recalling the journey I had traveled up to that point. I just let the thoughts rise up and fall away naturally.

I recalled that as my awareness was slowly deepening over the years, I had started noticing that there were things I enjoyed and loved to do. For the most part, the things I enjoyed had no obvious connection to my career and were not related to the things that society told me I should be doing at that stage of my life. As my understanding of my true nature increased, I found that I had more courage to step out and pursue the things I loved to do, despite what I knew society expected from me. I also noticed that it became easier for me to attract circumstances that allowed me to spend time doing the things that I loved to do.

Over the past few years, I had spent many hours accumulating knowledge on the topics of awareness, spirituality, and mystical experiences. This interest was completely unrelated to my career path. Even with the wildest imagination one could have, there was no room for mysticism in the drug discovery space, I thought. I saw the focus in that space to be solely on scientific theory and proof, objective explanations for observed phenomena, and the practical applications of scientific discoveries. The emphasis was on things that we can see, things that we can measure, and things that we can analyze.

I had often thought that this very fact is probably where most of us, as humans in general and scientists in particular, miss the point when it comes to science. Most of us focus on seeing, measuring, and analyzing the small portion of creation that we can detect with our limited physical senses and our even more limited instruments. But, we ignore the vast majority of creation that can't be seen, measured, or analyzed, which is the rest of reality that exists as the invisible part of Source. Most of us forget that what we see, measure, or analyze arises from the deeper invisible dimension. We forget that what we "discover" is already there, having been created by Source. In reality, when we invent the new forms that we bring into the world—new drugs, new gadgets, new spaceships—we in fact co-create with Source, using the laws of nature that are governed by Source. Yet most of us go on discounting the existence of Source. This is something I find a bit puzzling.

As I continued with my reflections, I realized that the fact that I had made my career in science had not dampened my enthusiasm for seeking and accumulating spiritual knowledge. I didn't spend time analyzing how incompatible my interest in spiritual matters and my career were.

That was the point at which I had stretched on the bed and dozed off to sleep.

The next day started with an hour of guided meditation in the sanctuary, followed by breakfast served in the cafeteria. When we reconvened in the sanctuary around nine, the leader made a few announcements and then asked us to take the morning to continue with the individual meditation and contemplation exercises we had begun the evening before.

Some participants stayed in the sanctuary, each finding a nook where they could be alone. Some went to the meditation room, next door to the sanctuary. But most of us spread out onto the grounds of the property.

I followed a path up a small mount and found a comfortable wooden bench at the top. I sat down and set the intention to continue with the contemplation I had started the night before.

Bringing my attention to my current surroundings, I took a deep breath. Sitting on the mount afforded me an expansive view of the grounds around the spiritual center. The landscape was dominated by cactuses. They stood upright, rising from the dry sandy soil of the desert. My eyes focused on a cactus plant a few feet in front of me. The plant had small pink flowers at the ends of broad, fleshy leaves. The delicate pink flowers, set against the desert landscape, were an unusual sight.

As I moved into contemplation, I put my attention on one pink flower at the top of the cactus plant, becoming aware of the fragility of the bloom against the harsh desert terrain. I allowed a sense of appreciation for the beauty of the flower to rise up in me. I allowed a sense of gratitude to fill me. I was grateful that I had the opportunity to witness the beauty of the flower in that moment, knowing how fleeting its existence was. With that sense of appreciation and gratitude as my background, I let the thoughts from the night before flood my mind. Then I asked a number of questions. What does it all mean? What is it that I am supposed to do for the rest of my life that would incorporate the knowledge I am gaining? How am I going to serve? Who am I going to serve? I knew that despite what might have appeared to be some wrong paths I had taken along the way, despite what might have appeared to be some misguided choices along my journey, and despite what might have appeared to be chances I let slip by, there had to be a higher purpose to everything. I had started to believe there was a perfect pattern to my life that was yet to be revealed to me.

I let the thoughts and questions freely rise and fall in my mind without attempting to control, judge, or, in any way, limit them. I held that mental posture for a while—about half an hour or so—then I went into meditation. Closing my eyes, I took several deep breaths, letting my mind slowly follow my breath as it moved in and out of my body. Then I put my focus inside my chest, becoming aware of my heart space. Within moments, I felt subtle waves of energy rising in my chest and spreading throughout my body, giving me a buzzing sensation all over. Then the buzzing energy was surrounding me, merging into the energy of the environment. I felt surrounded by the energy. I felt cradled and supported by the energy. I felt soothed and comforted by the energy. And I felt my mind letting go as I relaxed into the energy. I lost track of time, fading into a half-doze.

I started to slowly emerge from the lull I had fallen into. As I was regaining my bearings, I sensed an impulse rising from somewhere deep within me, coming through my heart space and bursting into my mind, crystalizing into a stream of thoughts. The thoughts carried a message. And the message was clear as a bell.

Continue to deepen your connection to Source, the creator of all that is seen and unseen, and allow the love from it to flow through your heart and bathe your mind, emotional energy system, and physical body.

Continue to strengthen your trust in Source, and allow the energy from it to keep your human form safe, secure, and protected.

Continue to expand your faith in Source, and allow the energy from it to provide you with everything you need.

Live your life rooted in Source, and practice the truth that you have come to know about the love, joy, and creative energy that surround us all in every moment.

And then share with others the truth that you have come to know and experience.

Some of the people you encounter will be drawn to the truth and may start to turn back to Source to heal the chaos and confusion in their lives.

This is your purpose at this time, and if you choose to fulfill it, you will enter into the flow, and your life will be guided and your needs met at every step of the way.

I opened my eyes and stared at the pink flower on the cactus plant in front of me. I took a deep breath in and let the breath out slowly, with my gaze still focused on the delicate bloom. Then I broke the gaze and took in the larger surroundings, first the rest of the plant with its broad fleshy leaves, then the rest of the sprawling landscape. The beauty of the landscape stirred something in me. It was as if I was seeing it for the first time. The scattered cactuses appeared to be releasing subtle energy waves that radiated outward into the surrounding. It was mesmerizing to see the waves dance in and out against the blue background of a clear desert sky. I remained seated in my spot for another half-hour or so, enjoying the desert and letting thoughts come in and out of my mind.

My thoughts drifted to the time I had spent on the hillside with my grandmother. She had told me to go to my heart with the questions I had for my life and to listen to my heart for the answers. This message had been repeated to me in the vision by her graveside. The retreat leader had delivered the same message, saying the answers that I was seeking were already in my heart.

Then I realized the importance of the message that I had just received. I realized that I was being asked to first live the truth of life as shown to me in the lessons that my grandmother had taught me and then to share that truth of life with others. My grandmother had said that she was passing the knowledge to me so that when the time was right I could pass on this knowledge to others who were ready for it.

I said a short prayer in gratitude for what had been revealed and for guidance in what was going to follow. Then I ended my period of contemplation.

Glancing back at the buildings, I noticed that people had started to congregate by the cafeteria doors. It must be close to lunchtime, I thought, so I got up and headed in that direction. My body still had the slight buzz that I had noticed during meditation.

After a quick lunch, we gathered in the sanctuary for the last session of the retreat. Following a short, guided meditation, the leader asked if any of us wanted to share experiences that had come during the individual meditation and contemplation exercises. I saw the hands of almost half the people in the room shoot up in the air. I was amazed. I hadn't expected this many people to want to share their experiences. To my surprise, I had raised my hand and wanted to share my experience with the group.

Each of us took about four to five minutes to share with the group. The more I listened to others recount their stories, the more I felt encouraged that what I had experienced was real.

When my time to speak came, I briefly summarized my journey up to that point, including the teachings from my grandmother. I shared how the words that the leader had spoken and the exercises he had asked us to do had touched me and opened my mind. Then I spoke of the revelation that had come to me at the end of my meditation, and how I perceived it as a call to share the life lessons that my grandmother had taught me. I did mention though that I had not yet figured out the next steps needed to follow-up on the call, but said I was open to what was to come.

I noticed that during the whole time that I was speaking to the group, sharing my story, I felt at ease. I wasn't self-conscious, and I didn't worry about being ridiculed. As I looked around and met the gazes of the people sitting close to me, I only saw compassion and kindness reflected back to me.

A few other participants shared their experiences after me. It seemed a lot of people had experienced breakthroughs of some kind during the course of the retreat. It seemed a lot had happened at the energy level. I could tell by the glowing smile on the leader's face that he was pleased with the results.

At the end of the testimonies, the leader held a moment of silence, his eyes closed, and his hands in a prayer position by his chest. Then he opened his eyes, his hands settling in his lap. With his gaze slowly moving across the room, he started to speak.

"Thank you all for taking the time to be here at this retreat," he said. "And I also thank those who have shared their revelations with us. This meeting is important, not just for you as individuals or for us as a group, but for humanity as a race and the universe as a whole. What just happened, judging by what has been shared, has cosmic implications. I heard you share powerful testimonies of minds falling back into hearts and opening for Divine Love to flow through and manifest in this world." The beaming smile on his face radiated his joy.

"I urge you to keep those minds focused on your hearts and open to Divine Love as you go back to your daily lives," he went on. "The breakthroughs that you have experienced here are wonderful and exciting and exhilarating and important. But this is just the beginning. The crucial work is in the days and months and years ahead as you hold onto the energy that you tapped into at this gathering and then pull in the manifestations that you have seen in your visions. You have to keep evolving your consciousness and keep opening up to more and more energy and keep pulling in more and more manifestations. That is how it works." I could feel the buzz in my body intensifying as I continued to listen.

"If you go back home and slide back into your old life without making any changes, then the experience you had here is just a 'high' and nothing will come out of it. That 'high' is Divine Love letting you know the possibilities that lie ahead for you, if you follow the guidance and the visions. You have to start changing your life according to the visions you have been shown. It is only then that things will change for you," he said, his face now luminous.

"And when the change starts to happen, it will be visible to you and to those around you. Where you were experiencing chaos and confusion, you will begin experiencing peace and harmony. Where you were experiencing loneliness and isolation, you will begin experiencing love and a sense of connection. Where you were experiencing lack and limitation, you will begin experiencing abundance and flow. That is how you will know you are aligned to your higher purpose, and that you are doing what you came here to do in this world."

Closing his eyes again, and with his arms outstretched wide above his head, the leader gave an invocation, saying, "I see blessings pouring into the lives of all of us gathered here, right now. I see blessings of peace and harmony. I see blessings of love and connection. I see blessings of abundance and flow. I see the consciousness in each and every one of us continuing to evolve at the individual level. As each and every one of us is evolving his or her individual consciousness, I see us contributing to the evolution of our communities, the evolution of human consciousness, and the evolution of our planet. I see us positively impacting what our world is becoming. This is what I allow to be established in Divine Love. And in Divine Love, I surrender this vision. So be it."

He slowly lowered his arms, letting his hands rest in his lap. Then he opened his eyes, his gaze moving across the room. I noticed he was making brief eye contact with each participant. When his gaze rested on me, I held it for a few seconds and felt the warmth and kindness in his eyes again. Then his gaze continued on to the other participants.

After a while, the leader asked us to hold a moment of meditative silence in gratitude for what had transpired at the meeting. After the meditation, he made a few more announcements and said some closing remarks to end the meeting. We gave him a huge round of applause. I thought this had been an amazing gathering in general, and a particularly helpful one for me considering where I was in my life.

The participants stood up and started gathering in small groups to share what had taken place or to say their goodbyes to the people they had briefly connected with. I noticed a small group of people chatting with the leader, who was now standing at the front of the sanctuary. I felt compelled to join the group by the leader. I wanted a chance to personally thank him for the very powerful gathering he had led. I walked over and waited my turn to speak with him.

After a few moments, the leader turned to me and took my right hand in both his hands, looking deep into my eyes. "I was very moved by your testimony," he said. "As you were speaking, I started having visions of you carrying out your assignment of spreading the teachings of your grandmother. I saw you receiving everything you need to assist you in your assignment, and I saw you making a positive impact in the lives of others."

He let go of my hand, but continued to speak. "Do not feel overwhelmed by what you are being called to do. The path has already been cleared for you. Remember to always go to your heart to find the answers to the questions you have about the next steps that you have to take. And then take action according to the guidance you receive."

I was astounded at what the leader was saying to me. All I could think of was that his words were further confirmation that the call I had received was real.

"If ever you think I can be of help to you in your assignment," he continued, "don't hesitate to contact me. You have my contact information in the package you received." He gave me a soft pat on the back and then moved on to the next person.

Then I remembered that I hadn't thanked the leader as I had wanted to. I saw that there was now a long line of people waiting for a chance to speak with him. I stood still for a while, not quite knowing what to do. I thought of joining the back of the line to wait another turn to speak to him, but discounted that as being a little silly. I decided it would be best if I sent my thank-you message in an email. I realized that I had been given an opportunity to keep in contact with one of the very few clear-minded human beings I had met in my life. And I was going to follow-up on that opportunity.

After Monica and I said our goodbyes to the other participants, we left. The drive home was uneventful. I still felt a faint buzz in my body from what had unfolded that day. We chatted for an hour or so about some of the things we had learned, but were quiet for the rest of the drive.

Over the following weeks, I continued the meditation and contemplation exercises that I had learned at the retreat, focusing on the revelation that had come to me then. Those sessions brought additional insights that shed light on my life journey.

It became clear to me that I had been given an opportunity to awaken to the truth about life in the lessons I had received from my grandmother, but I had not heeded those lessons. As a result, I had lived with no clue as to what life was about and what my role in it was. I had stumbled blindly and spun my wheels and stayed in one place. But, by the grace and mercy from Source, my grandmother's teachings were rising up in me again in many forms—in my meditations and contemplations and in the knowledge I gleaned from the teachers I met along the way.

When I looked all around me, I could see most people focused on ego pursuits and material delusions, completely oblivious to what life was about. I could imagine some of them would come to the realization that no answers were to be found in the things they were pursuing, just like I had come to that realization in my own life. I could imagine some starting to search for the truth of life, ready to be shown the way. By pursuing the revelation that had come to me—that is, by practicing and then sharing what I was learning on my journey as a seeker of truth—perhaps I could be of some help to some of the people who crossed my path.

Before the doubts even arose as to who would be willing to listen to what I had to share, the answers came to me. I was reminded of the movie *Field of Dreams*.[25] I thought if I started sharing what I was learning, those who needed to hear what I had to say would be drawn to the message.

I was to remember where I came from. I was to remember those I left behind.

What I had experienced when I visited Zimbabwe was still in my mind. And things in my country hadn't gotten better with the passing years. In fact, things had gotten worse. In 2008, a bitterly contested election led to politically motivated violence with people being abducted, tortured, or murdered. This violence occurred even in rural areas where people who had lived in peace as neighbors for decades suddenly started attacking each other and burning each other's houses because they belonged to different political parties. When it was all said and done, those in power retained control and the country continued to decline. The poor continued to face hardships.

I had kept on helping my family in the best ways I could over the years. However, I could not stop thinking about the other people who were not fortunate enough to have someone to help them. I asked myself: Was there anything I could do to bring relief to the suffering of the poor in my country? When I asked this question, an image of Mako, the girl lying on a death mat in her grandmother's hut, came to me. This was a girl who seemed to have known nothing but suffering in her short life. And I knew there were many more like her. More questions came to my mind. Did my life and her life cross paths for a reason? Was I being called to do something to help children in situations similar to hers? An image of her grandmother, *Mbuya* Svosve, came to mind. During my youth, I had known this woman to be a dignified, hardworking, proud, and self-sufficient person. Now, her life was reduced to just slightly above that of a beggar. I knew that sense of dignity, strong work ethic, pride, and self-sufficiency was still in her. And I knew there were many others like her. And again I asked myself some more questions. Did my life and her life cross paths for a reason? Was I being called to do something to help women in situations similar to hers?

I thought of the young fathers who had families to feed but had no jobs, no money, no land, and no prospects. I knew that given an opportunity, they would work to feed and support their families. I thought of the young mothers who had to watch their children go to bed hungry. They were prepared to work hard for their families, if only the opportunities to work were there. Was I being called to do something to help men and women facing these types of desperate situations? I thought of the young boys and girls I had met in the villages who could no longer attend school because no one could afford to pay the few dollars a year in tuition to give them an education that might change their futures for the better. Was I being called to do something to help those boys and girls? More images and more questions kept coming into my mind.

As I continued to contemplate my life, I thought of how I could share the truth of life that I had been shown and that was continuing to be revealed to me. I thought of the practical skills that I had that could be of help in sharing the knowledge that I was gleaning along my life journey. And a realization came to me. Over the course of my life, I had accumulated the skills I needed to do the work I was being called to do. As an example, I love writing.

For me, writing is a spiritual practice. It is one of the avenues I use to access my deeper self, rooted in Source. Each time I sit down to write, I take a few moments to breathe in and out to quiet my mind. This helps me to gather my scattered attention and to focus it on my intention on the task in front of me.

Now it seemed that perhaps writing could be one of the tools that I could use to share the lessons that I was learning on my life journey.

Gratitude Prayer

Divine Love
I thank you for revealing to me
The gift I came to share with the world
I thank you for the courage and confidence to share my gift
And I thank you for lighting the way for me to follow
My solemn vow and commitment today and every day
Is to stay connected to you

To draw strength, energy, and inspiration from you
As I express in the world
Serving others and serving you
In you, Divine Love, I surrender my life
Until the day I return home into you
Amen

PRACTICES FOR POSITIVE CHANGE

After the desert retreat, I had made a commitment to living and sharing the lessons I was learning on my life journey, in accordance with the guidance of the message I had received there. However, I had enough awareness to know that I would face challenges along the way.

The biggest challenge I struggled with was keeping negative energies in the form of negative thoughts and negative emotions from rising and overtaking my life. All my life, I had struggled with fear, anxiety, doubt, and a sense of unworthiness. Even as I started to gain a clear understanding of the connection between my thoughts, my emotions, and the experiences that show up as my life, I still struggled with these negative energies. I knew that I didn't have effective practices for managing the negative energies so I could stop them from attracting negative experiences into my life.

The one thing that I had understood from the many teachers that I had come across on my journey is the importance of following practices that allow one to keep in alignment with Source. I realized I needed to find practices that I could use in situations whenever negative energies threatened to overwhelm me, so that I could keep my sense of connection to Source, and be able to do what I was called to do. I started combining and adapting practices that I had learned from various sources, making them my own.

The practice that I find to be the most effective in managing negative energies that arise in my life is a process of emotional release that centers on using meditation, visualization, and prayer. This practice is based on allowing the negative energies to rise up and express until they subside and pass. With this practice, I go into a meditative state as soon as I become aware of negative thoughts rising in my mind or negative emotions expressing in my body. The reason for going into a meditative state is not to avoid feeling the negative energies, but rather to allow myself to be fully present and aware as the negative energies express themselves.

In this practice, I first focus on my breath to quiet my mind, calm my emotions, and relax my body. As my grandmother taught me, I then focus on my heart and feel my way into a sense of connection with Source within, which I feel as an energy, as an aliveness, as an alertness within my body. Once I can feel this sense of connection with Source, I surrender into it. I let go of any sense of separation, lack, or limitation. And I relax into the space within, where all needs are met and everything is perfect as it is. I relax into the space that is unchanging, no matter what else is going on in my life. I relax into my divine self. And I stay in this state of communion for some time, bathed in the love of Source.

From this state of communion with Source, I then consciously invite the situation triggering the negative energies to rise in my mind and my emotions. I use visualization to allow images related to the situation to flood my mind and to allow the negative emotional reactions to flow through my body as the negative energies tell their stories.

One of the reactions I might experience as I visualize the situation causing the negative energies to play out is a wave of fear. I usually recognize fear as bodily sensations such as contraction of muscles in my body, tenseness, constriction in my chest that makes it difficult to breathe, increased heart rate, excessive sweating, or as feelings of agitation, dizziness, or nausea. I watch these bodily sensations play out, witnessing the experience in a detached manner. The ability to detach from the experience in any situation and to watch the experience as it unfolds helps me to keep what is happening in perspective. I stay aware and alert so that I do not get overtaken by the negative thoughts and emotional reactions. I can stay calm in these situations because of what I now know about life: that everything that rises does eventually subside and pass. I keep reminding myself that these sensations will subside and pass.

Once I feel the negative energies subsiding and passing, I relax as much as I can, and, still in this meditative state, I offer a prayer. From that space of communion with Source, I sometimes recite the words of a standard prayer such as The Lord's Prayer or the Hail Mary, or I sometimes allow words of a new prayer to rise up in me. And once I finish reciting the prayer, I surrender both the prayer and the situation that triggered the negative energies into Source.

Sometimes I write down the prayers that arise as I allow myself to consciously process negative thoughts and emotions. Below is a prayer that came at a time when I was processing negative energies of confusion and illusion resulting from a situation that I was experiencing at that time.

Ending Confusion and Illusion (Part 1)

I am ready, willing, and prepared
To end the mental confusion and illusion
That come with identification with the things of this world
But offer no insight and no salvation
Except to add to the confusion and illusion
That keep me trapped in a cycle of slow death and decay

With a yearning in my heart
And a desire in my outstretched hand
I reach out to you for the salvation
That will once and for all put an end
To the confusion and illusion
That keep me trapped in a cycle of slow death and decay

In complete surrender
I wait for your answer

Knowing that the relief I seek is near
And the relief will stop and put an end
To the confusion and illusion
That keep me trapped in a cycle of slow death and decay

It's not always the case that when I process negative energies prayers rise from me with clarity. But as I continue with the practice of facing challenging situations in a meditative state followed by visualization and prayer, I have started to notice that this now happens with more frequency. I think the shift has to do with three things: The first is that I now allow the negative energies to express in a state in which my awareness watches the unfolding of the thoughts and emotional reactions, but is not embroiled in the experiences. The second is that rather than just pleading with Source to take me out of the challenging experience, I now use visualization to bring specific images that apply to that particular situation and use prayer to bring specific language to specify the experiences I no longer wish to experience. The third is that I now wait for the answers in awareness. It doesn't mean that I stop all activities and sit to wait for the answers to come to me. It means that I continue with my day doing what needs to be done, but—as my grandmother taught me—I keep a part of myself rooted in Source at all times. I let a part of me stay alert to any answers that may come in the "most ordinary and extraordinary ways."

One day, as I was walking along a path in a forest, listening to the calls of wild birds and animals, letting those sounds permeate my heart, the words of a prayer started rising up. I sat on a log nearby, keeping my focus on my heart. I listened carefully, and below is the prayer that arose from that experience.

Ending Confusion and Illusion (Part 2)

Divine Presence
I hear your answer to my prayer and I listen
As this is the only way
To end the confusion and illusion
That hide the truth of who I am as spirit

From deep within my heart
I perceive your guidance and I obey
I raise my awareness beyond thought, belief, and experience
To reach my true nature as spirit
Connected to you, the Highest Spirit

With my awareness beyond thought
I rise above all mental projections
Above fear, anxiety, worry, and doubt
Above the sense of lack, limitation, separation, and abandonment
For these are only thought forms with no substance of their own

With my awareness beyond belief
I rise above judgment of myself, others, and circumstances
Above the need to blame, condemn, and punish
Above guilt, shame, and a sense of humiliation
For these are only beliefs with no substance of their own

With my awareness beyond the human form
I rise above uneasiness, dissatisfaction, pain, and mental anguish
Above all mental, emotional, and physical suffering
Above all confusion and illusion
For these are only experiences with no substance of their own

As I rise above all negative thoughts, beliefs, and experiences
I reclaim my divine spiritual qualities
Courage, confidence, and calmness rise up in me
Kindness, compassion, and respect too
And, at last, I gain clarity of mind beyond all confusion and illusion

Whenever I become aware of confusion in my mind, I go into a meditative state and recite this prayer to raise my awareness beyond thought, belief, and human experience so that I reach the energy of Source. With everything that I have begun to understand on my spiritual journey, I now know that I can draw upon the healing energy of Source to resolve the confusion.

I find this to be a powerful practice in my life.

Beyond just the general confusion and illusion that may cause negativity to arise in our human experiences, there may be specific issues that we battle with. For me, I had struggled for a long time with the fact that I was alone, with no husband and no children. Through poor choices and paths not taken, I ended up alone. There had been offers, and even commitments, made for marriage; but, for one reason or another, none had come to pass.

It wasn't so much the marriage part that caused me the most suffering. It was not having children of my own that did. There were times when I used to get up in the early hours of the morning filled with a heavy sense of sadness. The thoughts that circled in my mind in those moments were that I had missed out on the joys of sharing the love between a mother and a child. I felt as if something in me was stunted. I felt as if some aspect of my being wasn't allowed to grow and flourish. I would experience a wave of self-judgment that I didn't take the time to raise a family. I felt that I cheated myself on playing a role that I was meant to play in this world. This used to stir feelings of emptiness, unworthiness, regret, guilt, and a sense of a loss that cannot be reversed.

As a way of coping with these negative thoughts and emotions, I turned to the practice of meditation, visualization, and prayer. Again, not so much to avoid or dull the pain from the tormenting thoughts and emotions, but rather to allow myself to be present and to feel the pain as the negative energies expressed, and to surrender the pain to Source. Toward the end of each session, I would say a prayer of gratitude, knowing that the negative energies were subsiding.

Each time I sat with the negative energies and experienced the pain in awareness and surrendered the pain to Source, the intensity of the pain diminished. After a few months of diligently practicing this process of emotional release, I realized that this experience carried a message for me.

The message became clearer with each sitting. The first part of the message was that I needed to accept my life as it was—not to wish that my life was different in any way, shape, or form from what it was. The second part of the message was that I needed to ask my heart what I desired to happen in my life, starting from exactly where I was—not wishing that I could start from someplace different from where I was.

One thing that kept rising from my heart into my mind was that I wanted to be involved in helping children in need, especially orphaned children and those from poor families. Again, I thought of the young boys and girls in my home country who had to leave school because no one had the few dollars to pay tuition for them to continue with their education. I wanted to help children in such circumstances by providing resources that would enable them to receive a good education and offer them an opportunity to express their gifts in the world and become contributing adults.

In the end, my struggle to come to terms with not having children of my own appeared to have been the conduit of my passion for helping children in need. In the silence of meditation and the reverence that I gave them, the thoughts, the emotions, and the pain delivered their message to me. With that understanding, I accepted my life situation with grace and dignity. The prayer below is what came out of that experience.

To Love and Be Loved

I buried the emotions deep down long ago
Where they could not surface and express
My longing for you in my life
My yearning to hold you, and to love you
With no reservation and no withhold

When you disappeared that long ago
What I didn't know then that I know now
Is that in your own quiet way
You yearned to love me too
With no reservation and no withhold

Even though you may not be here with me
To express in the world of the seen and heard
Deep down in my heart
I feel you quietly loving me
With no reservation and no withhold

You disappeared long ago
Leaving me with an empty heart
But you now return to fill my heart
As the children of this world that I now love
With no reservation and no withhold

You whisper softly in my heart
That I too can be counted as a mother
Who raised the children of this world
When I love the children left behind
With no reservation and no withhold

Gone are the tears I shed for your absence in my arms
Gone is the silence you left in your wake
Replaced by the cries, the shouts, and the laughter
Of the children of this world that I now love
With no reservation and no withhold

You whisper softly in my heart
That I love you each time I love another
What I did not understand then that I understand now
Is that to love is to love all
With no reservation and no withhold

When given and when received
Love knows no boundaries
Of who should give and who should receive
When allowed, love flows, flourishes, and nourishes all
With no reservation and no withhold

Love, joy, and peace fill my heart
And the yearning for you subsides
As the longing is now fulfilled by those children left behind
Who turn to me for love and who love me back
With no reservation and no withhold

As you wave goodbye as you did long ago
I watch you disappear with one difference this time
The grief and sorrow that was there before
Is now peace and understanding of the way it is to love
With no reservation and no withhold

I lay you to sleep, my loving child
A sleep of eternal peace and everlasting life
Till we meet again when I join you
After my love is all used up loving those around me
With no reservation and no withhold

As the words of this prayer rose up in me, the turmoil subsided. The tirades of "what ifs" diminished. The yearnings for "that which I do not have and can never have" receded. The aching for "what could have been but can never be" faded away. Whenever the negative energies return, I recite this prayer to myself and surround them with the loving energy of Source in meditation and in prayer. Putting my love, trust, and faith in Source through this practice helped me to move past this emotional block that had caused me a lot of pain and suffering and had kept me in bondage for a very long time.

In a different scenario, perhaps we ourselves may not be directly experiencing negative energies, but we may be witnessing another person struggling with them. We may have a loved one who is battling deep emotional issues that show up in his or her life as an addiction of some kind—an addiction to alcohol, illegal drugs, or sex. We see how the addiction is destroying the life of our loved one, and how the negativity spills over into our life and into the lives of others around that person.

In the early days of my journey, in my ignorance, I used to focus on how the addictive behavior of that person was affecting my life. As such, I would implore that person to stop their addictive behavior. I would tell them how their behavior was causing pain in my life and in the lives of others. I didn't know enough to consider the kind of pain that my loved one was experiencing that would make him or her resort to destructive addictive behavior as a coping mechanism. I didn't know that it was the wounds in that person's heart that led to the negative behavior, which was an attempt to seek relief from the torment and the turmoil he or she was experiencing. I didn't know that it was the pain in that person that I needed to focus on, not the negative behavior or the inconvenience that it was causing in my life or in the lives of others.

Now I have a different approach to situations like this. That approach is centered on showing compassion and kindness to the person exhibiting the negative behavior. I now have an understanding that pain is what leads to the addictive behavior. Again, I use the practice of meditation, visualization, and prayer. I go deep into mediation to commune with Source, and then I bring the image of that person to my mind. In a state of communion with Source, the first thing I seek to do is to feel the truth about that person; that is, I try to see the person as a spiritual being, as a soul that is a part of the invisible whole. I see that the person has lost his or her sense of connection to Source, blocked by the negative energies and pain of whatever condition that triggers the addictive behavior.

I don't need to know the details of the situation triggering the negative energies and the pain that triggers the addictive behavior in my loved one—that is not important. All I do is visualize a mass of negative energies blocking the free flow of unconditional love from Source to my loved one. Then I visualize the negative energies lifting from my loved one and dissolving into nothingness. Following that, I visualize a stream of unconditional love and creative energy, flowing from Source, through the heart, through the mind, through the emotions, and through the body of my loved one and overflowing into the world. I hold that mental posture and continue to visualize my loved one moving into the world, doing what they do with love, with joy, and with creativity. I see my loved one being creative and productive. I see the person spreading blessings to people that he or she meets. I move away from seeing my loved one tormented and tortured by negativity, and I start imagining unconditional love and creative energy flowing through his or her being into the world. I then say a prayer of gratitude and appreciation, and I surrender the situation to Source.

This process may not be an easy thing to do in all situations, and it may not lead to a resolution of the addictive behavior in the other person, but I have seen it yield positive results a number of times in my life. At the very least, this practice helps me to keep my attention focused on Source, and I avoid being drawn into the role of the victim who is negatively impacted by the other person's behavior. Because if I see myself as a victim, then all I can do is resent the person, complain about the situation, and implore that person to change their behavior—exercises that, of course, don't yield any relief for me or my loved one. By following the practice I just described, there is the opportunity to surrender the situation into Source, and also the possibility that, somehow, the pain and suffering that a loved one is experiencing may be relieved in some way.

I used this meditation, visualization, and prayer practice with a loved one who had a drug addiction that was literally destroying him and causing people close to him to distance themselves, not wanting to be exposed to such destructive behavior. For a few weeks, I would set aside about ten to fifteen minutes a day for meditation, visualization, and prayer for a resolution of the condition that was causing the emotional turmoil and pain in my loved one, in due time. I left it open as to when that due time was, because that was not for me to know or to determine. I saw my role as holding that outcome in my awareness and keeping the faith that one day, when the time was right, that outcome would be revealed. Below is the prayer that came to me during the sessions that I was working on behalf of my loved one.

A Prayer for Resolution

I am aware of my true nature as spirit
Connected to the Highest Spirit that you are, Divine Presence
In this awareness, I sense my wholeness as a part of all creation
Connected to the source of my power that you are, Divine Love
The spiritual energy that flows from you, the Invisible Power
Through my heart, mind, emotions, and body, and overflows into the world
To do that which I came here to do
To reveal truth, to radiate love, and to live with compassion and kindness
Blessing all the forms that you are that I encounter on my journey
In you I surrender this prayer

In my own awareness, I sense the true nature of my loved one as spirit
Connected to the Highest Spirit that you are, Divine Presence
I sense his wholeness as a part of all creation
Connected to the source of his power that you are, Divine Love

The spiritual energy that flows from you, the Invisible Power
Through his heart, mind, emotions, and body, overflowing into the world
To remind him of that which he came here to do
To reveal truth, to radiate love, and to live with compassion and kindness
Blessing all the forms that you are that he encounters on his journey
In you I surrender this prayer

In my awareness of his true nature as spirit
Connected to the Highest Spirit that you are, Divine Presence
The fear, anxiety, doubt, grief, and despair in him dissolve and disappear
To be replaced by a sense of peace and well-being, Divine Love
That allows spiritual energy to flow from you, the Invisible Power
Through his heart, mind, emotions, and body, and overflow into the world
To remind him of that which he came here to do
To reveal truth, to radiate love, and to live with compassion and kindness
Blessing all the forms that you are that he encounters on his journey
In you I surrender this prayer

In my awareness, I sense him gaining awareness of his true nature as spirit
Connected to the Highest Spirit that you are, Divine Presence
I see courage, confidence, and a sense of empowerment
Flowing into his being and revitalizing his mind, his emotions, and his body
He is filled with a sense of adequacy and self-expression
He is enthusiastic, motivated, and driven
He gets up and picks his tools to fulfill his purpose in the world
As he remembers what he came here to do
To reveal truth, to radiate love, and to live with compassion and kindness
Blessing all the forms that you are that he encounters on his journey
In you I surrender this prayer
Amen

With time, this person found a resolution to the emotional turmoil that was driving him to drugs. I did eventually tell him about the work I had done on his behalf, and he was very thankful. He also said that he wished I had told him at the time I was working on his behalf. He said that knowing someone cared enough to set aside time to assist with seeking a resolution of his condition would have been a great comfort as most of his tormenting thoughts stemmed from a perception that he was abandoned, isolated, and alone.

I have used the practice of meditation, visualization, and prayer in situations where I was trying to bring a resolution of an illness in someone. In this case, instead of holding the dissolution of negative energies in the other person, I held the dissolution of the condition that was causing the disease to manifest in the person. And I have also used this practice in situations where I was seeking to create specific outcomes in areas of my life involving finances, relationships, and so on.

To create a specific outcome, I go into my heart and connect to Source in meditation and visualize the outcome I want to experience, and then "speak the words" on the desired outcome in the form of a prayer. I find the teachings in *The Art of Life*[26] by Ernest Holmes to be the most inspiring when it comes to "speaking the word" on situations. These teachings follow the example described in the opening passages of the Bible where we are told that God created the light, sky, seas, land, plants, animals, and human beings by "speaking the word" (Genesis 1:1–26).[27] As extensions of Source, we human beings also have this power to "speak the word" on any situation and can believe that the word we speak will bring about the specific outcomes we desire.

I used to falsely believe that only certain people who had "attained a certain level of spiritual enlightenment" could "speak the word" on events and manifest desired outcomes. This, of course, excluded me as I knew that I had not attained that "certain level of spiritual enlightenment"—not that I claimed to know what that expression really meant. I therefore never used to think of myself as having the power to "speak the word" on anything. However, I now know that any one of us can access Source through our hearts. I now access Source in meditation and visualize specific outcomes, and then in prayer "speak the word" of my desires into the infinite intelligence of Source. I pray in faith, and with no doubt, that what I ask for will be granted to me. I take the words of the Bible to heart that say: "Ask and it will be given to you" (Matthew 7:7).[28] I continue to focus on the desired outcomes and make sure I do not offer any contradictory thoughts. Then I accept whatever comes, with no resistance.

Below is a version of a prayer that I often use when accessing Source and "speaking the word" on specific outcomes that I desire to experience.

Accessing the Creative Energy

I quiet my mind, calm my emotions, and relax my body
And I enter my heart space
In awareness of my wholeness as the spirit that I am
I raise my consciousness into the spiritual realm, to unite with Divine Presence
As I move my consciousness higher and higher
I rise above the confusion of my life situation
I let go of any sense of struggle, stress, or strain within me
I let go of any sense of burden from this world
I release the feelings of fear, anxiety and worry; for there is nothing to
    hurt me here
I release the feelings of doubt for I am guided by the knower within
Who knows all there is to know about everything in creation
As I continue to climb higher and higher within
I reach a place of deep silence, stillness, and peace
In this place, I merge with the life energy of my Creator
And I allow this life energy to rise in me
As the courage to do what I am called to do
As the confidence to let go and allow Divine Love to flow through me
As the clarity of thought that guides me forward

As I continue to climb even higher and higher within
The words I speak are creative forces
That bring manifestations into being
I speak the words of my desires quietly and clearly
Knowing they are moving and shaping creative energies
Into that which I yearn to experience
With my mind's eye, I see the images of my desires
I breathe into the images and bring them to life

Across the screen of my mind I let the images play out and unfold
So shall it come to fruition in my physical experience
For this is the simple process of creation I have come to know
As bestowed upon me by Divine Love
In this I know I have accessed the creative energies of Divine Presence
I, the created, have become the co-creator with Divine Love
In grace and in gratitude I let it be
Amen

As I say the words, I allow myself to feel them taking effect in me. When I say, "I release the feelings of fear, anxiety, and worry; for there is nothing to hurt me here," I actually let go of fear, anxiety, and worry. As I continue with the prayer, I access an energy within my body, which I know is Source. In this state, I know that I can mold and shift energies into the shapes and forms of the outcomes I desire. And I focus on a specific desire and bring the images related to that desire into my mind and I use specific words related to that desire to speak exactly what I want to manifest. The more specific I can be, the more likely that I will manifest the outcomes I want.

Sometimes prayers come to me in moments of silence and I write them down as I know they contain powerful messages from Source. The next prayer came to me as a simple and very ordinary revelation one day as I sat on a city park bench and watched people going about their business. The subject of human connections had been on my mind at that time. I had been in deep inquiry about human relations on a spiritual level, not just the blood relations that we usually pay so much attention to as humans. My quest was to understand how it is that as humans we are all connected, and how we are supposed to live together and help each other. Through the words of the prayer, I learned that when we go deep beyond what we see and what we believe, we can experience the connectedness from which we create the world.

Together Me and You

I may see myself and not think much
You may see yourself and not think much

We may see ourselves and not think much
But who we are me and you
Is the very force that creates the world around us

I may say to myself how can that be
You may say to yourself how can that be
We may say to ourselves how can that be
But the answer though simple and out in the open
Appears to be hidden as we continue the search

I will ask myself what I am
You will ask yourself what you are
We will ask ourselves what we are
Even though the answer may come
The answer cannot be heard with our human ears

I will ask how then can I know
You will ask how then can you know
We will ask how then can we know
And the answer will come
By listening to a place deep in our hearts
Only will we come to hear that which we seek to hear

I will stop and listen to my heart
You will stop and listen to your heart
We will stop and listen to our hearts
And only then will we know
That we hear the same voice from within telling us we are one

I will hear the voice calling me to serve you
You will hear the voice calling you to serve me
We will hear the voice calling us to serve the world
And only then will we come to know
That the voice from within is the essence of who we are as Divine Love

I serve you when I emanate love
You serve me when you emanate love
We serve the world when we emanate love
It is only then will we come to realize
That in our sacred union, we emanate love into the world

I will look at you with a knowing smile
You will look at me with a knowing smile
We will look at the world with a knowing smile
For only then will we come to know, that together all of us
We are the force that creates the world we see and experience

I will see myself and think much
You will see yourself and think much
We will see ourselves and think much
For only then will we know that together all of us
We are the force that creates the world we see and experience

I will reach for your hand in mine
You will reach for my hand in yours
We will join our hands in sacred union
For by then we will know that as we join our hands, we form a mighty force
That nurtures and sustains love in this world

I also know that when people or situations show up in my life, there is a bigger meaning behind it. I may not know the meaning in that moment, but more often than not, that meaning is revealed to me as I reflect back on situations. I may not know why a challenge shows up in my life at a particular time, but when I look back and reflect on it long after the challenge has passed, its meaning is oftentimes revealed to me. It may become clear that the challenge showed up in my life so that I had the opportunity to learn the skills needed for the next phase of my evolution as I grow into the person who will make the type of contributions that I desire to leave in the world as my legacy. With this awareness, it is becoming easier to accept all experiences that show up in my life and to surrender to what is in front of me at any given moment. With this awareness, I can even sing the praises of Source in all my life situations, regardless of whether I call them good or bad experiences. Through the words of the praises, I raise my energy level, the energy level of the people around me, and the energy level of the whole.

I Sing Praises to You My Source

I sing praises to you my Source
Right here where I stand
Knowing that even though I may seem alone
I am never alone because you are here with me
Surrounding me with your tender and warm caress
That I feel as a gentle breeze across my face
Reminding me of your everlasting presence

I sing praises to you my Source
You are the life that energizes my body
You are the force that invigorates my mind
You are the love that envelops my heart
You are the grace that makes my spirit soar
To the higher plane where you dwell
Where all is well exactly as it is

THANK YOU

I t has been a long day. The sun is now setting, appearing as a golden yellow globe suspended over the low hills on the western horizon. Wisps of white clouds streak the blue sky, adding to the magic of the moment. The beauty of it captures my heart.

I wonder how many people are witnessing the same magical moment that I am seeing. I wonder how many people even know enough to pay attention to the miracles of life that are there for us to witness in every moment. I wonder how many of us stop our busy activities, from time to time, to really notice the simple unfolding of life around us.

Today has been a day of contemplation. Except for the half-hour I took to eat a cereal-and-fruit breakfast and another half-hour to eat a sandwich lunch, the whole day has been about reflecting on my life journey that I have recounted to you, sitting on this bench. I thank you for allowing me to share my journey with you. I thank you for caring enough to listen. We all need someone to listen to what we have to say. We all need to know that we matter.

I have often realized that whenever I take long periods of time to reflect on my life, I clear my mind for new thoughts and insights to emerge. I have also noticed that sometimes, these new thoughts and insights point me to new experiences that propel my life in interesting directions.

Mind you, I still have a lot of unanswered questions. Why have visions of my grandmother been appearing to me of late? Is there a reason why the visions started appearing on December 21, 2012—the day that life on earth as we know it was supposed to end, according to various sources? Are there hidden messages in the timing of the visions? Are these visions pointing to something that I am supposed to know or something that I am supposed to do?

But even as these questions are rolling in my mind, I sense a part of me that already knows that any hidden messages behind the visions will be revealed when I am ready for what they bring.

What I know, beyond any doubt, is that today's reflections have helped to clarify a lot of things in my mind.

I know that it was my grandmother who planted the seed that started the process of opening my mind to the realm of Source. But, to use my grandmother's analogy, for many years, I had not given that seed what it needed to grow and flourish. I had not provided it with sufficient nutrients, water, and light that it needed. But the seed had not died; it had remained dormant.

I also know that it was the memory of my grandmother and the lessons she taught me that came to my rescue when I was living a life of chaos and confusion. It was that memory that led me to embark on a journey to search for the meaning and purpose of my life in this world. That quest led me to seek and receive knowledge from spiritual and motivational teachers, from ancient texts, from other cultures across the globe, and from simply being present to the unfolding of life in each moment.

Through study, focus, intention, and by grace, I have been given the opportunity to learn the truth about my true nature. And this truth has allowed my mind to open up to a much larger dimension, beyond where I used to live my life before. The seed that my grandmother planted with her lessons finally sprouted and continues to grow as the understanding of my true nature continues to deepen. However, what I have also discovered is that all that learning has really been a relearning of the simple message that my grandmother shared with me many years ago; that is, to seek the answers for my life within me.

It is by turning within that I started to receive the answers to the questions: Who am I? Where do I come from? Why am I here?

I have learned that I am an individualized extension of Source expressing in this physical world in human form; that is, expressing through a mind, an emotional energy system, and a physical body. And that when I maintain an awareness of my true nature as the formless spirit rooted in Source, my life becomes a guided journey in every step of the way. I have learned that by focusing on love, on expressing my gifts in the world, and on serving others I become a co-creator with Source, and I gain the ability to create the outcomes that I desire to experience. In doing so, I contribute to the growth and expansion of the world in my own unique way. Finally, I have learned to live my life forgiving at every step of the way. Whenever I forgive, I no longer allow the past to steal away my joy in the present moment and I no longer allow the past to cast shadows on my future.

I know that the evolution of my consciousness is an ongoing process that has no defined end. I know I will continue to deepen my connection to Source, to strengthen my trust in Source, and to expand my faith in Source. And I know my mind will continue to expand and to gain powers to manifest desired outcomes that are focused on expressing my gifts and on serving others and the world.

Through meditation, visualization, prayer, and contemplation, I will strive to live my life emanating love, joy, and creativity. It doesn't mean that I emanate these qualities all the time. Unfortunately, at times negative energies still overcome me, and in those moments my behavior reverts to that of the ego. But there is a difference between my behavior in the past and my behavior now. The difference is that now I can more quickly recognize what is happening, and I am able to bring myself back into alignment with Source by sitting in meditation, using visualization, saying a prayer, or going into contemplation. I now have practices that I can use to release the negative energies and to focus my attention back on Source and the unconditional love and creative energy that flow from it.

I now understand that my grandmother was a representation of Source in my life, just as everyone and everything is a representation of Source in my life. I now understand that my grandmother delivered a message from Source, just as other people around me and the situations that I experience deliver messages from Source. I now also understand that I am a representation of Source in the lives of others around me, and that I also am here to deliver messages to those around me.

With the clarity I now have as I continue on my life journey, I am very excited about embarking on the next phase of my life. I see myself pursuing the revelation that came to me in the desert. I see myself sharing with others the life lessons that I learned, to pass on the wisdom. I know that I will be guided in finding the most effective ways to spread the knowledge entrusted to me and the knowledge that will continue coming to me.

As I said this morning, there is an urgent need for a shift in human consciousness so that we put a stop to the chaotic conditions of today's world that lead to endless human suffering. I feel compelled to share the wisdom I have gathered and continue to gather on my journey, to encourage others to seek clarity regarding their own purpose, and to take action to fulfill that purpose in the world. We all need to find our own answers to the questions of life: Who am I? Where do I come from? Why am I here? I want to encourage others to discover their own unique ways that allow them to access Source—as they define it for themselves—and to be guided and fueled by the unconditional love and creative energy from it as they go through their days.

I strongly believe that by consciously cultivating a sense of connection to Source we gain the ability to stay alert as we go through our days. Through this alertness, we are able to perceive the messages that flow through our hearts, through others, and through conditions and situations around us. As we take action according to the messages we receive, we start living our purpose in this world. When each of us starts living a purposeful life, then together we will come to the realization of humanity's oneness with each other, oneness with nature, and oneness with everything in creation. And in that oneness, we will create a world that is focused on love, joy, and creativity.

The sun has sunk behind the hills, leaving a gray hue across the sky. The magical feel of the moment still lingers.

As I think of the possibilities that lie ahead of me, I am filled with a sense of awe. I breathe in deeply and breathe out slowly. I close my eyes, quiet my mind, calm my emotions, relax my body, and focus on my heart space. I feel Source around me. I feel a sense of peace, knowing that my life will continue to unfold, one moment to the next. I know that what I need at every step of the way will come to me in the moment that I need it. And I simply let it be.

In this very moment, I commit to living my life in this new way. It starts by being aware of what I need to do in this moment, trusting that I will know what I need to do in the next moment, and trusting that I will know what I need to do in the moment after that. The sum of the moments from now on are what will become my legacy.

What is it that I need to do in this moment to mark this new beginning? What is it that Source needs to express through me in this moment? What is in my heart right now?

I know to listen to my heart and to follow the guidance from my heart, as my grandmother taught me. I have a lot to give to the world, and I know that any impulse to give that I feel is coming from Source. It doesn't matter whether what I am compelled to give is big or small, for there is no big or small in Source. In Source, there is only what needs to be expressed in each moment for the purpose of the unfolding of the whole.

I continue to focus on my heart.

I feel gratitude and appreciation for the precious gift that my grandmother gave me, in the life lessons she taught me. With my inner eye, I see my grandmother sitting beside me, as if we are back on the hillside. With my inner ear, I hear her words. "Yeukai, my child, I knew you would come to understand the teachings I shared with you," she says.

I feel this overwhelming urge to express my gratitude and appreciation to my grandmother, and to do so in a way that would be meaningful to her. And I know what I will do. I will recite a praise poem to my grandmother. This is the gift I will give to her, so that her spirit can dance in ecstasy.

And the words of praise come effortlessly.

Maita, Mbuya

Maita Mbuya Debwe Renyoka Mutandiranwa
Maita Mhara, maita Varizvihota Nzangare
Maita Manyuka, vari Rare, vari Renje
Vari kumukwidza kwaHokonya

Vari kuchipendere kwakapendera nyika
Maita Mbuya Chikonamombe
Vanokohwa nyemba dzisigapfutwi
Maita vaera Mhara
Vane unyoro hunenge hwemembwe
Asi kunzi hezvo zvikara zvouya, munodauka semaputi ari murwaenga
Pakumhanya mosiya mhepo shure
Zororai murugare Mbuya Debwe Renyoka
Zororai murugare mbuya vangu
Kuzosvika zuva ratichasangana kuna Musiki

English translation of the praise poem for my grandmother:

Thank You, Grandma

Thank you Grandma *Debwe Renyoka Mutandiranwa*
Thank you, a member of the Mhara totem, thank you *Varizvihota Nzangare*
Thank you *Manyuka,* those in Rare, those in Range
Those on the steep slope in Hokonya
Those at the edges of the world, where the earth folds back into itself
Thank you, member of the *Mbuya Chikonamombe* clan
Of those who harvest beans that resist damage by weevils
Thank you, those of the *Mhara* totem
With the docility of a deer
But when predators come, you jump like popping corn in a roasting pan
When it comes to running, you leave the wind behind
Rest in peace Grandma *Debwe Renyoka*
Rest in peace my beloved grandmother
Till the day we meet again in Source

ABOUT THE AUTHOR

Martha Mutomba was born and raised in Zimbabwe. Martha's narrative storytelling interweaves her fascination with the mysterious nature of life, her deep roots in her Shona culture, and her curiosity in the cultures of the people she has met as she has travelled and lived in different parts of the world. Martha earned a PhD degree from Cambridge University in England and then worked in the biotechnology industry in the United States for many years. She currently volunteers for Munhu Inc. (www.munhu.org), a US-registered 501(c)(3) organization dedicated to helping orphaned children in rural areas of her native land of Zimbabwe. Martha's writing and charitable work give her the opportunity to combine her two passions of telling stories and serving others. Martha is donating a portion of sales of this book to Munhu Inc.

ACKNOWLEDGMENTS

It is with great enthusiasm that I express my sincere gratitude and appreciation to all those who contributed, in one form or another, to the completion of the story told in this book. As we say in Shona, *"Kusatenda huroi* (Not expressing gratitude is like practicing witchcraft)." Let it not be said that I practiced witchcraft.

I am grateful to the many teachers who have crossed my path. I thank the teachers in the spiritual realm: the benevolent spirits that work to sustain our world, the ancestral spirits that protect and counsel us in our daily lives, and most especially the spirit of my grandmother that inspired the story told in this book. I thank the teachers whose works are cited in this book. I commend you for being at the forefront to spread the word about human consciousness and the need for us, as human beings, to awaken to our true nature as emanations of Source expressing in the physical world.

A big thank you goes to members of the publishing team at Morgan James Publishing for their professionalism and dedication in bringing this book to print. Your guidance and encouragement was invaluable as I navigated the book publishing arena.

I am deeply indebted to my friends and colleagues who kindly and generously gave of their time, attention, and energy to reviewing this work during its various phases of development. I particularly thank Susanna Mac, Dikran Toroser, Kim Cremers, and Linda Rice who provided invaluable feedback that was incorporated in the book. A big thank you goes to Edward Mancini for his amazing editorial support during the development of this book. Another big thank you goes to Angie Kiesling for her outstanding line editing support.

A very special thank you goes to my friend Sungmi Um for the many conversations that were instrumental in clarifying my thoughts on what I wanted to share. And thank you Sungmi for the lunches and teas as well.

A heartfelt thank you goes to my "consultants" on aspects of Shona traditions and perspectives on Zimbabwe: my brother Wilbert Mutomba and my friends and colleagues Sipho Gumbo and Bothwell Fundira. Your comments and corrections were instrumental in keeping the narrator's story authentic.

I am grateful to my friend Mary Pablo for creating the inspired art that graces the front cover of this book. I am honored that you chose my book to be the medium to showcase your beautiful piece of art.

I thank my family and friends for being there for me. I thank my parents for supporting me in everything I have ever wanted to do, and for believing in me at all times. I thank you *Mai*—my mother—for reading the book during its development, despite failing eyes. *Ndinotenda Shava, ndinotenda VaChihera vangu*—the book is richer for it!

And I thank you Zimbabwe, my motherland—you are forever in my heart.

I wrote this story with you, the reader, in mind, and I thank you for choosing to read this book. I feel blessed that the circle is complete. I believe that through our collective efforts—each and every one of us—we can raise the energy of this world to be a heaven on earth for all.

Above all, I thank you Source for my life and the lives of all the forms in creation—human or otherwise. We are all a part of the dance of life in you. And what a dance!

NOTES

Village Celebration

1. Bongo Man, Kanda. "Zing Zong." *Zing Zong.* Hannibal, 1991. CD, digital download

Facing and Releasing the False Self

2. Godman, David (Editor). *Be As You Are: The Teachings of Sri Ramana Maharshi.* New York: Arkana Penguin Books, 1985
3. Holmes, Ernest. *The Art of Life.* New York: Penguin Group, 2004
4. Tolle, Eckhart. *The Power of Now.* Vancouver, Canada: Namaste Publishing, 1997
5. Tolle, Eckhart. *A New Earth.* New York: Penguin Group, 2005
6. Redfield, James. *The Celestine Prophecy.* New York: Grand Central Publishing, 1993
7. Redfield, James. *The Secret of Shambhala.* New York: Grand Central Publishing, 1999
8. Brown, Michael. *The Presence Process.* Vancouver, Canada: Namaste Publishing, 2010
9. Brown, Michael. *Alchemy of the Heart.* Vancouver, Canada: Namaste Publishing, 2008

10. Chopra, Deepak. *The Book of Secrets*. New York: Random House, 2004
11. Chopra, Deepak. *The Path to Love*. New York: Random House, 1997
12. Beckwith, Michael. *Spiritual Liberation*. New York: Simon & Schuster, 2008
13. Ruiz, Miguel. *The Four Agreements*. San Rafael: Amber-Allen Publishing, 1997
14. Somé, Malidoma P. *The Healing Wisdom of Africa*. New York: Penguin Putnam Inc., 1999
15. Goleman, Daniel. *Emotional Intelligence*. New York: Bantam Dell, 1995
16. Holden, Robert. *Success Intelligence*. London: Hodder & Stoughton, 2005
17. Sharma, Robin. *The Leader Who Had No Title*. New York: Simon & Schuster, 2010
18. Hicks, Esther and Hicks, Jerry. *Ask and It Is Given*. Part I and Part II (read by Jerry Hicks). Hay House Inc., 2005. CD sets
19. Hicks, Esther and Hicks, Jerry. *The Teachings of Abraham: The Master Course Audio*. Hay House Inc., 2007. 11-CD set

Finding Your Passion and Making It Your Gift to the World

20. Bocelli, Andrea. Schubert's "Ave Maria." *Sacred Arias*. Philips, 1999. CD
21. Belafonte, Harry. "Jamaican Farewell." *Calypso*. RCA Victor, 1956. LP, digital download
22. Hammer, MC. "U Can't Touch This." From the album *Please Hammer, Don't Hurt 'Em*. Capitol (US), 1990. CD single, digital download
23. Psy. "Gangnam Style." From the album *Psy 6 (Six Rules), Part 1*. YG, Universal Republic, School Boy, 2012. CD single, digital download
24. Bongo Man, Kanda. "Zing Zong." *Zing Zong*. Hannibal, 1991. CD, digital download
25. *Field of Dreams*. By WP Kinsella. Dir. Phil Alden Robinson. With Kevin Costner. Universal Studios, 1989. DVD

Practices for Positive Change

26. Holmes, Ernest. *The Art of Life*. New York: Penguin Group, 2004
27. Genesis 1:1–26. The Holy Bible (New International Version)
28. Matthew 7:7. The Holy Bible (New International Version)

GLOSSARY OF SHONA WORDS

Ave mangwana	Till tomorrow; a parting greeting to say good night and see you the next day
baba	father
chidawo	principal praise name, which is one of the social identifiers used in the Shona clan system
Chihera	name of a Shona clan
Chikonamombe	principal praise name for the Mbuya Chikonamombe clan; term of respect or endearment used in addressing a man belonging to the Mbuya Chikonamombe clan
gudo	baboon
guyo	large rectangular stone used as a grinding tool, it is used together with the huyo
hove	fish
hozi	type of granary found at a typical homestead in the rural areas of Zimbabwe

huva	built-in earthen platform usually found at the front of a typical cooking hut in rural areas of Zimbabwe
huyo	small stone used as a grinding tool, it is used together with the guyo
ishe	king
madzitateguru	ancestors
mai	mother
maiguru	relational term used in addressing the wife of one's elder brother
Maiweee!	common expression that translates to "Mother!" and is used to express surprise, disbelief, sympathy, sorrow, or pain, depending on the intonation
Makadini?	How are you?
Makomborero	Blessings (Shona name)
maMoyo	term of respect or endearment used in addressing a woman belonging to the Rozvi clan
Mamuka sei?	How did you wake up?
Mangwanani!	Good morning!
Masikati!	Good afternoon!
Maswera sei?	How did you spend your afternoon or day?
Mavambo	Source
mbuya	grandmother
Mbuya Chikonamombe	name of a Shona clan
Mhara	totem of the Mbuya Chikonamombe clan; term of respect or endearment used in addressing a man or woman belonging to the Mbuya Chikonamombe clan

Moyo	totem of the Rozvi and Njanja clans; term of respect or endearment used in addressing a man or woman belonging to the Rozvi or Njanja clan
Moyondizvo	principal praise name for the Rozvi clan; term of respect or endearment used in addressing a man belonging to the Rozvi clan
Mufakose	principal praise name for the Chihera clan; term of respect or endearment used in addressing a man belonging to the Chihera clan
Mugumo	Last born (Shona name)
mukoma	relational term used in addressing one's elder brother
musha	homestead
mushandira pamwe	working as a team
Musiki	The Creator
mutsago	pillow
mutupo	totem, a social identifier used in the Shona clan system—the totem can be an animal, an object, or an organ of the body
muzukuru	grandchild
ngoto	a type of traditional beer enjoyed in some rural areas of Zimbabwe
nguwani	hat
Njanja	name of a Shona clan
njuzu	mermaid
Pasipanodya	The ground consumes (Shona name)

roora	money and other items that a man pays to his in-laws in a traditional Shona marriage—similar to bride price
Rozvi	name of a Shona clan
rusero	a round-shaped tray-like utensil woven out of river reeds and has many uses in the traditional Shona kitchen
ruware	low-lying flat granite surface
rwaenga	roasting utensil made from a broken clay pot
sadza	staple food of the people of Zimbabwe that is made from cornmeal and has a consistency similar to polenta
sekuru	grandfather
Shava	totem of the Chihera clan; term of respect or endearment used in addressing a man or woman belonging to the Chihera clan
shumba	lion
simba	strength
Sinyoro	principal praise name for the Njanja clan; term of respect or endearment used in addressing a man belonging to the Njanja clan
Tatenda	We are thankful (Shona name)
tsuro	hare
vadzimu	spirits of deceased ancestors
varungu	Shona term used to refer to white people or Caucasians
wesango	of the forest
Yeukai	Remember (Shona name)

Morgan James
Speakers Group

www.TheMorganJamesSpeakersGroup.com

We connect Morgan James published
authors with live and online events
and audiences who will benefit
from their expertise.